Never Touched

Laney Wylde

THIS book is a work of fiction. Names, characters, places and incidents are the product of the author's imagination or are used fictitiously. Any resemblance to actual persons, living or dead, business establishments, events or locales is entirely coincidental.

No part of this book may be reproduced, scanned, or distributed in any printed or electronic form without permission. Please do not participate in or encourage piracy of copyrighted materials in violation of the author's rights. Purchase only authorized editions.

NEVER TOUCHED
Copyright ©2018 Laney Wylde
All rights reserved.
Printed in the United States of America
First Edition: November 2018

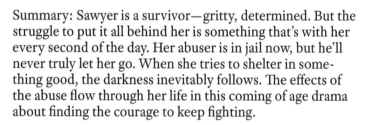

Crimson Tree Publishing
WWW.CRIMSONTREEPUBLISHING.COM

Summary: Sawyer is a survivor—gritty, determined. But the struggle to put it all behind her is something that's with her every second of the day. Her abuser is in jail now, but he'll never truly let her go. When she tries to shelter in something good, the darkness inevitably follows. The effects of the abuse flow through her life in this coming of age drama about finding the courage to keep fighting.

ISBN: 978-1-63422-312-6 (paperback)
ISBN: 978-1-63422-313-3 (e-book)
Cover Design by: Marya Heidel
Typography by: Courtney Knight
Editing by: Cynthia Shepp

COVER ART
© CHAOSS / FOTOLIA

Fiction / Romance / New Adult
Fiction / Coming of Age
Fiction / Romance / Contemporary
Fiction / Romance / Suspense

For Caroline, Elizabeth, and Susan who helped me find my voice by listening even when I spoke with it.

To hell with them. Nothing hurts if you don't let it.
~Ernest Hemingway

January 2018

My soul is crooked and dark, depraved and destined for hell. At least, that's what Pastor Jeff told me...

*S*MILE, SAWYER. I COULDN'T. *STOP CRYING.* I TRIED TO stop. *You're defiant.* I had to be. *Don't you love me?* No. *Don't you love Jesus?* I didn't know anymore. *Why can't you obey like Simone?* Because I'd rather go to hell. *Simone, show Sawyer how to be good.* I didn't want to watch. *Sawyer, open your eyes.* I did. To Simone's—blue, clear like shattered glass. Shattered by the threat of hell. Shattered by Jeff.

The therapist I was forced to see wanted me to talk about this, I presumed, since she wanted me to talk about my childhood, about anything that could have led to my December *incident.*

Bitch, please.

"Is there anything on your mind, Sawyer?" Dr. Harper started each session with the same wordless stare before crumbling into this question. She had two personas: soft, sweet therapist with a gentle manner, and assertive pain in my ass. I imagined her psyching herself up for our forty-five minutes twice each week. I liked to picture

1

her in front of the mirror saying some kind of Sawyer-specific mantra—*I will make it through the whole session as sweet-therapist. I will not break character.* I would have felt bad for her if she wasn't making so much money off my incarceration.

Her simple question, "Is there anything on your mind, Sawyer?" was already an admission of defeat. Every session was a game of Talk Chicken. Who would cave to fill the awkward silence first? The first time was the longest, a full six minutes before she broke. Our fourth round, the undefeated champion: me.

I shook my head.

"You've been here for two weeks now." Was that all? She crossed her legs and propped her delicate face in her spider-leg fingers with her elbow on the arm of the chair. "How have you been adjusting?"

I shrugged.

"Do you like your roommate?"

"I don't like that she has six pillows."

"Are you saying you don't have enough pillows?"

"I have one." Which wouldn't be a problem if it wasn't paper thin and my spine wasn't battered from years of gymnastics and cheer. "The second night I was here, I asked one of the nurses for a second one, and she said they were all out. But I knew where they were. She offered me a Trazodone to help me sleep."

"Did you take it?"

"No. I don't need medication."

"I have here in my notes," she started as she lifted a page in my file, "that you are on Effexor and Zoloft daily, Xanax as needed, and were given an injection of Haldol on the tenth. Are you saying you're not swallowing your medication?"

"Haldol? Is that booty juice?"

"Yes. Did something happen on the tenth?"

"Sure." I switched my bare feet to squish under the opposite knees. "Some nurses pushed me face down on the solitary room bed, then pulled off my leggings and panties."

"I'm sorry if the shot was triggering for you."

I scoffed. "It's not a trigger. Nothing's a trigger. It's just normal instinct to fight someone when they pin you down and take your clothes off, isn't it?"

"What led up to the 'booty juice?'" she asked, but she already knew. She had the file.

"I'm told I threw a chair at Louie..." I flicked my fingers as if this had yet to be proven to me. "During lunch, apparently."

"You don't remember?"

"Of course I remember," I lied.

"Okay." She lifted her chin from her palm, her brown hair swishing over her collarbone as she challenged me. "Where'd you hit him?"

"In the thigh." Lying again. And to a psychologist, which was basically lying to a mind reader.

"No, Sawyer, you missed."

Shit. Of course I missed. I should have guessed that. Dad always said I had terrible aim.

I crossed my arms. "Then why did I get booty juiced?"

"What was the last thing you remember before throwing the chair?"

"I don't know."

"Can you tell me why you did it?"

I shook my head, though I knew. Sure, I was violent,

but not without reason.

She softened her voice and leaned forward, her sharp elbows poking into her knees. "Sawyer, I know what he called you. Were you feeling unsafe?"

I snickered. "You all say that word a lot, you know? *Feeling.* Like everything I experience is some delusion, a deviation from fact. But if you know what he called me, you know I wasn't *feeling* unsafe. I *was* unsafe."

"I'm sorry. I didn't mean—"

"It's almost visiting hours. Can I leave now?" I asked as I dropped my feet to the carpet.

She sighed, her eyes moving past me at the clock on the wall. "You may, but do you understand the conditions of your hospitalization?"

"I'm here to pay my debt to society."

"You're here to get help—"

"Mandated by the courts."

"But if you don't let us help you, we can decide that it is in your best interest to stay longer. If you continue to cut your sessions short—"

"Okay." I sighed and bounced my toes against the floor. It was probably a psych patient thing; I'd scan any circle of us here and find a lot of restless legs and fingers. Or maybe it was just this place. It was January, and the AC was blasting. We were all bundled up in our drawstring-free hoodies, shaking to get warm. "Tell me what I need to do to get out of here."

"Basically, I can't sign off on your discharge until I have evidence you're not going to repeat the kind of behavior that got you arrested last month. Are you ready to tell me about that night?"

"Isn't everything in my file?"

"I meant talk about it for your sake, not mine."

"I've already told the story a hundred times: to the police, to my lawyer, to the shrink who evaluated me for the plea bargain—"

"Right, but you haven't talked about how you felt."

I summoned my most melodramatic eye roll yet. I could imagine Dr. Harper's view of it: the white of my eyes showing as my pupils revolved back into my head in slow motion. Contemptuous and gorgeous. I'd been working on it for years. "I *feel* that it wasn't my fault. I *feel* that I shouldn't be locked up here. I *feel* that it is unfair."

"Unfair, okay—"

"If I have to stay, can we talk about something else?" I sank back into the couch, crossed my arms, and kicked my bare feet onto the table, one ankle dropping onto the other.

"Of course, Sawyer. What's on your mind?"

"Nothing."

Dr. Harper sighed discreetly and flipped through my file. "Why don't we talk about your CBT assignment from yesterday?" She pulled out a stapled packet of papers, glanced at it, then dropped it on the coffee table between us. Her needlelike fingertips pivoted it my direction. "I was intrigued by how you filled it out." That was shrink talk for—*I was pissed to see that you didn't even try to follow the directions.*

I didn't have to see the Behavior Chain Analysis form, which was a diagram of blank bubbles representing links in a chain from a *trigger* to a bad behavior, to know what I wrote. The idea was for us to fill in all the bubbles, and then find the best link in the chain to break before we misbehaved again. Over the entire page, I had scrawled

JAKE in intricately filled bold letters.

"What was the problem behavior you were trying to address?"

"December 2."

She nodded. The date was more than enough to explain. "And who is Jake?"

September 2014

*I*NDIAN SUMMER WAS FIVE GLORIOUS DAYS OF actual warm weather in our southern Oregon shit town—sunny and over eighty degrees. Decadent. Glorious. Clear and present danger of suntan. My sophomore year, it landed the first week of school.

This, of course, meant that a lot of pale shoulders and pasty legs made their school debut, put on display by short dresses and tank tops. When I covered my semi-Cuban skin with a modest cheer tee shirt and jean shorts, I hoped Travis's eyes would lead him to another target. After all, he had me after school whenever he wanted. When the school bus stopped in his neighborhood since his license had been suspended again, I slouched and moved my backpack to occupy the seat beside me. Maybe he wouldn't even see me.

I couldn't ever be so lucky.

He chucked my backpack in my lap and sat down next to me. His clammy hand slid from my bare knee up my thigh where it rested, hidden beneath my bag. I tried to push him away by his forearm, but his fingers dug into my leg.

"Travis, back the hell off!"

He looked at me calmly, his words calculated. "You don't get to say that to me, or is the deal off?"

The deal being I let Travis do whatever he wanted to me...and he agreed not to leak a video of Simone and me on the "Overheard at BHHS" page, the anonymous gossip site everyone at our school followed. His friend Jeremy found the video four months ago, and he immediately showed it to Travis and two other basketball players. As far as any of us could tell, no one at school knew it existed. Until then, I didn't even know the video was out there. But now that I did, I knew it couldn't have been the only one.

And sure, I heard the rumors that circulated after those guys started screwing us. But rumors were just talk. It wasn't so bad being talked about. Even the stories those guys spread weren't all that shocking among the other cheerleaders. I was still popular. Being talked about did that. Being seen, though—I would never let it happen.

I dug my nails into the fleshy underside of Travis's wrist. He grimaced, but kept his hand sliding to the top of my shorts.

It was then I heard a voice from behind us. "Excuse me, is this guy bothering you?" Travis and I turned to see a guy with dirty-blond hair one row behind us resting his elbows on the back of our vinyl seat.

No, say no. No, no, no. But before I could, I was nodding—this involuntary motion like my body and mind were run by two different people.

"Okay." He scooted into the aisle, now only inches

from us, raking back the rogue hairs that fell in front of his eyes. "Stand up," he commanded Travis. "We're switching seats." Now that he was standing, I realized how small he was, especially compared to Travis, a six-four, two-hundred-plus-pound athlete. Travis could chew him up and spit him out in seconds.

"Fuck you," Travis spat before turning to me.

"Get up." The guy's eyes narrowed as if this would be threatening. Travis straightened to stand, about to swing his fist. Crap. Poor guy.

Before Travis had the chance to make contact, the shorter guy's fist smashed into Travis's face. His massive frame was blocking my view of most of the action, but from the crack I heard, I guessed it was his nose. His other jabbed Travis's gut. Travis crumpled into the seat.

There were gasps all around, and of course some idiot started chanting, "Fight! Fight! Fight!"

The guy put his hand on the back of our seat and stooped to meet Travis's eyeline. "Now, how about switching seats?" Travis stood again, obviously not to switch seats, but that guy kneed his groin before he could do anything.

Damn, how many times had I wanted to do that but never had the balls to?

The next thing I realized, the bus stopped, and the driver was escorting the blond to a seat at the back. Bruised ego and bleeding nose, Travis moved to the row behind me—had to have been his nose then.

So the fight was lame, but I got to ride the rest of the way to school alone. Bonus: I got to see someone half Travis's size beat the shit out of him in front of forty-plus people.

The bus stopped at the curb behind school. Students started filing out, throwing stares back at Travis, who had fat drops of blood falling from his nostrils and crusting in his tee shirt. I waited in my seat until Travis left and the kids in the back started down the narrow aisle. "Hey," I called the guy as he was about to pass me. I slid out to walk behind him. "Thanks."

"No problem." He flickered a half smile before heading down the steep steps to the sidewalk. I stood there beside the bus watching him walk toward school with his backpack slung over one shoulder. He disappeared behind the glass doors.

The twenty-eight hours after that were quiet, in that eerie calm-before-the-storm kind of way. I went from class to lunch to class to practice without seeing Travis at all. My phone was absent of booty calls. I didn't even see him on the bus. I spent the whole night refreshing the Overheard page on my phone, sure I'd find the video posted there. But I didn't. Maybe hell had finally frozen.

I left fourth-period Calculus the next day hesitant and hopeful. But once my locker was in sight, so was he. Travis leaned against it, glaring me down. My feet felt heavy, my progress down the hallway slowing. I convinced myself that the more time it took for me to get to him, the tougher I would be when I got there. It only kind of worked.

"You're in my way." I shoved past him to my locker.

"Hurry up," he said as he stepped aside. "We're going off campus for lunch." This meant Jeremy's house, a block away and always unlocked.

Jeremy and his other two friends opted out of our arrangement months ago, growing consciences after

Simone found her own way out. I could never decide if she was braver or weaker than I was for doing it. In the swirl of screams and stiff silences that followed, I was pissed at her. The little bitch *abandoned* me. Now I was just one girl left alone to protect the secrets of two. Every night, I fell asleep to the thought that I'd grow the courage Simone did, the strength or balls or foolishness to just say, "Fuck it, let the chips fall where they may." But each morning, I woke up to the cold reality of the currency she spent to keep her darkness locked up, safe underground. All she needed was for me to pay my share, a small price compared to hers. I could afford it. I owed her that much.

My stomach twisted as I pulled the books out of my backpack one at a time, slipping them into my locker as slowly as I could. Time. I just had to buy some time. I knew from experience this would do me no good, but I kept up my slug's pace anyway. I was about to pull my fifth-period Chemistry textbook out, when I jumped. There was an unfamiliar hand on my naked shoulder, one raised with callouses.

I turned my head to see the guy from the bus the day before. "Babe, are you ready for lunch?" he asked. We stared at each other, him straining to communicate something wordlessly that I couldn't understand. I went along with it anyway. Anything was better than *lunch* with Travis. His hand stayed on my shoulder until I threw my backpack over the other. Then his fingers slipped between mine.

I turned to Travis. He was *nervous*. And I loved it. So I let this guy lead me down the hall toward the quad. Before we made it outside, he yelled back to Travis,

"Keep icing that nose, bro." I would have laughed if I hadn't had so much adrenaline in my veins, if I knew what this guy wanted from me, what repaying him for my rescue would entail. He pushed through the door, dropping my hand once he found an empty table. "Sorry about that. I couldn't figure out another way to get you out of there. What is with that guy?"

Why did he care? And how did he appear out of thin air like that? Was he just expecting us to talk like we weren't strangers? "Thanks," I muttered. "It's a long story, but it's been like this for months."

"*Months?*"

I just then noticed he was sitting at the table and I should, too. "Yeah."

"Well, hopefully, he'll leave you alone now." He sifted through a plastic grocery bag, pulling out more food than it could reasonably contain.

I sighed. "It's not that simple."

"No?" he asked before taking a bite of an apple.

I didn't want to give this guy any more information. What was I supposed to do—tell him what I was willing to do to protect my reputation? Then he'd want the same thing, and I wouldn't be able say "no." No was never an option. I shook my head.

He took a bite of his turkey sandwich, then asked, "Are you guys dating or something?"

I couldn't contain the cackle. "Oh, *hell* no."

"Then there's no reason for him to keep hanging around you."

"Like I said, it's not that simple."

"Do you want to explain?"

"No," I said too quickly.

He stared at me with furrowed brows as he chewed his food. The long silence made my nerves fray. What did he want from me? "Are you hungry?"

"A little." I shrugged. My stomach was aching, but I forgot my lunch in my locker. I never had time or appetite when I spent lunch period with Travis.

He turned his bag toward me. "Here, take whatever you want, but leave me at least one Swiss Roll."

"Swiss Roll?"

His dark eyes widened. "You've never had one?"

"Is it this thing?" I asked, pulling out the pair of plastic-wrapped chocolate pastries.

"Yes. You *have* to have one. I don't usually share, but this is that important."

Who was this guy? Tiny fighter/junk-food connoisseur?

I opened them and took one of the rolls out. He watched as I took a bite. Kind of creepy. To my surprise, it was amazing—chocolate cake rolled around fluffy white frosting, covered in more chocolate. Exquisite, for something that could be bought at a gas station. "You're right. I've been missing out."

"See? I mean, you should eat some real food, too."

"Thanks, but you really don't have to."

He shot me a look that demanded I get something else from the bag. Frankly, he was kind of scary, so I did what I was told, a habit of mine I was eager to break. I found a bag of baby carrots, which I figured he wouldn't miss much.

"Why haven't I met you before?" I realized I should have asked for his name, but it was now to that awkward part of the acquaintanceship where he had already held my hand and called me "babe," so I was sort of hoping he would just volunteer it at some point.

"I just moved here from Medford."

"Why?" I asked it the way someone would ask why a person would move away from San Diego or to Texas. Medford was about three hours northeast, with actual chain stores and restaurants other than McDonalds. Everyone here made the winding drive there to shop for school clothes, go to Costco, or to just get the hell out of Dodge.

"My dad got hired as a firefighter."

"Well..." I crunched before swallowing. "A lot of old people do have heart attacks around here."

He laughed at my reduction of his dad's work to resuscitating the elderly. Fires didn't tend to be a big problem in our town. Sure, we had drunk beachgoers around poorly placed bonfires and the rare forest fire, but everything here was so damp it took a real effort to ignite.

"You've lived here a while?" he asked.

"My whole life, unfortunately."

"You don't like it?"

"What's there to like?"

"The ocean, the river, the hiking—"

"You know it's not usually this warm, right?"

"Seriously?"

I smirked. "You'll see what I mean."

His expression deflated as he took a bite out of an apple. "Well, I think you should give me your number."

"Yeah?" I asked, hoping for the opportunity to finally get his name.

"Clearly, that dick—"

"Travis."

"Won't leave you alone unless I'm around." He turned the bag around toward me. "Eat some more."

I handed him my phone and sifted through the rest of his lunch. "How did you do that by the way?"

He started tapping on the touchscreen. "Do what?"

"Beat him up so quickly. I mean, he's huge, and you're..." I felt my cheeks redden, realizing I was about to insult the guy who had inexplicably saved me twice.

"Not?"

"Well, yeah."

"Have you heard of Manny Pacquiao?"

"Who?"

"The welterweight boxer."

I bit my lip. "I have no idea what you just said."

"He's a little guy. Shorter than me, but heavier. He's amazing."

"Okay. What does this have to do—"

"I'm a boxer."

"Ooh." I examined him more carefully. His arms were muscular but not bulky enough to notice at first glance. A couple of bluish veins that popped in the crease of his elbows caught my attention, along with the defined shape of his shoulders and chest through his shirt. *Huh.*

He was rugged—like Disney prince buff—if there was such a thing as a short Disney prince. *Maybe* Simba counted when standing on all four paws. Poor short guys—woefully underrepresented.

Hot blood rushed to my cheeks when I realized I had been staring at him long enough for him to return my phone, run his fingers through his straight hair, and smirk at my gawking at him. Damn it, Simba. "Um..."

Um? That was the best I could do? "Thanks again for what you did. Twice."

"Don't worry about it. Text me your name. Or you could tell me now. Whichever." His lips curved into a smile that only sneaked up his left cheek.

You'll be fine. Just don't look directly at him.

I distracted my eyes with my phone, murmuring a shaky, "Sawyer." Smooth.

He reached out his hand to shake mine, which was now sweating. So embarrassing. Even my skin knew he was way out of my league. "Jake," he said as his rough palm surrounded mine. "Nice to meet you, Sawyer."

JAKE MET ME AT MY locker at the fourth-period dismissal bell every day for the rest of that week. If Travis was there, Jake would lace his fingers through mine, call me *babe*, and walk me out to our lunch table, where he would drop the façade. By the end of the week, Travis stopped hovering at school. With his license suspended, he couldn't pick me up at home or practice. He hadn't posted the video, either. It was over. It had to be.

Friday, Jake met me at my locker as usual. His expression changed the instant he saw me, like I was the most depressing site he had ever seen. "Hey, you okay?" I asked, twirling the combination lock.

"Yeah." He tried to smile.

"You going to the game tonight? I recommend it since it's the only time it won't be freezing."

"Well, I was going to ask if you wanted to go, but I guess you'll already be there." He dropped his gaze to my navy and gold cheer uniform, and my eyes followed his.

My heart drummed so loud I was pretty sure he could hear it. He was going to ask me out? No, not out. To a game. That wasn't a date. He wouldn't ask me out. He was teenage-Simba hot, way out of my sphere of realistic Disney suitors. "I'm sorry," I said, scrunching my face apologetically. "I mean, what would those football players do if we weren't on the track trying to distract the crowd?"

He laughed. "Well, what are you doing after?"

"Hmm...probably hanging out with you, babe." I smiled and pushed his shoulder. "Actually, Ronnie, one of the cheer captains, is having a party at her house up North Bank if you want to come. It's our last chance to swim in the river before it becomes unbearably cold. What do you think?" I asked, shutting my locker.

"That sounds tolerable," he said. Together, we started down the hall.

"Tolerable? We can do something else if you want."

"No, it's fine. I'm just not usually into parties and talking, or...you know, being around people."

"You're around me." I nudged his arm with mine.

"You're a person—singular."

"Well, hang out with *only* me tonight at the party up North Bank. I'm kind of obligated to go to make sure my flier, Tatum, doesn't get into too much trouble. She's ninety pounds and drinks like a linebacker."

"I'll meet you after the game, then?"

I smiled and nodded.

Indian summer ended abruptly with a forty-degree temperature drop that evening. At the beginning of the game, we were all sweating under our rayon uniforms. By the fourth, we were shivering, begging our coach to let us quit stunting so we could put our warm-ups on. But Coach Corinne was a hardass from Detroit who responded to our whining with anything but mercy. The game finally ended, Bruins—our school—winning by six. *Hooray.* I shivered into my warm-up pants and the flimsy matching jacket. They were damp from sitting out in the fog. I probably would have fared better without them.

I met Jake at the revolving chain-link gate after the game, where he was standing in the dust and gravel. All 5'7" of him was outfitted in jeans and a thick Carhartt jacket.

"Your lips are blue. Still want to swim?" he asked.

Through my chattering teeth, I stuttered, "If you swim with me."

He laughed. "Not a chance. Take my coat."

"No." I hugged myself. "Then you'll be cold." He ignored my protest, shedding his jacket and trading it for the bulky bag slung over my shoulder. The Sherpa lining of his coat was warm from his body, slowing my shaking. I watched goose bumps rise on his arms. "Jake, you're freezing!"

"We're at my car, so it doesn't really matter."

The drive to Ronnie's was long and tortuous. She lived twenty minutes away from town and officially off the grid. A dozen cars were already parked in the gravel lot in front of her log-cabin-style mansion when we got there. The house backed up to the river, huge windows overlooking the bank. In the darkness, though, the glass only revealed the dancing flames from the fire pit flickering light over the letterman-clad bunch circled around it.

We pressed through the warm bodies into the

woodsy house. The stuffiness gave me the chance to return Jake's coat, but not before Tatum saw me wearing it. She was leaving the kitchen with a red Solo cup, her blonde hair still bouncing in her cheer ponytail.

"Sawyer!" she shouted as she approached. "Well, well..." She scanned Jake up and down. "Is this the guy who got you out of your deal with the devil? You're right." She glanced at me. "He's hot for a short guy."

I took the cup from her hand and sniffed it. "Ew, Tatum, what is this?"

"Rum and coke."

"It doesn't smell like there's any coke in it." I handed it back to her. "Make me one." Turning to Jake, I said, "Want a beer or something?"

He shook his head, and Tatum weaved through a few people on her way back to the bottle-littered counter.

Jake leaned toward my ear to ask, "Your deal with the devil?"

I rolled my eyes, ignoring the cold fear in my chest. "Try to ignore Tatum until she's sober." As I led him by the hand to the sliding door, I yelled, "Tatum, meet us at the fire." She nodded as she poured cola into a cup. "Oh," I said to Jake as soon as we were on the back deck. "For the record, I never said you were short."

"Just hot." Pretending I didn't hear, I kept walking until he caught my arm. He pulled himself in front of me so we were nose to nose. My lungs forgot how to work as he brushed his hand from the top of his head to mine. "I'm taller than you."

"No, you're not. You're 5'7", and so am I."

"How do you know how tall I am?"

I shook my head. "Um—"

He crossed his arms over his chest, a smug expression crossing his face. "You looked up my stats."

Obviously, I had. Okay, I had never been in anything even resembling a romantic relationship before, so I was by no means a dating expert. But I knew one thing—I wasn't going to get into a car alone with a guy I hadn't internet-stalked. Neglecting to do so would be downright reckless, and I preferred to reserve my reckless behavior for when I was under the influence.

Based on my findings, Jake Lane was 5'7", 131 pounds, used to attend North Medford High School, had an older sister, Jenny, and owned a lean grey husky with bright blue eyes named Jamie. I found no evidence of a previous girlfriend, though people did tend to delete those kind of cuddly photos. From what I gathered, Jake didn't seem to be lying about not liking people, plural. Most of his pictures were of him with his dog or of him bruising other guys' faces in the ring while they sprayed blood and spit; all the violent ones were posted by his dad, who added braggadocious comments detailing the final score of each fight.

"Well, why didn't you tell me you were kind of amazing? Undefeated?"

He shrugged. "I'm not amazing. I just have a steel jaw."

"What?"

"Winners have steel jaws; losers have glass jaws. It's genetics."

"So..." I teased. "How do I find out what kind of jaw I have? Would they swab my cheek and do a DNA test to check for the steel-jaw gene or something?"

"Nah." He shook his head. "You'd just have to get

punched in the face and see what happened."

"That doesn't sound fun."

"It's not. Punching's the fun part."

Tatum appeared through the glass door with a drink in each hand. "Here, I put extra coke in yours." She handed me a cup.

Translation: "I made it with the normal rum-to-coke ratio." I was about to say, "Thank you," but she wrapped her arm around my waist and hugged me tight.

With her booze-sloshing hand, she pointed ferociously at Jake. "Let me tell you something about Sawyer." I drew a deep breath and winced while she started her drunken monologue. "She's my best friend—took a black eye for me. All you boys are such pricks to her, so you better be nice or I'll kick your ass." She kept pointing at Jake, her beverage spilling all over her hand.

"And that's as sweet as she gets." I said, unwinding from her embrace. "We're going to the fire. Are you going to join us or find Ocean?"

"Oshie and I were going to play quarters. Wanna?"

"No, but text me when you're puking." She tried to shove me, but my static weight was enough to make her stumble backward. I turned to Jake. "Remind me to check on her in an hour. I don't trust 'Oshie.'"

"She's pleasant."

"Right?"

"You took a black eye for her?"

We started down the porch steps. "I mean, technically, yeah. I'm her back-spot. She landed wrong at practice this summer and elbowed me in the face."

I handed him my drink so I could unfold the last available camping chair and add it to the circle around the fire. "You can take this." I offered the seat to him. He ignored me, and moved to sit on the ground in front of the chair. I stepped around him, slipping my legs behind his back.

I hugged myself, trying to warm up and forget everything Tatum blurted out. *My deal with the devil.* Shit. What if Travis told Jake? Or showed him? I hadn't held up my end, so why would Travis hold up his? I leaned to Jake's ear. "Hey, if Travis ever tries to send you anything—"

"Like a video?" He rested his shoulders against my knees.

I froze. Bile crept up my throat. "Did you watch—"

"Of course not."

I let my breath go. "It's not something I wanted—"

"You don't need to explain."

"Thank you," I breathed. Of course, he could have been lying. I'd never know. But if he did see it, it hadn't changed anything. And it could have changed *everything.*

Wait. Who else had Travis sent it to?

Jake turned his head to me and whispered, "Oh, I told him I'd paralyze him if I found out—and I *would* find out—he sent it to anyone else."

I took another gulp of my drink to calm the tremors in my fingers. Was I afraid of the right guy? "Paralyze? That's specific."

"Killing him would be too quick, don't you think?"

"Why, though? You don't even know me."

He glanced at me again. "But I'm going to." He stated it like a fact, like it was inevitable. I wasn't sure I liked that. There wasn't anything to know about me that wasn't stained somehow, muddied and dirty and impossible to clean. If he was going to know me, he'd eventually learn what I did to Simone, with Travis, with those other guys. Maybe he already did.

"But you've heard about me, right?"

He shifted to rest his arm across my thighs. "Yeah, I've heard some things."

"Go ahead. I can take it." I winked.

"All right. I heard you're the best tumbler on the cheer squad. That you actually did a standing back tuck at your tryout. Someone said you're the only sophomore in AP Calculus and I should go to you if I need any math help—thanks for the offer, by the way."

I chuckled nervously. "Anytime."

"A couple of guys told me you can out-drink them, shot for shot."

"Christian and Hunter? Total lightweights."

"Yeah, those guys," he said, laughing.

"Come on, Jake. What'd they really say?"

He stared ahead at the grass and took a deep breath. "That you're bi." He was quick to add, "Which doesn't bother me, by the—"

I shook my head. "It's not true. I like guys. Well, I hate most of them, but you know."

He smiled, but then whispered, "That you have every STD except HIV."

"It was nice of them to spare me that at least."

"That you had sex with the entire basketball team in one night."

"Varsity or JV?"

"Varsity, I want to say."

"In their dreams."

"That your dad is in prison. Child molester, I think

they—"

"*Fuckers*," I hissed. I scrubbed my fingers over my forehead.

"Yeah, I figured that one wasn't true either."

"No. My dad is definitely *not* in prison."

"Told ya I'd get to know you."

"You don't care you're hanging out with the school slut? That people will see you with—"

"You're not a slut," he interrupted.

"How do you know?"

"Because guys are dicks who lie about getting laid, and girls talk shit when they're jealous of girls like you."

"Envious."

"What?"

"Envious is the correct word for what you're suggesting. Jealousy implies a prior claim, like ownership or a relationship. Envious means wanting what someone else has but having no right to it."

"Are you correcting my grammar?"

"No, your semantics."

"*Semantics?* Are you serious?"

"And no one's envious of me." Or at least, they shouldn't be.

He shook his head. "You're an idiot."

I pushed his arm off my thighs. "You're an ass."

"Yep," he said with a nod. I pressed my lips together to keep from smiling at the pride he found in his flawed personality. Wrapping his arms around his bent knees, he stared at me, like he was gathering information for his next move. I held my ground—no smiling—though barely. After a long minute, he finally said, "You're cold."

I glanced down at my hands, which were a pale shade

of violet and reflexively quivering against each other to get warm. My body flinched when Jake took them between his, pressing them together and then making a hollow between his palms. He brought our hands to his lips and exhaled softly into the space between his thumbs, creating a small cave of warmth for my fingers. I swallowed past my suddenly dry throat at the cozy shivers racing up my arms.

Jake's dark eyes raised to mine, making me suddenly aware of the terror that was probably plain on my face. Parted lips, wide eyes, and my breath that had halted some time ago. Why was he touching me? What did he want from me?

Why did I feel *good* when he touched me?

It wasn't supposed to feel good, right? I shouldn't like the feel of his skin on mine. Men only touched to hurt. I shouldn't want that.

But when he said, "You might be warmer if we sat together," I nodded and stood, moving so he could take my chair, so I could curl up in his lap.

Huddling my arms against my chest, I rested my head on his shoulder. My eyes shut cautiously so I could take in the scent of his skin. He wrapped his coat over my back before relaxing his cheek into my hair. I kept my eyes closed, half from fear, half from the desperate need to feel what it was like to just be held.

I had felt nothing like it before.

October 2014

"You're not going to get punched in the face so many times you're going to turn into a dick like the football players, right?" I leaned my back against Jake's passenger window as he drove, curling my knees close to my chest.

"I'm a little insulted." He tickled my knee until I kicked at him. "How crappy of a boxer do you think I am?" He pulled the car into the driveway of my little blue house on Third Street, which was dark and empty with the curtains drawn.

"Thank God we lost." I shrugged off the Carhartt jacket he'd made me wear over my cheer uniform. Not that I wasn't grateful; I was frozen from the inside out after that game. "I'm so over football season."

"No, keep it. You know I have another one at home." I hid my smile as I pushed my arms back through it. I was now a girl with a boyfriend—a boyfriend who gave me his jacket, beat up an asshole for me, and did cute things like kiss me on the cheek and text me until he fell asleep each night. And he'd never brought up Travis again. Well,

26

except once.

We'd been together only a couple of weeks when Jake caught me tracing over the seven-shaped scar on my scalp in my sleep: my fingertips meeting at the vertex of the jagged pink tissue, sliding apart, and then together again—middle finger over the horizontal line, index over the vertical. It was this weird self-soothing habit I started after the stitches dissolved, like how kids sucked their thumbs or fingered a blankie. He took a picture of me the first time he saw it. Actually, it was a selfie of me slouched against him on the couch. My head was on his chest, late-night television reflecting blue off my eyelids, my hand in my hair like a monkey hunting down a rogue louse. The snapping effect on his phone had startled me awake and into a Pavlovian panic, where I'd promptly ripped his phone from his hands. "What are you doing?"

"Sorry, I didn't mean to wake you up. But look how cute you are." He pointed to the screen. "You twist your fingers through your hair when you sleep."

Monkey lice? How was that cute?

I tapped the little trash icon on his phone. "Don't ever take pictures of me, okay?"

"What? Ever?"

Crap. I'd embarrassed him. Poor guy. It wasn't his fault. "I'm sorry, Jake." I gave him his phone and nuzzled back into him. "I just don't take pictures."

"Why not? You're beautiful." He took a wave of my hair, then played with it between his fingers and thumb.

"It's nothing. Just..." I yawned. "Don't, okay? Please."

He leaned his head against the couch. I was almost asleep again when he whispered, "Travis?"

My eyes shot open, and nausea swirled in my gut.

A lifetime had passed in the days since I'd met Jake. The Sawyer from before was dead, buried deep, all her demons with her. Travis would not haunt me—would not haunt *us*. I sighed out, "Something like that." Those three words ended the conversation. As far as I was concerned, we'd never have to talk about it again.

Now, as I was about to get out of his car, I said, "Thanks for the ride. I can't do another bus ride with the football team."

"I don't blame you."

I pulled the door handle, feeling the rush of cool air through the crack in the door. "Do you want to come in and watch a movie or something?"

He studied the clock on the radio glowing blue in the darkness. It was eleven, and I could tell by the way he tilted his head he was calculating if his parents would buy that it took him longer than that to get home from the game. I didn't have that problem with my mom. She was working a twelve at the hospital tonight. He could stay until seven in the morning, and she would never know.

"Yeah," he said. Jake reached down to the lever to pop the trunk before getting out. He went to retrieve my duffel as I headed to the front door.

Inside the house was just as chilly as outside. I flipped on the lamp by the fireplace. When I knelt to ignite the flame with the gas switch, it roared to life, an instant fire. I stood and turned around when I heard the front door shut.

"How are your lips still purple?" Jake dropped my bag by the door. He strode toward me to warm them before I had a chance to reply. His rough fingers gripped my waist, rolling my hips and then chest against him. Then he pulled away. He *always* did that. Never any more. It drove me insane. I hadn't known guys had the self-control to tease, but Jake did. I couldn't take it anymore.

I ran my hands down his chest. "I'm going to change." I started toward my door. "Netflix is on the TV if you want to find something."

In my room, I stripped off the clingy navy polyester: shell, spandex undershirt, skirt, briefs, sports bra. The panties I could live with. My goose bumps cast shadows on my skin in the moonlight, so I pulled Jake's coat around my shoulders. I dug through my nightstand drawer for a condom. Setting it by the lamp, I glanced around. Everything was ready.

Except me. My hands trembled when I reached for the doorknob. I was just cold. That had to be why. I had done this a thousand times in my fifteen years. I knew what I was doing. I wasn't nervous. That'd be stupid.

I took a weak breath. Jake's scent lingering in his coat made me unravel from the inside—a rope too flimsy to hold my hands taut, to stop the shaking. Shit. I *was* nervous.

I opened the door to make it creak, so I wouldn't have an exit strategy. I *was* going through with this. What? Was I supposed to only have sex forced on me? Hell no.

Fuck you, Pastor *Jeff. And Travis. And his asshole friends.*

The glow of the fire flickered over Jake's face from his spot on the couch. His eyes scanned me as soon as I came into sight. "Hey?" The greeting was phrased more as a question, his trademark crooked smile flashing as his gaze ran down my bare legs.

"Hey," I whispered, and then bit my lip. Crap. What if he wasn't a tease? What if he just didn't want me? I hadn't thought this through. Maybe I could say, *Just kidding! I forgot my shirt and pants. Be right back.*

Before I could move, he set down the remote and slowly stood. He appeared cautious...like he thought any sudden movement would send me running.

A wave of relief rushed over me. Jake liked this idea. When he got close enough, he touched my cheek, his other hand reaching for mine. "Are you sure?"

I nodded, hoping I would be.

His fingers traced back and forth from my ear to my chin as he leaned in to kiss me. His hand slid under the jacket to my naked chest, brushing down my sternum and over my navel. His touch made me flinch. Sucking in my breath, I did everything in my power to kill the instinct to push him off and run like hell when he continued the caress to my hips and butt before starting to inch his way under the hem of my panties.

He pressed me against the wall, and I lifted my arms to twist my fingers through his hair. His mouth sent shivers down my neck.

I crept back when I felt him against my breasts, wishing I could escape into the drywall behind me. Every breath was panicked, too shallow to keep my vision crisp or my head clear.

You're fine. Pull it together!

His hands moved under my thighs, picking me up. I gripped my legs around his waist, and he carried me to my room. Each step he took closer to my bed made me dizzy, sick. The familiar dread that had filled this room for two years flooded me. I watched Jake as he lowered me to the mattress, reassuring myself of who I was with, so I could remember this time was my choice. This would be different—would *feel* different. It had to. Right?

Jake stood by the bed and took off his shirt. Even as the clouds obstructed the moonlight, I could see the outline of every muscle in his shoulders and torso. Even the thin scar over his right pec glowed with a muted sheen in the grey light. I sat up to taste his skin, to unzip his jeans, to feel the warmth beneath his boxers. He stepped out of them, then gently pushed me to the mattress. As he started to pull my panties down, his lips followed, pressing against my waist, hips, and then between my thighs as he did. I closed my eyes and swallowed hard, pretending this was okay, that I would be okay. He climbed onto the bed, his body crawling over mine. My heart scrambled faster with each inch he erased between us.

"Are you still cold?" Jake whispered, tugging on the coat I still wore.

"Not really." I laughed, or tried to, but it came out shaky and nervous when he peeled it from my arms.

"Just in case..." He threw the covers back, and we slipped under them. I laid on my pillow, goose bumps rising on my skin when his mouth found my ear. His fingers laced through mine, raising them to the mattress just above my head. He was hard between my thighs, the weight of his legs and chest on top of me. When I tried to take a breath, I realized I was pinned down.

Fear pulsed through me—that primal kind that made me fight before I could think. I pulled my face away and into the pillow, struggling against his hands, pushing and twisting. He was so much stronger than I was. Even though a hundred ways to escape flashed through my mind, I couldn't have unless he let me. And he wouldn't. Why would he? He was a man, and that was what men did. I was such an idiot. Had I actually willingly put myself in this position? I had, and there was no one to blame but myself. Squeezing my eyes shut, I braced for the inevitable.

"Sawyer, what's wrong?" His voice was breathy and foreign. Concerned. He was motionless, just staring down at me.

I clenched my hands into fists, but then released them. They were empty. Jake had untangled our fingers and straightened his arms, giving me room to breathe, to move, to go. My chest was heaving; his was, too. His dark eyes were wide as he waited for me to respond, a ribbon of dishwater hair blocking part of his view. "Yeah," I exhaled. "I'm fine."

My hand drifted over the nightstand until I found the condom. I tore it open. As I reached down to roll it on Jake, he grabbed my wrist. "Stop."

"Why?"

"Sawyer, you're shaking."

"So," I said, struggling to free my arm from his grasp.

"Are you sure you're okay?"

I didn't meet his eyes or answer, so he finally gave up, releasing my arm so I could finish. Once I had, I eased him into me.

He was slow at first, like he was afraid I'd break if he did what he wanted. I wouldn't break. Maybe I'd bleed or tear or bruise, but I'd never break. I hadn't yet.

"Is this okay?" he breathed in my ear as his body

moved forward and back over mine.

Closing my eyes, I forced out, "Yeah," hoping he'd just finish fast.

He did, his throbbing and gasping churning my stomach until I thought I'd vomit. That was normal though, right? I *didn't* puke and nothing hurt, so I'd call it a win, a successful re-losing of my virginity.

I was still trying to rein in the stomach acid gurgling up when he pulled the covers around me. He raked his fingers through my hair, brushing his lips against my temple. Why was he still touching me if he didn't have to anymore? I thought guys weren't into cuddling. Whatever he wanted, I guessed.

Laying my head on his chest, I listened to the beating of his heart as it slowed. I focused on each *thump-thump* as if it were some Morse code that would help me figure this guy out.

Thump-thump: He didn't hurt me.

Thump-thump: He hadn't hurt me.

Thump-thump: Maybe he wouldn't hurt me.

Curious, I asked, "Jake?"

"Yeah?" he answered on a sigh, still working to catch his breath.

"Had you ever had sex before?"

He held me tighter and kissed my forehead. "No. Had you?" It was sweet he asked even though he knew my reputation.

I sucked in my breath before murmuring, "Yeah." I was quick to add, "But you shouldn't be jealous or anything. It's not like I had a choice."

He rolled me away from him, confusion and then shock creeping over his face as he searched my eyes.

"What?"

"I don't like to talk—"

"Who?" Even in the dim light, I saw his eyes darken. It was a color I hadn't seen on him before, like charred wood or cooling lava. Rage.

"It's okay. He's in prison," I rushed to answer. It wasn't totally a lie. Jeff was in prison. Jake appeared capable of killing the others if he knew.

He pulled me into his chest. "Sawyer, I'm sorry. I shouldn't have—"

I touched three fingers to his lips. "No. I wanted to."

"Why didn't you tell me?"

"I don't know." I whispered the lie, hoping he'd buy it.

I nuzzled into his chest, searching for his heartbeat again. His calloused hand stroking my hair, I fell asleep.

I woke early the next morning, Jake's coat beside me and a note on top. Running my hand over my eyes to clear the blur, I read what he had scribbled in the dark.

Sawyer, I hated leaving without saying goodbye, but I knew you were out cold when you started doing your hair twisting thing. I couldn't stop thinking about what you told me. I know there's nothing I can say or do to make it better, but I'm not going to let it happen to you again. I'll pick you up at 11 tomorrow. Wear something you can get sweaty in. —Jake

Sweaty? *Um, no thank you.*

"OKAY," JAKE STARTED AS WE stepped into his garage. I was exhausted just looking at the boxing equipment in his home gym. "First, let's run a quick mile to warm up."

A quick mile? I cackled. "Look, friend, I'm a too-tall ballerina/gymnast turned cheerleader. What do all those activities have in common?"

"I don't know. Glitter? Subjective scoring? Twirling of some kind?"

I shot a glare his way. "Glitter? Excuse me?"

"Whatever. General girliness."

"There are guys in *all* of those sports."

"Straight guys?"

"Smart straight guys. You know those back spots get to grab the fliers' butts for libs, right?"

He smirked and lifted his fingers from his chin. "I honestly didn't understand a word you just said."

"Whatever. I am not *that* girly."

"Sawyer, there's a freaking bow in your hair."

Patting my hand over the base of my ponytail, I felt a half-inch satin ribbon. Damn it. I must have went into autopilot this morning. In my defense, there was no glitter anywhere near me. And the bow was blue—hella butch.

"What I'm trying to say is that none of them require running."

"Well, today is your first day as a fighter, so you're going to run."

I rolled my eyes, but I followed him down the driveway into the overcast morning. Forty-five seconds later, my lungs were chafing against the cold, humid air as I tried to keep up with his pace. Between pained breaths, I muttered any Spanish expletive that came to mind, making sure Jake knew each was directed at him. Eventually, I got into a rhythm that kept the side stitch plaguing me at bay. His street was finally back in sight.

Warm relief washed over me.

Then Jake said, "Let's go around the block one more time."

Oh, hell no. I pushed his back with both hands, partly because I was too winded to shout my objection, but more so because I wanted to hurl him to the ground for even thinking of making me run more. I stumbled into a sloppy jog before stopping. Bracing my hands against my knees, I watched black spots float over the sidewalk under me.

Jake was laughing. "Are you pissed enough to hit me for real now?"

I managed to tilt my face to see his while hyperventilating and nodded.

"Prove it." He tilted his head toward the garage.

I tried to kick his ass, I really did. In my mind, I was this sexy female version of Rocky, jabbing the punch mitts with a ferocity even Jake couldn't compete with. In reality, I probably looked like a clumsy kitten batting at a string. Wavy strands fell out of my ponytail and stuck to the sweat on my neck. My skin was well past girly glistening, covered in swollen beads of perspiration—after only fifteen minutes of training. I flopped backward onto the mat.

Jake dropped his knees to either side of my hips where I laid on the floor. My chest was surging as I tried to breathe. "My lesson's done, right?" I panted.

"Just about." He smiled and pressed his hands into the mat above my shoulders.

"I'm not going to be able to defend myself if you kill me."

"Okay, one more thing and we can be done. Here's

the most crucial rule of self-defense. Are you listening?"

I glowered and nodded, still taking short breaths.

"Go for the groin."

My eyebrows scrunched together.

"Seriously," Jake added. "There's *never* any shame in hitting below the belt. If someone's going to attack my gorgeous girlfriend, they don't deserve to have children."

"So, here?" I moved my hand over his shorts.

"Yeah." He laughed. "But we're not going to practice on me."

"How am I supposed to learn?"

He pushed my hand away, then leaned down for a sweaty kiss. As he pulled away, he said, "We should do this every Saturday if you really want to learn."

"Make out in the garage?" I winked. "I'm down, but I refuse to run more than half a mile."

"A mile."

"Three-quarters."

"Done."

December 2014

*J*AKE GOT A MOTORCYCLE. AS IF HE WASN'T HOT
enough.

He turned seventeen a month before my sixteenth
birthday, so he was my ride everywhere. Maybe his
parents were sick of him borrowing their Camry seven
days a week to see me, or maybe this deal had long been
established. Either way, a week before his December
birthday, his dad took him used car shopping. Jake's
parents kicked in two grand, and the rest came from what
he had saved up from doing yard work for neighbors for
years. In some flurry of testosterone and male bonding,
Jake and his dad purchased a 2005 Honda street bike
from a guy who lived south of the harbor.

I heard the *vroom* coming up Third while I was in
my garage. Like a good mechanic's daughter, I was
changing the oil in my mom's car. Okay, fine. Maybe I
was buttering her up, so she'd hand it down to me. When
I heard the engine cut in my driveway, I inched out from
beneath the car. I sat up in time to see him take off his
helmet, flick his hair out of his eyes, and then comb his

fingers back through it like a damn movie star.

"*Holy shit,*" I said under my breath.

He climbed off the bike. "What do you think?"

What did I think? I wasn't thinking about anything but taking off all his clothes—except for that collarless leather jacket.

Ah, crap. I did *not* just think that. Did not just become one of those girls who was infatuated with her boyfriend, who couldn't keep her hands off him, who felt like the sun wouldn't rise if he left her. But there I was, fifteen feet too far from him, unable to restrain myself from closing the space between us.

Had this been Jake's plan all along? Did I really get sucked into his nice-guy, *let's take it slow* act? I had been fine two months ago when he had suggested we start over, but now I wondered how I existed before him.

So nauseating.

"Really, Sawyer?" Jake hissed with his face inches from mine. This was our third time having sex, a few days after that last football game.

"What?" I snapped. Was it over yet? I felt him pull out of me, and my stomach settled. Three times and I only threw up once, and it wasn't even on him. I was killing it.

He sat back. "I can tell you don't like having sex with me."

I scooted to lean my back against the headboard, pulling the blanket with me. "What are you talking about?" Had he seen me wince every time his fingers slid under my clothes? Maybe he tried to tell me something, and I hadn't answered because I wasn't in my body. How would I even begin to explain...

Oh, shit. It was the puking last time. He'd heard. He must have.

I couldn't help it. It was some weird mix of disgust and motion sickness. Not disgust with Jake. Just disgust with any sound or sensation I registered.

Don't cry. Don't cry, this tiny voice repeated in my head when Jake pressed into me. *He doesn't like it when you cry.* But holding in those tears Sunday night had made my head pound and my muscles itch, taunting me to scratch them, to do anything to alleviate the urge to score my skin and scrub my hair until it was like it had all never happened. I couldn't cry, so my body purged itself of sex the only way it could.

But I kept volunteering for this. Guys left girls who didn't put out. And if Jake was gone, I'd be Travis's again, so I'd volunteer for this as many times as I needed to.

"It's okay," he said. Furrowing my eyebrows, I watched his hand stroke my thigh in a peculiarly asexual way. "I know it's not, you know, easy for you."

"It's fine." *Please don't make me talk about this. Please don't make me talk about this.* We hadn't talked about the abuse. I wasn't eager to share details or discuss it at all. With anyone. Ever. Especially not naked in bed with my boyfriend.

"Don't be mad, okay?"

Why did people say that? Those were the four most infuriating words.

"I read a couple of articles online about having sex after, you know, being—"

I glared at him during the uncomfortable pause. *Say*

it, asshole.

"—raped."

"What?" I seethed through gritted teeth. As if sex wasn't humiliating enough?

"And, well, basically, they said...um...that..."

I watched him sputter for a second before grabbing the pillow on my right and throwing it at him. Next, I clutched the one below it and beat his head with it.

"What?" I shouted. "I'm so fucked-up that you have to research how to have sex with me?" I smacked him again and again with the down pillow. "Go ahead! Tell me how I'm supposed to do it!"

He ripped it from my grip, and then took my face in his hands. His lips opened mine, drawing my lower lip with him as he pulled away. "No," he breathed against my skin. "I'm not having sex with you again. Definitely not tonight." He slid the condom off and threw it on the floor. Wow, so he just quit without coming? Guys could do that?

My voice caught in my throat, thick with hurt. Not again? What did that mean? Was he dumping me? *No, no, no, no.* "What? I'm sorry. I want to—"

"Lay back." His voice was a tender whisper, his hands still on my face.

A terrified pounding started in my chest. What was he going to do to me? I shook my head.

"Do you trust me?" he asked, sweeping my dark hair behind my shoulders.

I studied his chocolate eyes as they pleaded with mine. Finally, I forced out a quiet, "I don't know."

Letting out a defeated breath, he nodded.

My hand grazed his chest. I bit my bottom lip to try

to hide the desperation in my voice. "I can try."

A crooked smile flickered across his lips when I rolled my back down to the mattress. Jake slipped the pillow I hit him with under my head, then laid down on his side next to me. The sensation of his bare skin against mine pricked each of my nerves, setting my skin on fire with confused desire while leaving my muscles frozen with fear. My body was rigid next to his as I fought to keep it in place.

"Tell me when to stop," he said. His hard fingertips grazed the underside of my wrist, stroking it up and down, hand to elbow, elbow to hand, and back again. They did the same to my upper arm: back and forth from elbow to shoulder. Then my shoulder to earlobe. "This okay?"

I was warm. Warm and shivering somehow, slowly easing at his touch. "Yeah, I'm okay."

His lips pressed to my throat, soft on their way to my ear. "Is this okay?" he breathed.

I closed my eyes to inhale the scent of his skin. "Yes."

I was all too aware of his hand skimming over my collarbone, slowing at my breasts. My heart raced like it was trying to escape my body. I grabbed his wrist and jerked it away. After a few cutting breaths, I glanced up at Jake. His face was understanding, or at least pretending to be. Noticing my fingernails digging into his wrist, I gasped. "Sorry." I let go, too embarrassed to look at him.

He let out a light laugh, one that sounded as nervous as I was. "Don't apologize." He skipped down to my abdomen, his fingers drawing wide circles around my navel piercing.

"Umm..." I shook my head. "I'm sorry."

He flicked my arm. "Stop that."

I flinched away. "Ow!"

He smirked. "I said no apologizing." His hand moved lower.

My muscles seized up. *Please don't. Please stop. Please!*

"I'm guessing this is out, too?"

I tried to sound calm. "Right."

He lifted his hand from my hips. "Okay. Turn over."

I hugged the pillow into my chest as I rolled onto my stomach. Jake's hands brushed my long hair off my back. He kneaded into my shoulders and neck. I felt just his hands, never the weight of his body pinning me to the bed. My eyes closed as his calloused fingers pressed into my tight traps, the fibers of which slowly loosened.

His touch glided down my back to my thighs, his skin blazing a trail of sparks down my spine. That instinctive urge to bolt left me when I realized Jake would stop each time my muscles tensed, each time I was afraid. After a few minutes, he drew the covers over us and wrapped his arms around me. I relaxed into him.

"Now what?" I whispered into his chest.

"Whatever you want."

My hand crept down his torso, following the thin trail of hair below his navel. He inhaled sharply. "It's okay. You don't—"

I covered his mouth with mine, feeling inside his lip with my tongue. "You said whatever I want," I exhaled in his ear before pulling the skin of his neck gently between my lips. I wanted him to feel what I couldn't. Wanted him to know what that fifteen minutes of touch without pressure, expectation, or force meant to me. I wanted him to feel wanted. Because maybe I could eventually want him, really want him.

We pushed a little further each time. First my waist, then my breasts. First his hands, then his mouth. After a couple of weeks, I didn't have to tell him more than occasionally when something was too much. He heard my breath cut out or saw my fists clench and would stop.

I hadn't known any guy could have that kind of patience, that kind of discipline. And I wasn't sure why Jake was doing this for me. He could have dumped me after I took his virginity, left me for someone less complicated. Instead, he was spending most of his nights in bed with me—*not* getting laid. And I knew it wasn't okay, that it wasn't fair to him. But life had been so damn unfair to me, had me thirsting for something sweet and cool, something that could keep me alive, but had surrounded me with only oceans of undrinkable salt water. I couldn't say no when Jake offered me a sip of what I needed. Then another and another. Even though it felt like stealing, soaking up all that clear water when all I could offer him was my useless ocean of salt and sand, I was too deprived to abstain.

Which was probably why everything changed that night in December. His lips and tongue were hot between my legs. For the first time, I wasn't scared or nauseous. I was with Jake. He didn't stop, and I couldn't ask him to. And maybe I should have expected it, but it still struck me like lightning when warmth rose from his mouth and spread to my thighs, making them quiver. I gasped for air and gripped the sheets as that intense feeling flooded through me, causing my toes to curl and my fingertips to hum. The sounds that escaped my mouth and the stiff arch in my spine exposed me to him completely. When it ended, I was mortified. That had never happened before. Sure, I'd given more than my fair share of orgasms, but I hadn't had one in front of anyone.

Of course, I'd had plenty alone, my first when I was only ten. Jeff was in prison, but my body still expected to be fondled and entered. It was invaded by heat at every touch. When my gymnastics coach would spot me or correct my waist or shoulders, the sensation through my hips was sharp and warm. The same happened when my mom hugged me, or a friend wrapped her arm around my back for a photo. One night in the shower, I ran my hand down my swollen labia, soap sudsing between my fingers. My fingertips spread and softened and pressed and ventured inward until that sharpness spiked at their touch.

I was in the shower so long trying the textures of bar soap, shampoo, and conditioner, feeling what it was to be inside myself, that the water was running cold against my back when I finally shook and panted with relief. I collapsed weak and sick in the tub under the cold rain, waiting for the punishment for my pleasure. After all, I had learned by then that what Jeff did with us was bad, though no one ever told us so because no one ever knew. But I was a smart girl; I connected the dots.

At church, they said sex was bad, but Jeff said I needed to obey and have sex with him to be good. He said heaven and hell were between my legs. Heaven if I let him in. Hell if I didn't. He did everything to get me into heaven. Still, my unwilling heart bound me for hell. But then, Jeff was in prison, and the church said he was bad. Now nothing but hell lived between my legs. So, I huddled there, cold in the water but warm and whole inside, warm and whole because I had done something bad. I felt no shame. I couldn't have if I tried. It felt too good to stop, and I would burn in hell anyway because of what Jeff did—now because of what I did—so I'd be bad as many times as I wanted.

This time, though, I had been bad with Jake, really bad because it felt so good, so much better than it had without him, really bad because Jake saw and heard and knew just how good. It was one thing to know how much I loved sinning. It was another to revel in it with someone else.

I stared at the ceiling, the white bumps clouded by purple, while I fought to catch my breath and stifle the moaning still rising from my chest. I couldn't look at him after he had seen me naked from the inside out like that. Jake crawled to my side and tucked the covers around us.

"So—" I said without enough air. I took a second to catch my breath and tried again. "Do we get to have sex now?" Maybe seeing him the same way again would make me feel less like an idiot.

"Hell yeah." I heard the smile in his voice. I finally turned to see him on his back, his fingers combing through his straight hair. His dark cocoa irises met mine.

Nope. Too soon for eye contact. I buried my face under the covers.

"What are you doing?" He laughed.

I let out a long, muffled groan into the blankets. When he tried to pull the covers down, I fought against him and whined, "You're too cool for me to be around right now."

His voice was broken up by his laughter. "What the

does that mean? Are you embarrassed or something?"

I nodded under the covers.

"Sawyer..." He finally overpowered my grip on the comforter and stared straight into my wincing eyes. "That was hella hot."

"I don't believe you." I reached down for the blanket.

As I pulled it up to my neck, he caught my wrist. "Let me prove it then." He leaned in to kiss me and rolled me on top of him—a position he knew kept me from feeling trapped.

I pulled my face away. "Jake, I'm sorry. How did you do that? I must taste disgusting."

His tongue sliding along my nipple, he breathed, "Shut up. You taste amazing."

I eased onto him, trembling as he pushed into me. My eyes closed, and a gasp escaped my lips at the sensation rippling under my skin. *This* was what it was supposed to feel like to have a man inside me. Not pain, not a numbness to shut out, but *this*—this sort of safety and wholeness I hadn't known existed in any kind of touch.

Those rough hands skimmed my ribs. "Sawyer, you okay?"

I opened my eyes and lowered my face to his, my hair meeting the pillow before our skin touched. After guiding his lips open with mine, I whispered, "Perfect."

JAKE SHOWED UP WITH HIS motorcycle the next afternoon. I pulled him against me by the open zipper of his leather jacket and drew a deep kiss from his lips, like taking a first drag of a cigarette. "So..." I drawled with his arms still around the small of my back. "*This* is how your dad rewards you for not getting home until seven this morning?"

Apparently, I fell asleep right after Jake and I had sex, because the next things I remember were Jake's kiss on my cheek and his voice soft in my ear saying, "I'll be back in a few hours." I only managed to open my eyes long enough to smile at him and see dawn illuminating the clock on my wall, which read 6:45. Then I melted into the warmth from his body that remained in the sheets.

He laughed. "He told me as long as we use a condom every time and I'm respectful of you, it's fine."

My eyebrows furrowed. "What?"

"Oh, and that I swear not to tell Mom he said that to me."

I grunted a laugh. Jake's mom was a devout, though new, Christian, so she could never find out about our sleepovers.

"Also, he bought you an early Christmas present."

"*He* did?"

Jake pulled the bulky backpack from his around his shoulders. "He said, 'always use protection.'"

I took the black leather jacket and helmet from Jake. "He did *not* say that."

"It was awkward for me, too." He smirked.

I laughed. "I'm never going to be able to look him in the eyes again." I slipped each arm into the coat and pulled my hair out from under it. "I know you haven't lived here a whole year, but it rains. A lot." The fact it was overcast and not pouring right now was a fluke for a December afternoon.

He adjusted my jacket at the top of the zipper. "That

looks so sexy on you." Was he even listening to me?

I bit my lower lip. "What are you going to do when it rains? Or hails? Or the one day a year it snows?" I raised my eyebrows and gave him a little shove.

"Come on." He intertwined his fingers with mine and took a step toward the bike.

But I didn't want to go near it. And I didn't want to admit I was scared to. My mom had seen her fair share of accidents in the ER. She called motorcycles *donorcycles*. And I knew what it was like to watch someone bleed out in a crash. It wasn't a moment I was eager to relive, so I stalled. "Don't you need a special license for this?"

"Yeah, I'll get one. My dad knows all the cops since the fire station's right next door to them. They'll leave me alone." Damn this tiny shit town.

I pulled the helmet over my hair, and Jake faced me to buckle it under my jaw. "Does your mom know about this?"

"Dad and I are going for an 'ask for forgiveness, not for permission' thing. Are you done with your interrogation now?" He swung his leg over the bike. "Get on."

I wrapped my arms around his waist and closed my eyes when the engine roared to life. This was Jake. I could trust him. I did trust him. He'd keep me safe. He had so far.

I ducked behind him to dodge the misty air rushing at us on the coastal highway, my hands staying warm by stroking the skin under his shirt. The grey Pacific was ominous on our left. It was bound to rain. We were just out of city limits when it started.

February 2015

"WHAT THE HELL?" I SHOUTED TOWARD Michael, Jake's dad. The crowd was roaring, and Jake looked like shit. He staggered in the ring, half his face shimmering with blood. There was no way he'd be standing five seconds from now, and the round still had fifteen seconds left. Why wouldn't the ref just call it? "If this isn't time for a TKO, I don't know what is!"

"No, no," Michael said in that patronizing tone he always used with me. "He's got plenty of fight left in him. He's fine." Men and their sons and their stupid egos. I was about to point this out when Jake caught a second wind and knocked his opponent to the mat. He didn't get back up before the round ended. "Told ya." He winked at me.

Jake lifted his boxing gloves above his head in triumph, took two wobbly steps, and then collapsed. "Shit," I hissed, starting to push my way to the ring. I climbed through the ropes, onto the mat, and stroked Jake's dewy back. "Hey, babe, you're okay. You're okay." But he had blacked out, his face smearing red onto the mat. I pulled out my phone to call an ambulance. Why wasn't there one standing by like at our varsity football games? Stupid cheap fight. Michael went to roll him onto his back. I slapped his hand away. "Let the paramedics do that. Hi, I need an ambulance at—"

Michael glowered at me. "I'm a *firefighter*," he retorted before he continued to move his son. I rolled my eyes. As far as I was concerned, this was his fault, so he wasn't allowed to touch him.

Jake came to just before the ambulance arrived. I swept his sweat-saturated hair off his forehead. "Hey, Jake. How you feeling?"

"Sawyer." He smiled, his hand moving cautiously to cup my cheek. "You're so pretty."

"Oh, wow." I let out a hesitant laugh. "You musta got hit pretty hard."

His throat jumped with a labored swallow. "Did I win?"

"What do you think?" I smirked. My fingertips skimmed his supposedly steel jaw. I couldn't feel the bone through the swelling. Two paramedics stomped into the ring. "You're bleeding pretty bad, and your dad says you have a concussion. They're going to put you in an ambulance, okay?"

"Why?"

"Um...for the reasons I just listed."

"Do I have to?" Jake's voice was small, his chocolate eyes wide as he tried to sit up to prove he was fine.

"Hey, try not to move," the EMT said with his hand pushing Jake's shoulder back down.

"You're coming with me, right?" He grabbed my hand as the paramedics inspected him. Apparently, he was too injured to keep up the cocky fighter act all boxers did with an audience.

"Of course, babe."

"How's your pain?" the female paramedic asked Jake. "On a scale of one to ten?"

"Which part of me?"

"Which hurts the worst?"

"My head. It's like a seven." Then he squeezed his eyes shut. "Maybe an eight."

"Do you want something for it?"

Jake nodded slightly.

Once we were in the ambulance, she hooked up an IV bag. I patted his hand. "Hey, you're going to get some fun pain meds!"

He grunted, eyeing the needle in the paramedic's hand. "Uh, no." He cleared his throat and deepened his voice, "No, I'm fine." He tried to lift his head, but then grimaced.

I shoved his chest down. "Don't be stupid, Jake. This will make you feel better."

"I don't like needles," he whispered, moving his right hand to cover the vein in the crook of his left arm.

"Are you serious? Your face has like a pint of blood crusted on it, and you're afraid of a little needle?"

"Hold my hand," he whimpered when the paramedic pried his arm free from his right hand's grasp. I laughed and intertwined our fingers. What happened to my ass-kicking boyfriend? His grip on my hand relaxed when the morphine kicked in.

"Sawyer?"

I nodded and leaned toward his face.

"You look more Cuban than usual today."

"Thank you?"

"I think I should start calling you my Latin lover."

I bit my lip and shook my head. "Nope. Nope. Please, never ever call me that." Lover? Grossest. Word. Ever. Right up there with *semen* and *moist*. Disgusting.

"Why isn't your name Cuban if *you're* so Cuban?"

"My dad loved Mark Twain. I was doomed to be Sawyer if I was a boy or a girl." Of course, he knew this already, but the memory had apparently been knocked from his head.

He took a hard-earned breath, before letting it out. "Did you know you're beautiful?"

I smiled. "You are, too, Jake."

"I like your nose a lot." His finger poked at it. I tried my best not to flinch, harder not to laugh.

"I like your nose, too. Don't let anyone break it, okay?"

His eyes floated to the ceiling where they lingered. A few long blinks interrupted his view. I thought for sure he'd doze off, so I jumped when he yelled a panicked, "Sawyer!"

"What?"

"I haven't kissed you in so long! I can't even remember the last—"

"A couple of hours ago, Jake."

"But I can't remember."

I snickered at his puppy-dog eyes, but still took his lips between mine, the bottom one bleeding and swelling fast. His hand caressed the nape of my neck as he brought me closer. When I pulled away, I could still taste that rusty flavor on my tongue. "I love you," he whispered, his fingers tangled in my hair.

"Jake, you're so sweet, but maybe you should wait until you don't have a traumatic brain injury to say that. And until you aren't high."

"No." His expression turned intense. "I've known for months, since, like, the week after we got together. Remember? We were on the beach, and it was so cold. I'll never forget because you took your clothes off and had a bikini on under them, which was insane. You *planned* to swim. You got in the water and complained I wouldn't join you, like *I* was weird for being bundled up on the sand. When you were soaking wet, you ran to me and curled into a ball in my lap. I called you an idiot, and you said, 'Piss off,' then hugged me tighter and said, 'No, please don't. I'm freezing. Stay here.'" He tightened his fingers around mine.

How did he say so many coherent words in a row just now? I stared at his dark eyes—well, what I could see of them through the bruising. One was okay, but the other was swollen to a slit.

I leaned toward him to brush my lips over his fingers laced through mine. "I'm pretty sure I said fuck off. Piss off is so British."

"Fuck is a bad word, Sawyer."

I snickered, and his voice broke into a chuckle.

"That's the moment, though?"

He nodded.

"Interesting." I pursed my lips and searched the ceiling. "For me, it was right before Thanksgiving. We were doing homework on the floor in your room. Well, I was. You were asleep on your back in that army-green Henley you wear like every other day."

He interrupted with an affectionate, "I love that

shirt." Maybe he just loved everything on morphine. This was the worst time to be having this conversation.

I breathed a laugh. "I know. Anyway, I dropped my pencil and laid my head on your chest. And I just remember realizing I never wanted to be with anyone else. It was too late for me, you know? I was yours." His eyes softened as he listened, and not from the drugs. Ah, crap. So embarrassing. *Deny. Take it back.* "And I'm only telling you all this because you won't remember tomorrow."

Half his mouth curled into that crooked smile as he closed his eyes. "I'm always going to remember that."

Unfortunately, he did. Though he forgot the Latin lover thing, thank God.

We stayed overnight in the ER so they could make sure Jake hadn't sustained any brain damage, which was never what anybody wanted to have to wait to find out about their boyfriend. I woke up the next morning stiff from sleeping in a chair, with red indents on my forehead and cheek from having my face pressed against my arm for hours. I rubbed my eyes and checked my phone to find out the time. There was a group text from Michael to Jake and me.

I opened it to find a picture of us.

Michael: *Jake, I sent this to your mom to show you were okay. She said it was cute, and I should send it to you. Sending to Sawyer, too.*

The photo quality wasn't great; the lighting was dim and cool in the emergency room. Jake's forehead was bandaged, his eyes tinging black, his jaw uneven with inflammation. He was asleep. I was sitting beside his bed in a chair, leaning forward with my head resting on one bent arm on the thin mattress, my other hand in my wavy hair—monkey on a lice quest again. Jake's hand was over mine. I was asleep, too, obviously, or the photo would have never happened.

I saved the picture to my phone. One photo couldn't hurt.

July 2015

*T*HE KNOCK AT THE DOOR CAME A HALF-HOUR after my food arrived. It was like a blurry echo. Had it really happened? I took another swig of Corona Extra and kept my eyes on *A League of Their Own*, the only light I could endure in the living room. The closed curtains blocked the brightness of the summer day. Hopefully if someone was there, they would just go away.

The doorbell rang.

I pried myself out of my nest of pillows on the couch, wrapping my dad's loose flannel around my bare midriff. My half-full bottle accompanied me to the door. Through the sheer curtains, I saw his familiar silhouette.

"Hey, babe," I said after cracking open the door. Even squinting, I couldn't see Jake clearly. "God, it's so bright." Why did it have to be sunny today? It was overcast and dreary every other day. Could the weather not cooperate for once in this shit town? "Come inside." I ushered him in and tipped my beer to my lips as I made my way back to the couch.

"I've been texting you all morning. Where's your phone?"

Geez, Jake wasn't usually such a girl.

"Uh..." I did a cursory search of the room and ruffled my matted ponytail, "I think it died. Beer?"

Jake closed the door behind him. He eyed the living room, taking in the empty bottles and partially eaten order of fish and chips. "No, it's two in the afternoon. Are you *drunk*?"

"No, I'm pacing myself. I'll be hammered in six hours if you want to stick around." I tilted my beer toward him, half-singing, "You'll get lucky once I break out the tequila."

"Sawyer, what's wrong with you?"

"You're mad that you're going to get to have sex?"

"I'm not having sex with you when you're like this."

"Really?" I raised an eyebrow and dropped my flannel to the ground, standing before him in just my black bra and matching cheeky lace panties.

"What's the matter with you?"

After I swallowed the rest of my beer, I slammed the bottle on the coffee table. "It's July 17," I declared as I popped open another beer.

"So?"

I dropped to the couch and kicked my heels on the table, crossing one over the other. "Have I ever told you how my dad died?"

He sat next to me and rested his elbow on the back of the couch. "Car accident, right?"

"Rock slide on Highway 199. He swerved around it, but the roads were slick because it was raining. The car rolled down the bank toward the river until it hit a tree.

Landed upside down. Dad was pinned in his seat, his gut sliced open by his seatbelt. He just kept saying, 'Todo va estar bien, mi niña. Todo va estar bien,' as he bled to death. I hung upside down in my booster seat watching him die as he told me everything would be okay. Over and over: everything is going to be okay, everything is going to be okay, everything is going to be *fucking* okay."

"Sawyer." Jake rubbed a lock of my hair between his fingers. "Why didn't you tell me you were in the car?"

I just shook my head as I took another sip, the neck of the bottle between my middle and ring finger.

"It was today?"

I nodded. "Ten years ago."

"Then why isn't your mom here?"

I sat up and swiped the bottle from the table. "Do you know how long she waited to get remarried?" Before Jake could answer, I stood and added, "Eleven months." I circled the room as I guzzled the beer, the sting of the bubbles dulled by the drinks that came before it. "She couldn't even wait a full year."

"You had a stepdad?"

"*Have.*"

"Where is he?"

"Prison. Oh, excuse me, *Dad* is in prison," I said with feigned endearment. "They started the adoption paperwork the week after he proposed. Changed my name and everything. Sawyer Emilia Lindley."

"De la Cruz isn't your last name?"

I shook my head as I drank the last inch.

"We went out to dinner when the adoption was finalized. Some bullshit about celebrating, I don't know. My mom had a shift afterward, so Jeff tucked me in that night, insisted on it, like I was incapable of getting under blankets by myself. I mean, really? I was almost eight. He brought his laptop. I thought maybe I'd get to watch a show before bed. Sometimes Mom would let me do that. But Jeff pulled up this video of a man and a girl my age."

I gazed down at the bottle, regretting its emptiness. "I couldn't understand what they were doing, but I knew I didn't want to watch. Jeff said, 'This is what we get to do now. This is what daddies and daughters do. Isn't it beautiful?' Then he prayed with me," I cackled. "After, he pushed this kiss on my lips the way he kissed my mom and said, 'Our secret, baby girl.'"

"God, I'm so sorry." He stood and brushed his hand down my arm. "He's in jail now, right? He can't hurt you any—"

"*Bullshit*," I screamed and threw the bottle at the wall. It shattered, the remaining liquid splattering sticky drops on the matte-yellow paint.

"What?"

"If you're going to be an ass, you should just leave!" I pointed at the door and yelled, "Go! I didn't invite you over. I don't even know why you're here."

"No, I'm not leaving you like this. And where the hell is your mom?"

"In Portland with her sister. She's been leaving me home alone every July 17 since I was eleven."

"Why?"

"So I can get drunk and she can pretend it doesn't happen." I reached for another beer on the coffee table.

Jake clutched my wrist. "*I* can't pretend it's not happening."

"Sure you can." I struggled to try to get free, but his

hand grasped me tighter.

"Let go of the bottle."

"I told you to fuck off!"

"Let go, babe," he said softly as his body eased closer to mine.

"Please." I choked on tears that ambushed me. "I don't want you here."

He pulled me into him and whispered, "I don't care." His fingers slid down my wrist to the beer in my fist, forcing me to release it into his hand. I huddled into his chest and sobbed. "I'm here," he breathed, "I'm here." And somehow, that was enough.

I WOKE UP UNDER A thin blanket on the couch. A clear glass of water and a bottle of ibuprofen stood on the table in front of me. All the beer bottles and trash were gone, and the curtains were open to let in the bearable evening sun. I sat halfway up and swallowed four pills to quiet the pounding in my head. All the broken glass and beer had been cleaned up from my tantrum.

There was a warm hand on my calf. "How are you feeling?" Jake's eyes were soft like milk chocolate, his expression expectant and anxious as he searched my face.

I wiped a tear from my cheek. "Jake, I can't..." I shook my head. "I'm so sorry."

"Don't think about it."

"You stayed?"

"Well, yeah. I had never seen *A League of Their Own* before. Tom Hanks was phenomenal." He smirked, and I laughed even though it stabbed pain through forehead. "Can I ask you something?"

I nodded.

"Where was your dad buried?"

"Uh, he wasn't. He was cremated. We scattered his ashes in the water at Harris Beach."

He glanced up and around to think, then nodded. "Okay, that'll work."

AT THE LATE RED SUNSET, we walked down to the beach, following the fallen tree my dad and I used to read against. Barefoot, I led Jake by the hand to the water where we said goodbye to my father. I took off my sweatshirt, then my jean shorts, throwing both in the sand. Then I slipped my fingers under Jake's shirt and pulled it over his head.

He followed me until I was hip-deep in the water, until the surf was too loud for me to hear anything on the shore. I dove under a shimmering wave as it crashed in front of me. The icy water rolled through my long hair and down my spine, arching the small of my back and bending my knees. I came up for air, watching the purple sky burn fuchsia at the horizon. Jake's shaking hand slid over my waist. Poor guy had no fat to keep him warm. I had never seen him put more than his feet in the ocean.

He combed his fingers through his hair and said, "Beat you to the next wave." He took off into the water in front of me and dove into a cresting wave, shaking his hair out like a dog when he resurfaced. I swam out to meet him, wrapping my legs around his waist and pulling my body close to his. Cold skin to skin, we shivered and laughed through chattering teeth as the waves rocked us and occasionally tumbled us to the sand.

Wrapped together in a towel on the shore, we

watched the violet sky darken to black and the stars appear one by one. "This will be July 17 from now on," Jake whispered against my cheek.

"Every year?"

"Every year."

May 2016

"BABE, FOR THE THOUSANDTH TIME, NO," JAKE hissed, shutting the door to his bedroom and closing us inside. He stepped over a half-filled cardboard box on his way across the room, which was pretty much the only thing he had packed for his move in three weeks.

A few of his older friends had been renting a house for almost a year now, and they were counting on Jake to take the recently vacated third bedroom. Jake was eager to get out of his parents' house so he could have me sleep over without parking two blocks away and climbing out the window in the morning. His mom caught us naked and asleep in his bed a couple of months back. It could have been worse, especially as Jake didn't have a lock on his door. But a screaming match erupted between Jake and her with Michael caught in the crossfire. I was bad for Jake, according to his mom, dragging him down or corrupting him or something like that. It was hard to hear her exact words from Jake's room. All that to say it was time for him to have his own place.

"Jake, I need a legitimate reason." I slapped the back of one hand against the palm of the other. "And not, 'Oh, I'm Jake. All I do is box and brood and ride my motorcycle because I'm too cool for everything.'"

"First," he pointed my way, "that was a terrible impression of me."

"No. That was spot-on." It was. I did an excellent Jake.

"Second, I told you when we started dating that I'm just not into dances and all that high school shit."

"I asked for a legitimate reason."

He pulled his shirt over his head. "Uh, how about: *I don't want to go*," he said as he threw his shirt at the pile of laundry in the corner of his room.

"In the last year and a half, when have I *ever* asked you to go to a dance? I'm only asking this time because I *have* to go. I'm on court."

"Yeah, so you'll have a date built in." He raised an eyebrow, crossing his arms over his bare chest.

"Are you serious? Is that what this is about? You're jealous of Ryan?"

"Of course not."

My eyes fell to his chest. "Why aren't you wearing a shirt?"

"Sawyer, really? You haven't figured this out by now?"

I threw up my hands. "Figured what out?"

"I shouldn't tell you this, but..." He ran his hands over his face and groaned. "This is the only way I win fights with you."

I snorted. "By taking your clothes off? Don't flatter yourself, Jake. That would never work on me."

He raised an eyebrow.

Oh shit.

65

I flipped back through our recent arguments. They'd all ended without clothes, without resolution. *Oh, no, no, no, no. Oh, hell no.* How long had he been doing this? He reached for the button on his jeans.

"Damn it, Jake!" I picked up a shirt from his floor and threw it at him. "Leave your pants on!"

He crossed his arms again, letting the shirt bounce off him and fall to the floor. "I'm not going to prom."

I grabbed my backpack and sweater off the bed, then stomped toward the door. Jake acted all tough and obstinate, but I had him wrapped around my finger. In a battle of wills, mine always came out triumphant. Unless he got naked, apparently. Such a cheap move. And I fell for it every time?

But he didn't chase after me. Or cave to my cold shoulder. Twenty-four hours and no word—a record for us. No. I wouldn't be the one to reach out first. I would out-stubborn him. I had that unflappable Cuban determination that got my dad in this country even after he and his family got caught in the water and sent back. I could go days, weeks even.

Saturday afternoon, Tatum came over to my house to get ready for prom. She had a date who asked her all cute by decorating her car in the school parking lot. And I had an asshole of a boyfriend. She had just zipped up my little white dress when the doorbell rang. I answered, so she could do the cute walk-out-blushing thing for her date. I swung open the door. "Damn," I breathed.

Jake's dirty blonde hair was combed back, his hands behind his back, and he was wearing a tailored blue suit. "I know," he said with a smirk. "I look incredible."

I regained my composure and pissy attitude. With

one hand on the door and the other on the frame, I inched it closer around me. "What are you doing here?"

"Did you really think I wouldn't take you to prom?" he asked, like I was some kind of idiot.

"Uh, obviously, I thought that. You use your abs for evil. What else are you capable of?" I shifted to stand on one foot with my toes tapping the floor behind me. "And maybe someone else asked me."

"Oh, really? Since yesterday?"

"I'm in high demand. But..." I tilted my head and flipped my hair in front of my left shoulder. "I'll consider going with you if you grovel a little."

He brought his hand in front of him. In it was a corsage made of white roses.

I raised an eyebrow.

"Hardball, huh?"

"Oh, babe, you can do better than that."

Jake sighed. "Okay, this was going to be a surprise, but apparently, those are wasted on you." He reached for a plastic card in his pocket. "I got us an ocean-view room. It's technically a suite since I know how having a couch in your hotel room makes you feel fancy."

"Okay, getting better." I nodded.

"And I'll do that thing you like with—" I covered his mouth with my hand.

"Shut up!" I laughed. "I'll go to prom with you, just stop talking." I pulled my hand from his face.

"What? You don't want—" I kissed him this time.

I leaned back. "Please, shut up!"

LATER THAT NIGHT, I WOKE naked with my face

smashed against white hotel sheets. I turned my head to see Jake reclined beside me, watching highlights of the Trail Blazers losing on TV. My head hurt, my throat was dry, and my eyes were squinting against the warm light of the lamp beside him.

"Hey! Look who's awake." Jake smiled.

"Water," I groaned in a hoarse whisper.

He chuckled and handed me a glass from the nightstand, clearly already prepared for this. How drunk was I?

That tumbler of water wasn't close to enough, rolling over my parched throat without soaking in at all. It was then I realized how nauseous I was. "What time is it?"

"11:15."

"What?" I snickered, rolling on my side to hold my angry gut. "Did we even go to prom?"

Jake laughed, the roaring kind from his belly. "You don't remember?"

"I remember being there, but we must have left crazy early."

"Do you remember why?"

I shook my head, my messy curls falling around my face. Even without a mirror, I knew I was not cute, nothing like the girl he picked up at the beginning of the night.

He laughed again and rolled to his side, propping his head in his hand. "Kayla Moss was crowned queen, which, for whatever reason, made you want to cheer, then jump off the stage into my arms and start macking on me."

Oh, yeah! That memory was clear. "You don't understand. I was thrilled to be relieved of the pressure of prom queen duties." Whatever those were.

"Then you didn't want to dance. You just kept making out with me."

"In my defense, that was an undetermined but significant amount of tequila into the evening." Significant for sure. I was feeling it now.

"Then you started saying filthy things in my ear, though not as quietly as I would have hoped."

"Well, the music was loud."

"When I said you were way too loud, you switched to Spanish."

"What did you expect? You were in a blue suit!"

"Not for very long."

"Sounds about right."

"So, we've been here since 9:30."

"We were at prom for only an hour?"

"Yep." He smiled and took the empty glass from me. "Let me get you some more water."

I grabbed his arm. "Sorry I dragged you to prom and got ugly drunk."

"It's okay." He ran his hand down the back of my hair and kissed my forehead. "And you're never ugly."

February 2017

*T*HE ALTERNATING LAUGHTER AND OUTBURSTS of *Ooh!* were so loud I could hear them from the street in front of Jake's house. I swung open his front door to the stuffy odor of guy stink, beer, and pizza, enhanced by the old furnace cranking heat into the duplex. Jake, his roommates, Hunter, Sean, Christian, along with Hannah, the girl Christian was trying to sleep with, and Hunter's girlfriend whose name was so *unique* I never remembered it surrounded the coffee table playing *Scrawl*, the crass child of *Telephone* and *Pictionary*.

"Hey!" a few of them echoed off each other when they saw me. "It's Sawyer!"

"She's got the dirtiest mind here," Hunter said as he scooted down the couch. "Move over."

I stripped off my zip up. "It's boiling in here."

"Yeah, but it's getting you to take your clothes off," Christian said as he tipped his beer to me.

"Oh, sweetie, we could be in hell and it wouldn't be hot enough for Hannah to take her clothes off for you."

Everyone but Christian laughed as Jake stood and

wrapped his arm around my waist. I took a sip of the beer in his hand before pressing my chest into his. "Can we go to your room for a sec?"

There were a few shouts of "Ow, *ow*!" and "Get it, Jake!" as we climbed the stairs to his room. He closed the door behind us, and I started digging through his closet.

"What are you doing?"

"We're running away together." After pulling a rolling suitcase from the farthest corner of his closet, I dropped it on the bed and then opened his dresser drawer.

"Like for the weekend?"

"No, like for forever."

"What?"

"How do you feel about LA?"

"Umm…"

"Or Miami? You'll like it there. The gulf water is warm. And their sand is white. It's crazy. Though, you're not going to need all these Henleys—"

"I don't want to go anywhere I won't need my Henleys."

"Fine!" I plopped a pile of long sleeves into his suitcase. "Colorado then."

Jake grabbed my arm and turned me to face him. "Sawyer, you have three months left of school."

"I'll get my GED."

"No. You're not going to be a high school dropout with a 4.2 GPA."

I cleared out his sock and underwear drawer, then shoved the contents in the bag. "I'll enroll in Miami."

"Colorado."

"Sorry, right."

"Can you tell me what's going on?"

I didn't stop packing his clothes when I said, "Jeff's getting released early."

"What? Why?"

"I don't know, but he's coming home tomorrow. I'm sure as hell not going to be there when he does."

"He was only in jail what, nine years? That's not very long for raping you."

"That's not what he went to jail for."

"What? Why did—"

"Forget it." I snapped. "Do you need these?" I held up a second pair of boxing gloves.

"Yeah."

I threw them in the suitcase.

"Don't you have nationals in a few weeks?"

"Three weeks. I don't care."

Jake opened the pants drawer of his dresser. "What about OSU? Will it mess up your acceptance or your scholarships if you switch schools in the middle of your last semester?"

"Maybe, I don't know."

"Sawyer," he said as he took me by the shoulders and turned me to him. "I can't just let you throw away everything you worked for."

"Fine. I'll go by myself." Clutching his shirt in my fists, I kissed him hard and deep before pushing him away. "I love you. Take care of yourself, okay?"

"Sawyer!" His fingers wrapped around my hand and yanked me back. "You're not leaving me. Have you tried talking to your mom?"

"She doesn't believe me. She's never believed me."

"What?"

"I have to go."

"Move in with me." The words just spilled out of his mouth, but I knew he meant them.

I stared at his eyes a long time. They were warm but serious. "I can't afford rent. And I'm on my mom's cell plan and car insurance. She's not going to pay for all that if I move in with you." Jake and I held each other's gaze, silently realizing this would be the case in Colorado or Miami or Los Angeles—anywhere but home. I was trapped.

"Then just stay here every night. Sneak out or something." His rough hands ran up and down my arms. "I'm not going to let anything happen to you."

I rested my forehead against his and closed my eyes, doing everything in my power to believe him.

April 2017

A RIVER RAN DOWN THE STREET. JAKE'S motorcycle was hardly visible through the horizontal April shower. What a stupid purchase. How many times had I told him it rained here all the fucking time? Whatever. Just a few more months and we'd be out of here. Not that it rained less in Corvallis.

The puddles soaked through the canvas of my Converse until my socks were soggy. I didn't even bother with the hood of my Bruins pullover on my way to his door. My hair was still wet from my shower. And what the hell? Maybe the rain would wash off what the shower couldn't.

I forgot to knock. I just stood half in the rain and half under the dripping roof, the fat drops rolling off the edge onto my cold scalp, and stared at the blue door, the indents carved in it, the mud stains, the rust-spotted handle. Jake and I had an argument Friday, hadn't we? What was it about? It had to have been bad. I skipped his fight last night, and I never missed a fight.

I jumped backward when the door swung open.

"Sawyer, what's up?" It was Hunter. "Jake's upstairs. Hang on. Jake!" he shouted. "Your girlfriend's here!" He brushed past me, ducking into the rain.

Jake's bare feet tread gingerly down the stairs. He never moved quite right after a fight. His hand leaned against the doorframe as he took in the sight of me, continuing the silent treatment we had persisted in the last forty-eight hours. Messy hair fell over his battered face, only half of it combed back into place. His eye was purple and swollen, a wide but shallow cut in the bruise. I scanned his bare chest. His collarbone was inflamed, red from icing it probably. Grey sweatpants hugged his hips, hiding where his muscles tapered to a "V."

What was I thinking? How was I supposed to tell him this? This was a mistake. I turned around to the cement steps and headed toward my car.

"Wait!" His fingers gripped my arm, pressing the cold fabric into my tender skin. Air squeezed into my lungs to relieve the pain of his touch. "I miss you. Come inside." Jake took my hand and led me up the stairs to his room. "How long did you stand in the rain? You're dripping." His warm fingers crept under my sweatshirt. I swallowed hard as he pulled it over my head. He unbuttoned my jeans and slid them down to my ankles before digging through his dresser. I stepped out of my pants and shoes, then stood frozen in my bra and underwear, hugging myself.

"Here," he said as he pulled a grey thermal from his drawer. "Put this—" His eyes scanned my body, spotting the finger marks on my upper arm and the round bruise above my breast. That one was from an elbow, I thought. Jake took my arm in one hand and turned me around to find swelling under my shoulder blade. Another elbow. I remembered that. "What happened to you?"

I opened my mouth to answer, but then felt my throat burn. The bathroom was just across the hall, so all of my vomit made it into the toilet after I sprinted there. Jake closed us in and combed my hair back as I puked up the remaining alcohol from the night before. His hard fingertips grazed the scar on my scalp: that tender seven-shaped mark. With that touch, I was hanging upside down again in my booster seat, hearing my dad say, "Todo va estar bien, mi niña. Todo va estar bien." But he was wrong. It wasn't going to be okay. It never could be.

Hot tears rolled down my cheeks as I sat back against the tub, the cold surface a shock to my bare skin. I reached for the thermal at Jake's feet. "Jake, I'm so sorry. I should have gone to your fight," I said before pulling the shirt on.

"No, no. Don't worry about that." He squatted down in front of me. "What's going on?"

I pressed my palms into my eyes. "I should have been there. I should have been there."

"Babe, stop." He pulled my wrist away from my face. "It's okay."

"Did you win?"

He raised his shoulders as if to say, *obviously*. Right. Steel jaw. "Just tell me what happened."

"I went to that stupid party up South Bank. At Kyle's house."

"Okay?"

"Well, his parents came home, and I was too drunk to drive. They called my house, and Jeff answered."

"Shit," Jake hissed, brushing his hair back out of his

eyes.

"I'm sorry. I tried, Jake. I was *so* hammered. I just... I couldn't—" I pulled my knees to my chest. That rape was just vindictive. I knew Jeff didn't want me anymore now I was a D-cup with hips and an athletic body. I wasn't flat and helpless enough for his taste. But this was what I got for protesting his move home—proof he was in control, that he still owned me. Clearly, he did.

Jake's brown eyes darkened to that homicidal coal color. "Hang out in my room for a while, okay?" It wasn't a request. He had already scooped me up and was headed through the door.

"Wait? What are you going to do?"

He laid me on his bed and tucked the covers around me. Crouching to my eye level, he asked, "Do you need some water or ibuprofen?"

"Both," I whispered.

He pulled a shirt on. I heard him trot down the stairs at twice the speed he had before. A glass of water in his right hand, two pills tucked in his fingers, and my keys in his left hand, he returned and announced, "I'm going to take your car." Oh, now he wanted a car.

When he set the glass down on his side table, I ripped the keys from his grasp. "Jake, no. Don't go near him."

"Are you kidding me, Sawyer?" he shouted, like I was the one acting crazy.

"Please! You're not thinking. You get like this when—"

"I'm not going to get hurt. I can handle myself."

"Not if you get arrested!"

"What the hell am I supposed to do then, huh?"

"I don't know," I mumbled.

He ran his hands over his face while he shook his head. "Okay, well, if I'm not allowed to kill him, then we should throw his ass back in jail."

I buried my face under the covers. "Does that mean I have to talk to a cop?"

He sat on the bed and rested his hand on my back. "What's the alternative? Going home and letting him do it again?"

I shut my eyes and sucked in my breath.

"I'll take you. Everything will be okay."

That was what my dad said.

Jake drove me to the tiny station with two black-and-whites parked outside. My stomach twisted. Just being in the parking lot was humiliating, exposing. Jake held my hand as we approached the front desk, a high ledge with thick glass to protect the plump middle-aged woman behind it from people like me. "What can I do for you?" she asked, like we were at the bank.

I stammered out the words, "I, uh, I need to speak to an officer."

"Regarding?"

"Um." I darted my eyes to Jake, who squeezed my hand tighter. "I just need to report a crime."

The woman shuffled to the back to find the rotund, mustached officer to introduce to us. The cop pulled me into a bare room with a table and four chairs before dismissing Jake from our company. Why couldn't Jake be here? I needed him.

The officer started as soon as the door was closed, a legal pad in hand. "So, Ms.—"

"de la Cruz."

"What happened?" he asked as he sat across from me.

"Um..." I hesitated, peering out the window of the door with the crisscrossed wires threaded through it. Jake was out there, but I couldn't see him. "I was raped. I think."

"You *think*?" He raised his eyebrows as if I was distracting him from his very important game of solitaire. Really, though, what else was going on in this town? Maybe someone was going five miles over the speed limit on the highway, which, they pulled people over for, by the way.

"Yeah," I pushed myself to continue. "Last night, my stepdad picked me up from a party. I woke up this morning naked and sore with blood and—" I couldn't keep going. For all I knew, this guy was just as creepy as Jeff.

"And?" he asked with a hint of impatience.

I swallowed, forcing myself to say the word without vomiting. "Semen on my thighs and on my sheets." I hated that word. *Semen.*

The officer took a couple of notes on the form before meeting my eyes. "Were you under the influence of anything, miss?"

"Well, yeah, but—"

"So you don't remember the alleged assault?"

Alleged? Asshole.

I raised my voice, "Well, not all of it, but I'm covered in bruises."

"Miss." His tone was gruff. If he was trying to calm me down, he sucked at it. "I just asked if you remembered it."

"Bits and pieces."

He softened his voice and asked, "Did you have sex with anyone at the party? You can tell me. I know it can be hard to admit around Lane's kid—" Fuck this town. Of course this officer knew Jake and his dad.

"No! I didn't cheat on Jake," I hissed, my teeth gritting so tight I thought they'd grind to sand. "You *know* about my stepdad, Jeff Lindley. He's on the sex offenders' registry."

"Miss, it's a far jump from showing porn to a kid to raping an adult."

I squeezed my eyes shut. "So that's it? There's nothing you're going to do?"

"Go to the hospital. Have a rape kit done, the sooner the better, and we'll go from there."

"Will they do that in the ER?"

"Yeah," he answered as he tapped the back of the pen on the cold table.

"No, I can't go to the ER." I shook my head. "My mom's the charge nurse there."

"Ms. de la Cruz, that's the best way we can collect evidence to charge him. The longer you wait, the less likely it is that we will have what we need for an arrest." He scanned my sopping hair, pushing the pad aside and folding his fingers together. "Did you shower?"

"Well, yeah, it was all over me."

He took a slow inhale before sighing a drawn-out, "Okay. The rape kit probably won't do you much good since you washed most of the evidence away. You still need to go to the hospital for an exam—"

I scooted the chair out. Jake had the right idea— beating Jeff to death. That would have swift and final justice. And probably the best time Jake and I could have with Jeff. "I have to go," I muttered as I headed for the door. Jake shot me a confused expression from his waiting room chair. "Let's go." I nodded toward the exit. He stood and followed me, wrapping his arm around my waist.

"What happened?" Jake asked as he buckled his seatbelt. "Are they going to do anything?"

I met his searching eyes. "Can I stay with you for a while?"

He laced his fingers through mine. "Of course, babe, but—"

"Okay, let's go to my house and pack."

"Shouldn't you go to the hospital or some—"

"I'm fine. Can you just take me home?"

He nodded and started the car.

....

IF JAKE'S ROOMMATES OBJECTED TO the new freeloader in their house, I never heard about it. I was sure Jake crushed any fight they put up with his dark look that made my blood run cold. And he had never, would never, hurt me, so I could only imagine the effect those ominous eyes had on them.

Still, I wasn't eager to live in a hostile environment, even if it was infinitely safer than home. That Monday after my fourth, and last, class of the day, I headed to the grocery and liquor stores. Fake IDs didn't work when someone Mom knew from church could spot me with beer in the checkout line at Fred Meyer. I filled the fridge with produce and Coronas, the cabinets with cereal and Swiss Rolls, and the oven with two take-and-bake pizzas by the time Jake came home from training.

Oh, and I cleaned, making use of the supplies I

stocked the house with back in June when Jake moved in. They had remained untouched except when I used them over the year to wash Jake's sheets—that I got naked in—along with a huge pile of sweaty clothes he left in the corner of his room—that I smelled when I got naked in his sheets—and his bathroom—where Jake tried to get me naked. I did my homework at the dining table that night and watched the guys come into the kitchen to grab a few slices and beers. Hunter found strawberries in the fridge and acted like he had died and gone to heaven. I was in.

All the guys had jobs, part or full time, or per boxing match or construction job in Jake's case, to pay rent for the three-bedroom house only four blocks from school. I didn't. So I helped around the house. A lot. Besides, with cheer over and only morning classes to attend, I had the time. And no one else was doing it. It was all very sexist 1950s. Wait. Or racist. Should I have been offended?

Anyway, it was nothing out of the ordinary that I was folding Jake's laundry after school two Thursdays after I moved in. Or maybe it was extraordinary. Maybe he was hella lucky to have a girl like me. Sexy, smart, and able to operate a washing machine? I was the whole package.

I was putting his tee shirts in the dresser when I spotted it. I had a choice in that moment: put the clothes on top of it, feign ignorance, and let the curiosity fester inside me until I exploded and died, or... No, I knew I shouldn't open it. On the other hand, if the little velvet box just had earrings, a necklace, or some other benign jewelry, I shouldn't get my hopes up. It was better that I found out now, right? Right.

It was anything but benign. Wedged in the center of the box was a fat green gem surrounded by diamonds on a white-gold band. Again, I was well aware I shouldn't, but I slipped it on my left hand. Come on. It was staring right at me! It fit a little snugly, but close enough. How had Jake known my ring size? I heard the front door open and shut. *Please be one of the guys. Please be one of the guys. Any guy.* Footsteps plodded up the stairs. *No, no, no, no.* I tried to pull the ring off, but it stuck on my knuckle. *Shit!* I turned it around so just the band would show—as if that would help—then shoved the box under the shirts in the dresser and slammed the drawer shut.

"Hey, babe," Jake said as he dropped his gym bag on the carpet and wrapped his arms around me.

"Gross, Jake, you're all sweaty."

"What? Do I smell?" He lifted his arms above his head and puffed his chest toward me.

I pushed him away by his hips. "I don't know why you think that's so funny." He pulled his damp shirt over his head and threw it at the hamper, which was a new addition since I moved in. He missed. Eh, he wasn't a basketball player. "Please go shower."

He pulled me toward him, running his hand down my spine until my body was flush against his, then he kissed his way up my neck. "Shower with me?" he breathed in my ear, sending chills down my spine.

The fingers of my right hand slipped under the waistband of his shorts. I was about to run my left hand up his neck when I snapped out of it. I shoved him away and tucked the damning evidence behind my back. "Nah, you go ahead."

Jake put both hands on my arms and scanned my nervous face. "You okay?"

Ugh! Why couldn't I be a normal female and say "no"

to sex regularly so the *I'm not in the mood* cover would work?

"Yeah, I just don't want to mess up my makeup."

He narrowed his eyes. "You're the worst liar." His hands ran down my arms. I slipped my left hand in my back pocket. "Sawyer, what's going on?"

My face was burning red. I bit my lip and closed my eyes when I spread the fingers of my left hand in front of my chest.

"Damn it, Sawyer!" He laughed. I squinted one eye open to see him smiling and shaking his head, his hair falling across his forehead.

"I'm sorry." I cringed. "I was putting clothes away when I found it, then I had to know, so—"

"I get that, but why did you put it on?"

"Because," I exhaled, "it's beautiful."

"You like it?"

"Seriously? I love it. Do I have to give it back?"

He laughed again. "Don't you want me to propose?"

Just the word made my heart trip. "Do it now."

"Here? I had it all planned—"

"Tell me about it later. In the shower?" I raised an eyebrow. He grinned. "Ask me now." I put my hands on his shoulders when he lowered himself to one knee, then I gave him both my hands.

"Sawyer Emilia de la Cruz, will you marry me?"

"If only because I can't get the ring off." I laughed.

"Really? That's the story we're going to tell for the rest of our—"

"Yes!" I threw my head back and shouted. "Of course I'll marry you!" He pulled me into him as he stood to kiss me.

*T*HREE MINUTES. I TAPPED THE START BUTTON on my phone's timer.

The night I made him propose, Jake laid on his side in bed and twirled a piece of my hair through his fingers as he told me all about the proposal I ruined. He had saved up for months for the ring, an emerald because, as he said, even it could never compete with my green eyes. That was what he first noticed about me, besides the fact that a pervy senior was groping me. He told me it took everything in his power not to stare at them. He couldn't figure out if they were real or if I was just shitting everyone with contacts. He figured they must be mine, because, according to him, they were audacious and haunting, like me.

Two minutes left.

He had tickets to *An Ideal Husband* at that fancy theatre in Ashland. Cute, right? I had read the script and seen the movie, but this would be my first time seeing it in person. We would still go in June; he just wouldn't propose after.

We hadn't picked a date. I liked the idea of getting married before I went off to Oregon State in the fall, but that gave us little time to pull together a wedding. We were dirt poor, too, and I wondered if his parents would foot the bill since I wasn't exactly speaking to my mom. Maybe eloping would be more our style anyway.

One minute left.

We might as well just elope. We were already living together. And I had already learned more about Jake this past month than I had in our two and a half years of dating.

First, he left dirty washcloths in the shallow bathroom sink—not in the tub or laundry room. The sink. So I was always spitting toothpaste out on a mildewy pile of rags. *Why, Jake?*

Second, if he ran out of body wash, he'd just use shampoo instead of buying more. Then, when he ran out of shampoo, he'd use hand soap. I didn't wait to find out what he'd use once that ran out.

Third, he had trouble falling asleep unless we had sex right before bed or he had Netflix on. And, since Netflix kept me awake, he was sweet enough to sacrifice that option. Those few nights we were chaste, he would lie awake on his back, brushing his hands through his hair and staring at the ceiling. Then, like a kid at a sleepover, he would whisper, "Sawyer, are you awake?"

I would grunt to confirm as his fingers slid so gently up my back it tickled.

Then I'd get to hear whatever thought was bouncing around his head. "We should take the motorcycle down the coast of California this summer. Maybe to the Bay Area? Then to Santa Barbara and San Diego? What do you think?" Or, "My trainer says I need to run more, but I just don't know if it's worth it on my knee, with that old injury, you know?" Or, "What are you going to major in next year? I know you think math is more practical, but think how much you'd get to read if you majored in English or something? You know your dad would love it if you did English." Or, "Do you ever want to have kids? I think three would be cool."

Then we'd be up for another hour, and I'd doze off in second period American Government the next day.

My phone buzzed. Time was up.

I was already on my knees with my head hanging over the toilet as the timer ticked off the passing seconds. All I knew was that I was sick. And late. My arms, shaky and weak from the nausea, pushed me off the toilet seat so I could see the pregnancy test on the counter to my right.

Two pink lines.

I grabbed it and peered closer just to make sure. Positive.

Pregnant.

It didn't sink in, especially when all I wanted in that moment, perhaps more than I wanted anything else, was to throw up. My body, that stubborn bitch, wouldn't cooperate. So I just let my face hover over the toilet, watching the still, clear water in it in case my will beat her.

I tried to think while I waited to hurl.

First, I needed to count. When was my last period? During spring break? So, a month and a half ago? Before I moved in with Jake, right? My stash of tampons under the bathroom sink was untouched, so definitely before then. How far along would that make me?

Second, how did this happen? Jake and I were so careful; we used condoms every time. Maybe I was just crazy fertile like my mom. My conception had been a condom failure. I guessed it happened sometimes.

Third, would my scholarships still be good if I postponed a year or took a semester off to have the baby?

Fourth, could I be any more of a small-town cliché—

Wait. Shit.

Shit. Shit. *Shit!*

Jeff hadn't used a condom.

I sat back against the bathtub, my head in my hands and that damn plastic stick pinned between my fingers.

Jeff's baby was growing inside me.

That was enough to finally make me barf. I angry hurled into the bowl, the kind of puking that popped the capillaries in my cheeks and eyelids. I flushed the toilet and sat back on the floor, my face clammy and sweaty, my mouth bitter with sickness.

I heard a knock.

"Sawyer? You okay?" Jake asked from outside the door.

I wiped my mouth with the back of my hand. "Fine." What was I supposed to tell Jake? He had done everything in his power *not* to murder my stepdad. I wasn't sure anything would stop him now.

"Are you sick?"

"Yeah, but—"

"Can I come in?"

"You want to see me puking?"

He laughed. "Can I get you anything?"

A time machine would be wonderful, thank you.

"No," I moaned again. I shoved the pregnancy test back in the box, then the box into the pouch pocket of my pullover hoodie. From the floor, I reached for the door to crack it open. "I need to run to the store. Do you need anything?"

"No." He stared down at my pitiful position on the linoleum. "Let me do that. You should lie down. What do you need?"

"Ginger ale, please."

"Sure, babe." He squatted in front of me to kiss my forehead. "Do you want me to help you into bed or something?"

I shook my head. "I'm okay here."

I waited until I heard his motorcycle drive out of earshot before making my way down the stairs. I hunched over my tightening gut through the garage to the side yard to dispose of my little secret in the outside trash can, even burying it underneath a couple of bags of trash just to be safe. After, I went inside and trudged up the stairs to bed.

It wasn't until my head felt the relief of the soft pillow and the weight of the covers over me that I realized how tired I was. Exhausted. I wanted to just huddle there and sleep—wake up to find none of this had happened. If only life were that gentle. But it wasn't. It was harsh, unrelenting, and cruel, and I had to do something to get Jeff's spawn the hell out of me.

I searched for the nearest Planned Parenthood on my phone. Seventy-five miles away for one that offered abortions. Great. How was I supposed to drive the three hours back from Ashland after an abortion? I scanned their site further. Abortion pill. Okay, that could work. I could just bring it home and take it. No big deal. Okay, I clicked on the tab titled, "What can I expect if I take the abortion pill?" I scanned the long list of symptoms on the page. Yikes. That seemed miserable. Jake would find out. Unless I stayed with Tatum. Or in a hotel in Ashland. There had to be a way.

I heard the front door creak open, and Jake walk up the stairs. I blackened my phone and shoved it under the pillow. He knocked on the already-open door. "How are you feeling?"

"Not much better." He put a cold twenty-ounce bottle of ginger ale on the bedside table, just in my line of site. I envied the drops of condensation sliding down the icy plastic, needing that coolness on my forehead, on the nape of my sweaty neck. The nausea returned with Jake's presence and the flare of panic he induced in me. What was I going to tell him? What would he do if he found out I hid an abortion from him? Should I just tell him? No, that was stupid. I was just sick. That was all he needed to know.

He pushed the hair back from my cheek. "Babe, you look awful." When he said that, I realized I was still hunkered around my abdomen with my eyes shut. "You don't feel warm, so I doubt you have a fever..."

I felt my fingers for my ring and twisted it around. Jake and I didn't have secrets, except a few he let me keep about my past. This wasn't a good one to start with. I didn't think I could bear living with it for the rest of my life. So, I just blurted out a pathetic, "I'm pregnant."

Jake's eyes widened, the brown in them melting almost to liquid. He ran his hand over his face, then let it cover his mouth as he stared at me. A few seconds passed.

Was he going to say something? Anything?

"But—" I started.

He interrupted, "Holy shit." He dropped his hand from his chin. "We're having a baby?" His voice was soft—scared and shocked and full of hope. I could tell his mind was racing like mine, but his was over the next few years instead of just the next couple of days.

"Jake..." I shook my head and cringed.

"What's wrong? Is it college? We'll figure it out so you can—"

"No, Jake." I raised my voice. "It's not—" I took a deep breath. "I think it's Jeff's."

He crossed his arms and didn't hesitate to object. "No, no. It's not Jeff's. No way. You and I have sex all the time, and he—" Jake squeezed his eyes shut and shook his head. "No." He dropped his hands to his thighs with a clap. "It's mine. I'm sure of it."

Ah, that irritating optimism of the unbroken. It was hard to argue with.

"Okay, fine. That's a nice thought, but what if it's not?"

"There's no 'if'—"

"Jake!"

"Fine." He sat on the edge of the bed, and then leaned his hand on the other side of my hips. "I'd never ask you to give up your baby. I'll be there if you keep it. For all of it. I'll change diapers and wake up in the middle of the night and rock it to sleep. I can sell my bike to help us pay for the baby stuff we'll need. Don't they need a lot of stuff?" he asked as if I knew more than he did. "Look, it's mine even if it's not, okay? But..." he breathed. "If that's too hard for you, I totally understand. We can find a family or an agency or—I don't know how it all works, but I can learn. If you don't want to deal with any of it, I'll take care of everything. I promise."

I bit my lip. "Jake, I can't do eight more months of this."

His face fell. "Sawyer, no." It was a plea, but it was firm. It was obvious in that moment he would hold his ground.

I sat up. "Think for a second, please! You really think we'll be able to give this baby up without Jeff knowing? Without him fighting for custody?"

"You think any judge in their right mind would give him cust—"

"Yes! He's charming. Everyone gives him the benefit of the doubt. There's no proof he raped me. They'll just have proof it's his."

"*If* it's his."

"It's his. Having this baby could mean being stuck with Jeff for the rest of my life."

"Sawyer, you're being totally irrational. That's not going to happen."

"And what if he abuses her, too? I'm not putting my kid through that."

"So it's better to kill her?"

"Rather than her grow up with Jeff as her dad, yes."

Jake stroked my waist. "Babe, I know you've been through hell—"

"You don't know anything about hell."

"Then tell me!"

"I've told you enough for you to be on my side. I can't believe you're asking me to do this."

"I'm just asking you to do what your parents did for you."

"What?"

"Seriously, Sawyer, you of all people should know better! You were a condom accident, right?"

"So?"

"So, first, you know they happen. You know it could be mine. And if it is, I get a say. Second, your dad gave up everything to be your dad. I bet he never even thought about aborting you, but they could have. They were younger than us."

"*My dad?* Really, Jake?"

"It's not an option." He crossed his arms across his chest again. "I can't believe we're even having this discussion," he said with a flicking shrug of his shoulders.

"I can't believe you're making me keep a baby from a rape that was your fault."

"*My fault?*"

"You said..." Cue Jake imitation. "'Oh, babe, stay in town. Finish high school. I'm not going to let anything bad happen to you.' You really fucked that one up."

"How is it my fault that *you* refused to move in with me in February, that *you* didn't go to my fight, or that *you* got shitfaced at that party?"

"Oh, so it's *my* fault?"

His whole face tightened with regret, his eyes and mouth closing as he dragged his hand from forehead to chin. "Of course not. You don't think I feel awful I didn't stop this? But I *couldn't.*"

I stared down at my hands a long time before whispering, "I know." After a quivering inhale, I added, "I'm sorry."

"It's not the baby's fault, either." He took my hand in his. "Please, Sawyer, please don't do this."

"I can't have another reminder of that night. Or of those two years."

"You think killing it is going to make you forget?" He brushed my hair behind my shoulder. "You have a chance to make something beautiful out of this horrible thing that happened to you. Please, babe, take it."

....

I'D FORGOTTEN WHAT IT FELT like—loneliness. But it was the only thing I was guaranteed as I lay in the Ashland motel bleeding.

Childless.

What a strange feeling to regret something even as I did it—the sheer denial that masked itself as courage, the rush of relief once the decision was final, and the cavernous sorrow that sank in within the hour.

Part of me didn't believe it was real. I was gone. Jake probably got home from training a couple of hours ago and found his room cleared of my stuff, my existence erased except the emerald ring I left on his nightstand, my phone in his kitchen trash, and a note saying, "I love you, but I can't keep it."

We had done nothing but fight for two weeks, spending our nights silent in the same bed, me making a Plan B that excluded him, his thoughts shut away. It made me feel better thinking he probably expected I'd leave the day after graduation—better as in it felt better to stand in fire for four seconds than for five.

June 2017

A WEEK PASSED, AND THE BLOOD TURNED from red to pink. I was in a questionably clean Los Angeles motel with bars on the window, trying to decide how to fill my summer before the school year started. My bank account was dwindling with the cost of lodging, food, and hooch. I would need a job soon, preferably one that would help me pay the out-of-state tuition during the school year.

I called Jake twice last night from my burner—a burner to erase my trail from Jeff and my mom. Jake didn't answer the first time, so I left a voicemail to let him know that was my new number. He didn't call back. I called again a couple of hours and a half bottle of tequila later, weeping and begging for forgiveness. No word.

I GOT A STUDIO APARTMENT for the summer in South Central. There were iron bars over the windows here, too. There was just enough money left to get through July. After that, I would be on the streets.

Every day that I searched for jobs, I drove past a nude strip club. And every day that I got turned down as a barista, tutor, or assistant, a grey thought lingered in my mind. Stripping was just dancing, right? I was a great dancer. I was busty, athletic, and dull to the sensation of being degraded. Oh, and in desperate need of cash. This would pay cash immediately. I could do it until I found something better. What was the big deal? I wouldn't *be* a stripper. It would just be something I did to get by for a few weeks. Then I'd go to school and kick ass at that like I always did. No one would know about the summer where I took my clothes off to pay rent.

After the fifteenth job rejection, I drank up the nerve to call Jake. That familiar voice rang through when it went to voicemail. "Hey, this is Jake. I can't come to the phone right now because I'm punching someone in the face. Leave a message!" Then the beep I knew was coming but still made my heart race.

I sat there a long moment deciding what to say. Out tumbled, "Jake, if you want me back, call me by eight tomorrow night. I love you. I'm sorry for what I did and for what I have to do now." I hung up.

September 2017

"You're Cash, right?" I asked the guy sitting against the wall as I slowed down on my way through the hall of our dorm. I had lived here now for two weeks, and I still felt like a dripping-in-diamonds heiress popping champagne off the back of a yacht. There were no roaches lurking by the bathroom sink here like at my South Central apartment, no bars on the windows, and high-pressure hot water for every shower. I couldn't think of anything better, because there wasn't anything better. The first shower I took here, I must have stood in the stall for forty-five minutes until my skin was bright red and pruny. Turned out, Los Angeles wasn't all homeless addicts, sweaty air, and midnight gunshots. This must be how the other half live.

"Yeah." My neighbor cocked his head as he searched my face. "I'm so sorry, but—"

"Sawyer." I winked. "It's okay. We're all meeting a ton of new people." To be fair, the first time we met, I was in a towel, wet hair clinging to my bare skin after one of those decadent showers. He was in his jammies, his short, dark curls messy, doing a half-conscious shuffle to the bathroom for a three AM tinkle. And, as it was three AM, unarguably the worst hour of the twenty-four, he was quick to forget it.

This time, though, his lips curved sweetly, a boyish quirk on an otherwise masculine face, and stood to shake my hand. I hadn't noticed the first time we met how tall he was. "Nice to meet you, Sawyer." My name coated his lips like sticky brown sugar. Southerner for sure.

I smiled and shifted my book bag to my other shoulder. "Do you want to borrow my desk? You know, until you have access to yours?" I was feeling generous, after all, spoiled with dorm life. I had my own bed *and* desk now. There was plenty to go around.

"You don't mind?"

"Not at all." I waved my hand down, and then headed toward the door to unlock it. Tilting my head, I studied the loose leaf and textbook he was gathering. "Physics?"

"Yeah."

"Engineering or do you hope to be the next Stephen Hawking? I mean, without the crippling, degenerative disease."

He laughed. "Engineering. Aerospace, ideally."

"Sounds amazing."

"What about you?" He slung his backpack over his shoulder as we passed through my door.

"Haven't decided yet," I lied.

"First quarter?"

"Yep." I dropped my bag on my bare but made bed and hopped onto it.

"You've got time. Is this your desk?" He pointed to the one bordering my bed, the one that wasn't covered in books, fast food wrappers, and half-empty coffee cups. Nicole, my roommate, was either a slob or conducting some sort of biological experiment with the dairy remaining in those paper cups. Or, possibly, a psychological one to see how long someone as uptight as me could survive in her natural habitat.

Within the first three minutes of our study session, it was obvious I would not be able to concentrate with Cash around. He started drumming on the desk with his mechanical pencil, the lead inside making a *shick-click* sound as it rattled against the plastic. It drove me nuts. Over and over—*thump-shick-click, thump-thump-shick-click*, as he tapped the eraser on the page with one hand and held his forehead in the other. It must have been what he did when he was stuck on a problem because his paper was covered in harsh indents and eraser shavings. I sent a sideways glance to his textbook from my bed, a different one than he had in the hall. Linear Algebra. Easiest class in the world. At least, easiest of all the algebras. "Cash?"

"Yeah?"

I took a breath to revel in the silence that followed. Ah. Two full seconds of no *thump-shick-click*." What problem are you stuck on?"

He narrowed his eyes on me. "You know how to do Linear Algebra?"

Doesn't everyone?

"Number fourteen?"

He nodded.

"Have you tried a 'suppose not' proof?"

"'S'pose not?'" In the south, it must be too much effort to pronounce all the syllables in a word. Was his sweet tea not strong enough today?

"Proof by contradiction." I reached out for his pencil and notebook. He surrendered both.

I wrote... *S'pose not,* and then the opposite of the statement he was trying to prove with the two-by-two matrices given in the text. "That'll get you the most elegant proof. Never do brute force when you can use 's'pose not.'" I winked and handed his notebook back, then took a hesitant breath before returning the pencil.

"Thanks?"

"I turned in that homework today, so let me know if you need more help."

He stared at me a moment with knitted eyebrows. "Thanks," he repeated. I was starting to get offended by his shocked expressions at my apparent intelligence. What about me looked stupid?

We both heard Cash's door open and someone leave. I whispered, "So, is it the same girl every time or—"

"So far this year. We'll see."

"You ever lock him out?"

"No, I don't hook up." Well, that was disappointing to hear. It had been months since I had sex with a decent guy. Cash was striking with perfect hair, and I could listen to him talk all day. He seemed like he would actually be nice to me, care if I liked his hands and lips on my skin, and not just see how fast he could get off.

"No, I mean, just for the hell of it. Even the scales, you know?"

He gathered up his books. "That's kind of a good idea. Thanks again, Sawyer."

"Anytime." I smiled.

By the way he smiled back, I could tell I was right about him.

October 2017

*I*SORTED ALL THE GUYS I MET INTO TWO categories: those who wanted to use me and those who wanted to protect me. Since I'd only met two men in the latter category, one of whom was dead and the other I was dead to, it was safer for me to assume Cash had been in my dorm room studying two or three times a week to get the chance to confirm that I was, in fact, hot naked. Maybe he just needed a few weeks to get to know me so he wouldn't feel like he was taking advantage, so he wouldn't consider sex between us a *hookup*.

Our third week of studying, he started that arrhythmic tapping on his Linear Algebra book again. I didn't let him break into a chorus before I asked, "Do you need any help?"

He leaned onto the back legs of the chair, lacing his fingers behind his neck. "How'd you know?"

I patted the space next to me on my bed. With little effort, he hopped next to me and pointed to the number eight on the page. I eyed his forearms, the veins rising from them. Was the rest of his body like that? "So, you're not a fan of proofs?"

He pushed back a few short curls. "This is what engineers pay mathematicians for."

"Well, I'm not getting paid enough."

"I thought you weren't a math major."

"Shh..." I pressed three fingers over Cash's smirking lips, then pored over the half-worked out proof. "Oh." I leaned against him as I pointed to the error. "You just made a mistake computing the adjugate. That should be a two and that," I scribbled a calculation in the margin, "should be a negative three."

"Really? That's it?"

"Yeah. Think you can handle the rest?" I nudged his thigh.

"I'd rather not."

I flashed my green eyes at him before saying, "Then take a break."

Cash closed the textbook over his homework without finishing the number he was writing. He turned to face me. "Sounds great."

I allowed that split second stare where his gaze trailed from my eyes to my mouth before closing the space between us. His lips were warm on mine, his hand moving to brush the dark hair that cascaded over my cheek—not the direction I expected it to take, but maybe that was a Southern gentleman thing. Please. I didn't need to be handled so gently.

I moved my fingers through his hair and around his neck until I could feel the top button of his shirt. My hand skimmed down his chest, where I slipped my index and middle finger between two of the buttons, tugging on the fabric as I climbed onto his lap. I brushed the surface of his abdomen, feeling the heat rising to the surface of his skin as I slid one button after another loose.

His hands were on my hips when he pulled his face away, thumping the back of his head against the wall. "Wait."

"For what?" I whispered heavily in his ear before tasting his earlobe between my teeth. My fingers still worked at the remaining buttons.

"I don't hook up," he breathed. Sure he didn't. He was just here to what—get to know me? Please, I had a terrible personality.

"Not even..." I ran my lips under the crook of his jaw to his throat. "Not even with me?" Done with the shirt buttons, I went for the one on his jeans. Once I crossed that border, he wouldn't change his mind. Rather, he couldn't.

Cash clutched both my wrists like he was blocking a strike and rolled me onto the mattress, ridding himself of me. He didn't say anything as he buttoned his shirt, his chest still heaving. For the record, the rest of his top half was like his arms. Such a waste. "No," he muttered. "Sorry."

My voice was cool when I said, "Then maybe you should go."

"Maybe." Cash shrugged as he collected his books. He left without a backward glance.

I hugged my knees to my chest and watched him shut the door behind him. What in the hell had just happened? Since when did guys turn down sex? Sure, I guessed sometimes I'd invite a guy back to the VIP room at the strip club and he couldn't afford the full very-important-person experience, but beyond that... seriously, what the hell? What did *I don't hook up* even mean? He had a penis, no? It pissed me off the rest of the day, all through Advanced Calculus and while I lined my eyes before work.

I showed up to the club early to fulfill my promise to Brandy that I would teach her how to work the pole. I wasn't sure why I had. She was beyond help. Maybe it was that I still saw her as the girl crying on her first day in the locker room. A couple of other dancers laughed as she shivered behind her open locker, as if the first day hadn't destroyed whatever part of them wasn't broken, too. I walked up to her and rested my hand on her bare shoulder. Brandy turned around and hugged me tight, crying hot tears down my back. I'd stood there limp, unsure what to do, before patting her back. "Tomorrow will be better," I lied, hoping the embrace would end.

Now, I watched her embarrassing attempt at the pole. She wasn't so much gliding around it as bracing herself on it as she fell. "Did you get a pull-up bar at home like I told you to?"

She just crossed her arms and stared at me. "Yeah, but that didn't make me magically stronger in a week."

"Did you use it?"

Brandy flipped me off before trying the move I showed her again. A little better. "Girl, how are you so strong?"

"Four years of varsity and competitive cheerleading. Before that, gymnastics and ballet. But I didn't stick with those because I'm just not built for either."

"Not with those boobs." Brandy pointed to my chest, compressed in a sports bra.

"Oh, I more meant because I'm too tall. But sure, those didn't help either." I shrugged. "Most recently, though, *pull-ups*."

"Fine," she sighed as she tried again.

"Hey..." I started, but then took a long breath before blurting out, "Has a guy ever turned you down before?"

"How? Like for a date? For sex?"

"Sex."

"No, but I may not be the best person to ask. I've only had two boyfriends, and those are the only guys I've slept with."

"Two? Aren't you like twenty-three?"

She laughed. "Are you saying I'm old?"

"There's not really a good way for me to answer that."

"Okay, what's *your* number, Baby Emmy?" Baby Emmy was the name some of the veterans gave me when I started taking a chunk out of their tips. Emerald was my stripper alias. Even Brandy didn't know my real name, and I doubted Brandy was hers. Anyway, it seemed as though I was supposed to be insulted because my coworkers were saying I was the youngest one here at the age of eighteen. Every time they talked down to me, I knew they were just threatened by my measurements, my lean power, my young skin. They could call me Baby Emmy all day. If it started to bother me, I'd just go home and count the money that used to be theirs.

I just shook my head. "I don't know. All those VIP-room guys kind of blur together."

"Hang on." She dropped to her feet. "You have sex with clients?" Brandy's baby blues grew wide.

"Why do you think I keep condoms in my locker?"

Her face was full of judgment. And what was she? A

nun?

"Look, I'm not in a financial position to turn down eight hundred dollars for twenty minutes." I truly wasn't. The night after I called Jake the third time, I walked into that nude strip club I drove by daily, told the manager I had a background in dance and gymnastics, and asked for a job. I'd never forget counting my tips on the kitchen counter of my shitty apartment after that first shift. Almost two hundred and fifty dollars. That was a quarter of the way to rent. It would have to work.

I decided then if I was going to do the cliched strip-my-way-through-college thing, I was going to do it right—go big so I'd never have to go home. I worked five days a week in the summer, sometimes double shifts. I practiced the pole until every movement was smooth, perfect, until I could do what none of the other girls could. Cue cheesy Rocky-esque training montage where I fell repeatedly in my sweaty gym clothes and heels before finally getting it right with a winded but triumphant smile.

But the cash really began to flow when I started letting men do what the other girls wouldn't—let them lick their way up me and tell me how good I tasted, pull my nipples between their teeth, let them between my legs, or put my mouth where they told me. And I'd pretend because I was good at pretending. I was raised to pretend. And I'd shut away the memories of Jake's hands and lips and what he said my skin tasted like. I'd pretend he never existed, we had never been, so I could make my living doing what I had been forced to do as a kid. And I'd tell myself it was different because this time, there were bouncers who took guys out who wouldn't stop when I said "no." This time, I got paid and not in promises to spare my life or my reputation. I got paid cash and lots of it, five times what I made my first night.

"Holy *shit*, Em," Brandy shouted, "What happens if one of them is a cop?"

"Shh!" If the cops didn't know before, they knew now. "You think the LAPD really has time for that?"

She shrugged. "Maybe."

"Plus, I pick out the clients, and I'm really careful. I only do favors for guys I actually want to hook up with." Or rather, guys I wouldn't vomit on if I hooked up with them. I tipped my chin toward the pole. "Try again." She pulled herself onto it, warming up slightly. "But this guy who lives in my dorm, Cash, we started making out and he stopped it because he says he won't hook up with anyone, like he lives in a Kelly Clarkson song."

"'I Do Not Hook Up?' Wow, that's an old one." Her feet landed on the floor with a thump. Was she even trying? "Do you like him?"

"Getting better. Are you ready to try it with heels?"

Brandy raised an eyebrow. "Do I look like I'm ready to try it in heels?"

I bent to the strappy stilettos by my feet, snagging them up and throwing both at her. "I believe in you."

"You're a taskmaster."

"You'll thank me." I winked.

Brandy sat down to put on her shoes. "You never answered my question. Do you like him?"

What a stupid question. It wasn't like I could date anyone while I had this job—or after—especially a prude like Cash. "No, he's just really hot." I checked my phone. "I've got to change. My shift starts in ten. Use that pull-up bar."

"Yeah, yeah," she mumbled as she clutched the pole.

THE SHRILL SCREAM OF THE fire alarm woke me that night. I couldn't have been asleep more than an hour when it did. A quick check of my phone confirmed that, yes, it was only four AM.

Nicole and I let out matching grumbles as the screeching persisted. We joined our equally pissed neighbors in the hallway, our RA herding us like cattle to the stairwell. Four flights of stairs at four in the morning. Couldn't I just take my chance with the elevator? What was the worst that could happen, really?

While I thought to check my phone when I heard the alarm, I didn't think to grab a blanket or a sweatshirt or even anticipate that it might be cold outside. The foggy air sent shivers through me as soon as I stepped through the glass doors. Goose bumps carved into my shoulder blades, down my wrists, and over every inch of my bare legs. My hair, still damp from my two AM shower, was icy on my back.

"Okay, everyone," the RA from the floor below us shouted, "line up by floor and room number. First floor over here," he pointed to his far left, "second here, and so on." As he said this, a fire engine pulled in front of the building. Those firefighters would be disappointed. This was obviously a case of a stoner forgetting to unplug his smoke detector before hotboxing.

Nicole and I gathered with the other fifth-floor residents. I was rubbing my hands over my arms, trying in vain to warm up, when Cash slid beside me. I kept my focus on hugging myself into a higher temperature, ignoring his presence entirely. Not even twenty-four hours had passed since he left me fully clothed on my bed. I felt like crap. Seeing him made me feel crappier.

I heard a long zip, cutting my eyes over to see Cash fidget out of the corner of my eye. I flinched when I felt a sweatshirt rest over my shoulders. I still refused to acknowledge him even as I felt his hands pull my wet hair out from under the fabric, draping it over the hood.

I bit my tongue, literally, to keep my irritation from spilling out. Really, what was his deal? What did he want from me?

I slipped my arms through the sweatshirt. The zipper was halfway down my thigh when I found it. Fine, I could admit I was warmer in it. I tugged the hem over my boxers so it would look to Cash like I was wearing just his jacket, which was a technique I knew from experience worked. Whatever this guy's game was, I'd win.

"Thank you," I whispered, then bit my bottom lip as I glanced his way.

He barely glanced at me as he said, "You're welcome."

November 2017

I NAPPED TOO LONG AND WAS IN A HURRY TO transform into Emerald before my Thursday night shift. I was fumbling with my hair when he knocked on my door. Flat iron still in hand, I opened it.

"Okay, I have a super last minute, crazy favor to ask you," Cash blurted. His hands were together in front of him as if in prayer, which he would need a lot of if he wanted anything from me. It had been three weeks since our last intentional interaction. He had chosen to sit in the hall and avoid eye contact or disappear entirely when Dylan's sock was tied around their doorknob. Now, here he was at my door, asking for help. I wasn't going to make this easy.

I smirked as I set the flat iron down and twisted up a portion of my hair. "Is it the kind of favor I already offered you?"

Cash sucked in his breath. Exhaling, he frowned. "No."

"Then I'm not sure I can help you." I reached to close the door.

"Wait!" His voice sped up. "My sister is getting into town today to visit campus, and she was supposed to stay with my aunt, but her whole family has the flu. I'd have her stay in our room, but I don't think she'd be comfortable with my pervy roommate."

"I heard that," Dylan's voice called, muffled from the room next door.

"But you're not denying it," Cash yelled back. I would have laughed if I hadn't noticed where this was going. "I know this is a lot to ask, but is there any way she could stay with you?"

"Umm...how long?"

"Tonight through Saturday night."

"I won't be around tonight or Saturday night. Is that okay?"

His blue eyes flickered. "Yeah, of course."

I let out a sigh before heading toward my desk. I was not a sucker. This wasn't for Cash. This was for his sister. No one should have to room with Dylan. I could never be that cruel. "Here's my key," I said as I worked it through the keychain. "I'll be knocking on your door a little before three tonight for it." I gave him a hard look and added, "Make sure you wake up. I'll be pissed if I get locked out."

"Thank you." He took the key and ambushed me with a hug. His shirt was smothering my face when he said, "Her name's Jolene. She's great. You'll love her."

I FIRST WOKE UP ON Friday to the squeak of an air mattress. But the other noises kept me from falling back to sleep: hands rummaging through a suitcase, a phone vibrating, then the solid door opening and shutting. I rolled over to face the wall, sure it couldn't yet be eight in the morning. If anyone was counting, that was only five hours of sleep. After the night I had, that wasn't even close to enough.

The door opened again about an hour later. "You can turn the light on," I said before throwing the covers back. The light flicked on, and a petite, rosy-cheeked teen walked toward me.

"Hey, it's nice to finally meet you." She reached her hand out to shake mine. She and Cash had the same curls, but hers were blonde and reached past her shoulders.

"Hi, Jolene, right?" I tried my best not to act irritated I was awake at such an ungodly hour. After all, it was Cash's fault, not hers.

"Yep!" She smiled before launching in with her own sugary accent. "Thank you so much for letting me crash. I felt just awful dropping this on you."

"No worries." I yawned.

"Do you have to work that late often?"

"Three nights a week."

"Oh, yeah? What do you do?"

I drew a deep breath, never quite sure how to answer this question. "I'm a dancer."

A snicker sounded from Nicole's bed. Great. She was awake for this.

"Really? What kind? Do you ever go on tour? You must have to rehearse all the time." Her blue eyes appeared more naive with each question she asked.

Nicole sat up to laugh this time, waiting for my answer.

"Exotic." Jolene's expression turned puzzled.

Nicole heard the pause and clarified, "She's a stripper."

"Oh." Jolene nodded in slow motion.

"I'm also just a good dancer," I added to Nicole, "or do you not need help with your little movie anymore?"

Nicole rolled her eyes and looped her thick red hair into a ponytail.

"Are you a film major?" Jolene asked Nicole.

"Yeah. My group is working on a project with a Latin dance scene that Sawyer choreographed."

"That's so cool! I'm here to check out the screenwriting program. What do you want to do?"

"Direct."

"They're shooting the scene this afternoon," I chimed in. "You should come with us." Nicole wasn't exactly the invite-a-wide-eyed-kid-along type, so I did it for her.

"Really?" Jolene's eyes got even bigger, like only-possible-in-a-cartoon-big.

"Yeah, you can be an extra. Right, Nicole?"

Nicole lifted one shoulder in reluctant agreement.

CASH DECIDED HE HAD NOTHING better to do than hang out with Jolene and us at the shoot. I half wondered if he didn't trust me with his little sister. He had that protective brother stance whenever he was around her. I didn't have a brother, but Jake was like that with his sister even though she was two years older than him. Once, Jake found a guy trying to undress her at a party when she was passed out, and he broke his nose with one jab. It was clear now why I hadn't told him everything about Travis and his friends. They would be dead, Jake would have gone to prison, and I had rather not see my boyfriend only through glass.

We had only an hour in the dance studio at school to get the scene perfect. My grade wasn't on the line, but I had sunk probably twenty hours into this stupid scene, so I was unhealthily invested. More invested than one of the actors.

"Jared," Nicole barked. "Where's Emma?"

"Hungover," Anne Marie, her roommate, announced from where she was stretching at the ballet bar.

"Shit. Sawyer, you have to fill in."

I glanced down at my cropped tee shirt over my shorts, my belly button ring peeking out. "I'm not in a dress."

"Cash." Nicole handed him her key. "I have a short black dress in my wardrobe. Can you run and get it?"

I grabbed his arm as he was heading out the door. "No, Nicole. I'm not going to be on camera."

"Why the hell not?" Her eyes narrowed. She was so pissed I thought her red hair might burst into flames.

"Why can't Jolene do it?" I pointed at the young girl trying to stay out of our way. "She could fit in your dress."

"She doesn't know what she's doing."

"I'll teach her."

"In ten minutes? No, it has to be you. Cash, go!"

"Only if you ask nicely." He crossed his arms and smirked.

She gritted her teeth. "Please."

Cash was out the door, leaving poor Jolene to watch us fight. "I'm not doing it. Jared?" I called, "Can you teach Jolene here the steps?" I turned to Jolene. "Is that okay with you?"

"Sure!" She strutted toward Jared, her curls bouncing on her way.

"What is your problem, Sawyer?" Nicole hissed.

"Come on, give Jolene her *Dirty Dancing* moment."

Jolene *was* good enough to be in *Dirty Dancing*. She had clearly crossed the border into Florida to salsa before. Which was a relief, because Nicole would have smothered me in my sleep if I screwed up her precious film.

"Does she pay you to help her?" Cash asked as we walked to the caf after the shoot.

"No, but we have a deal. Every time I help her, she owes me. When she's famous and getting into all the A-list events, she has to invite me until I meet one of the following Ryans: Eggold."

"Manageable," Nicole said.

"Gosling."

"More of a challenge."

"Tedder."

"Not even in the industry."

"Ryan Tedder?" Cash asked.

"Lead singer of OneRepublic. And a brilliant songwriter. And gorgeous. And married." I frowned.

"Cash," Jolene called from behind us, "he helped write 'I Know Places.'"

"Oh, got it," he said as if that cleared everything up.

"What song is that?" I asked.

"Taylor Swift," Jolene said.

I looked at Cash. "I've never heard that one. How do you know such an obscure—"

"You know, you really have a type," Nicole interrupted. "Those guys all look alike." It was true. They were all blue-eyed versions of Jake.

In the caf, Cash and I stood in the Korean barbecue line while Jo picked at the salad bar. I glanced across the room at her and asked Cash, "Do you guys have any fun plans while she's here?"

"Besides going to Diddy Riese?"

"Cash! She flew all the way out here and you're just taking her to ice cream?"

"First, not just ice cream. Diddy Riese."

I rolled my eyes. Ice cream sandwiches weren't a step up from ice cream in my mind.

"And," he laughed, "in my defense, Jo had plans with my cousins before they got the flu. I think they were going to go to Disneyland."

"Well, a bunch of us are going to this all-ages thing at the House of Blues tonight. It's Downtown Disney, so next best thing. You guys should come with us."

"Yeah?"

"Or we can just take Jo if you're not into that."

"Are y'all gonna be drinking?"

Obviously. "Probably."

"I better go."

"Oh, come on. We'll have a designated driver."

"Really?" He crossed his arms and stared down at me. "Who?"

I pursed my lips as I thought. "Yeah, you better go."

MY SHORT YELLOW DRESS SLIPPED up my thigh as I climbed onto the barstool. "Tequila shot, please," I called toward the bartender.

"You're doing a shot alone? Isn't that kind of sad?" Cash chuckled as he leaned his hand on the bar.

"I drink shots when I'm at a club or a party, so I don't have to keep my hand over my drink." The bartender slid the shot in front of me. I threw it back.

"Keep your hand over your drink?"

"So no one drugs it," I said with a flip of my hand. Did he not understand stranger danger?

"You won't be on camera even though you're stunning. You only drink shots, and this," he said, snatching my burner from the bar, "is your phone. How often do you switch these out?"

Stunning? "I'm sorry. Are you investigating me?" I grabbed my phone back.

"Where are you from again?"

"Out of state. I'm also a size seven shoe and a 32-D bra if you want to scribble that on your notepad."

"And your family. What are they like?"

I tilted my chin to my shoulder and gazed at him through my eyelashes. "What family?" I raised my hand for the bartender again. "Another tequila, please." When he set another glass in front of me, I said, "Thank you, baby," and winked as I leaned on the counter to twirl it between two fingers.

"You know," Cash said with narrowed eyes, "you can't keep him from drugging your drink."

"That'll be a short list of suspects, though, won't it, Holmes?"

He stared at me a minute. "What's your greatest fear?"

What the hell kind of conversation was this? I

deadpanned, "You're making me swoon."

"Just answer."

"You know, you've been asking me a lot of questions. How about you show me yours, and then I'll show you mine?"

"Fair enough." He nodded. "My greatest fear is watching someone I love die and being helpless to save them."

"Really?" I felt my eyebrows crinkle and the pitch of my voice betray my surprise. "More than spiders or heights or amounting to nothing?"

"Really. You go."

I swallowed the shot, squeezing my eyes shut as I did. Then I answered him, face to face, sure of the truth of my statement. "I'm not afraid of anything."

"No. You're afraid of something."

"I'm really not. Everything bad that can happen already has. There's nothing left to be afraid of."

His voice and eyes softened. "What happened?"

I leaned to whisper in his ear, "Are we going to waste all night at the bar?"

He watched my eyes as I stared at his. Then I felt his hand on my arm, warm even in the stuffy club. It eased passed my elbow down into my hand. He led me down the steps onto the sunken dance floor. Once we were in the sea of dancers, he spun me into him, my back to his, his hands on mine, one gliding over my hips and waist. His other hand outstretched mine before tracing up my arm.

"So, the white boy from Atlanta can dance?"

Cash's breath fogged up my neck when he said, "I'm not as terrible at everything as you think." He pressed my hips away, spinning me so I faced him, then cupped his hand around the nape of neck, dipping me back against his bent knee. I rolled to stand. Looping my hands behind his neck, I danced back into him. "For instance—" He pulled my chest into his. With his hands sliding down my back, he said, "I have a B in Linear Algebra."

"Cash." I tried not to laugh as I pressed his shoulders down so he'd take a knee. I stepped on either side of his thigh and lowered my face to his. "You'd know that'd impress me if I didn't have an A."

"Of course you do." He chuckled as he twirled my hips away from him. His hand caught mine when he stood and snapped me back against him. "So, how exactly am I supposed to impress you?"

I smoothed down the buttons on his chest. "You know you don't have to do anymore impressing." My hand found one of his belt loops, and I inched him closer. I kept one of my legs bent between his as we swayed. "I'm yours if you want me."

He leaned me back so I dipped from his right arm to his left, then pressed his lips against my ear. "No, you aren't. Not the way I want you."

"Please, there's only one way any of you want me."

"No. I want more than this. I know there's more to you."

"Not more that you want to know."

"I want to know what happened."

I was about to roll my eyes when I realized my opportunity. His resolve was crumbling as he danced hip to hip with me in that sweaty crowd. This was my chance to take control, maybe even demolish his will completely. I stared up at him with innocent, wide eyes and said, "I watched someone I love die."

"Who?" His voice was so sympathetic it was barely audible.

I searched his eyes as they pierced mine. They were blue, which I knew, but now I saw they tinted brown at the pupils, which were pulsing in the flashing lights, like waves crashing into an island. "It's a good thing to be afraid of," I said as my hand crept up the back of his neck to pull his face close. I tasted his breath, then his lips. He dug his fingers into my hair, his kiss rougher than before. My body caved into his. I clung to him with a hand behind his neck and one still hooked to his belt loop. For those few moments, I stopped breathing, stopped thinking, stopped hearing the bass from the speakers overhead. I could only feel—only feel him.

Without warning, he tore my face from his. He shook his head and said, "This isn't enough."

"Then we'll go to the bathroom. Or your car."

He glared at me. "Sawyer, stop. This isn't how I want you."

"Really? You don't want me sweaty and pressed against you?"

"When you decide to be real with me, I'll be here." He let me go and weaved through the crowd until he disappeared.

....

"WHAT ARE YOU GUYS UP to tonight?" I asked Jo the next evening as I swept eyeshadow into the crease of my lid.

"Cash is taking me to Third Street Promenade." She was sitting on my bed, swiping the screen of my phone.

"I love that place, all the buskers and stuff. I think I'd like it better if I had money to shop, though."

"I thought you made pretty good money." There was a twinge of judgment in her voice, or maybe just discomfort. It didn't bother me. She had been a good sport about her less-than-ideal Los Angeles accommodations.

"Yeah, but tuition is expensive."

"Your parents don't help?" What a cute question.

"Nope." I smacked my lips together to press the gloss in place. "I gotta go." I pushed my arms into my sweatshirt. "Tell Cash to buy me something pretty," I said. With a wink, I waved and slipped out the door.

Saturday night was always busy at the club. I spent half my shift bouncing between two bachelor parties before getting a VIP room request from a groomsman, a cute-enough guy in his thirties with paradoxical freckles and salt-and-pepper sideburns. I took him by the hand, leading him down the dark hall for his private show. We hadn't even passed through the curtain when he started pawing at my bare waist. He pulled me against him, scrabbling his fingers under the lace hem of my panties. I feigned a moan and added a breathy, "You have the cash for that?"

His finger was already inside me when he said, "I'll pay anything to fuck you, Delilah."

Delilah.

My breath stopped, and my body froze.

Then I laughed. It was this sick reflex—to laugh. But that was what people did, right? When they couldn't cry or scream because they couldn't feel enough to do either of those? They laughed. It was what happened to those too numb for pain, who instead sensed only a tickle.

They laughed.

It *was* funny, actually. I was so careful to protect my identity, to change my number when I moved, to have no internet presence, but I made my living stripping. I should have known better.

I should have known that we kiddie porn stars never got to grow up.

This job was just a mating call. And now that one had found me, they all could. I had basically shouted, *Hey, pedophiles! Delilah's over here! Like what you saw? Now you can screw the real thing! Sure, it's older and has boobs now, but it's probably better than jacking off to a video of someone else raping it.*

How had I not realized that any of them could recognize me? My face hardly changed in the last decade. It was this Cuban-cursed DNA drawn from the fountain of youth. Or maybe it was my inability to exorcise myself of that molested eight-year-old. Sometimes I wondered if I cut deep enough down my center, if I cracked my sternum and peeled open my ribcage, I'd find her clinging to my spine, digging her heels into my pelvic bone as I yanked at her. I saw her fingernails clawing at my lungs, her hands around my heart squeezing it to take my life with hers. But if I overtook her, if I rid myself of her, maybe the lingering freckles that bridged curved cheek to cheek would disappear. Cheekbones, stubborn and hard, would emerge beneath thinner skin. My viridescent eyes would dull like weathered rock. I would look older. Unrecognizable. Maybe then I'd be safe.

And that girl would die, along with all that happened to her.

I watched from the pole platform as the groomsman

pressed me face-down into the couch and shoved himself into me, thrusting fast and hard. That was how I had sex these days, watching from a few feet away, waiting for the panting and jerking that cued it was almost over. It was how I did it when I was a kid. How I got through it at work. Even from the stage, I could feel my vagina sting with tiny tears, cuts that would leave pink stains in my panties.

He was zipping up his pants when I realized I better piece myself together and get my money. A pang radiated between my thighs when I straightened my arms to rise from the couch. I searched for my underwear on the ground and said, "It's a thousand." Had to tack on an extra two-hundred for him calling me Delilah. Dick.

"I'm not paying more than six hundred. You didn't age well."

I saw the fingers on his left hand as he buttoned his shirt. Silver ring. "Too much of a woman for you now? Do you have to think about me to get it up for your wife?"

"You? No. That little blonde who was with you, though. I can't remember her—" *Simone.*

"Chomo," I muttered under my breath while searching the floor for my underwear.

There was a coldness in his voice when he said, "Whore." Then he added a self-justifying, "I've never touched a kid."

I scoffed. Right, because this wasn't him paying to rape the eight-year-old he wanted in those videos and pictures. "Whatever helps you sleep at night, baby." Found my panties. I stepped into them then crossed my arms over my chest while I waited for him to pay.

He pulled his wallet from his back pocket and sifted

through a wad of cash, dropping a handful of bills on the platform beside him.

I raised my eyebrow. "I said it's a thousand, or do you want me to tell your friends how you know me?" I had no idea how much he already doled out, but I wanted all he owed me. Not that he'd ever give me all he owed me. He pulled two more bills from his wallet and added them to the pile. I added a sultry and condescending, "Good boy," before folding the money and tucking it into my bra.

He raised his middle finger when he walked through the curtain. The feeling was mutual. I knew we'd both burn in hell, but, come on, his fire *had* to be hotter than mine.

Fully dressed—and by that I meant in damp panties and a bra functioning as a bank account—I crossed the club to the locker room to stash my earnings. I counted them behind the door of my locker. Huh. He actually had paid me a grand.

I wasn't sure why, but for the first time, it didn't feel right. Not that it hadn't felt wrong before in the—this is illegal; I might get caught; no guy's going to want me after this sort of way. But all those other nights, I knew who I was pimping out: an eighteen-year-old who screwed over everyone she cared about and was hiding in LA until the storm passed. The money was always dirty, but this—this money was repulsive. This was exploiting the eight-year-old who played out the vile fantasies of grown men, men who cowered behind their computer screens. This was child prostitution. This made my dinner come up.

I couldn't save my long hair from the vomit as

it poured into the toilet. My body shook all over. I crumpled on the locker room floor, trying to huddle it into submission. The stall wall, the inch-wide square tiles that made up the grungy floor, the air from the vent above—everything was cold, turning my shaking into near convulsing. *Get your shit together. You have two hours left.*

Music pulsed into the room. Someone had opened the door. "Emerald!" Derek, my manager, shouted. "I've got two guys in line for the VIP room, requesting you specifically. Hurry up!" Of course he did. I gripped the toilet seat, pulling myself over it just before I hurled again. "Uh, are you sick?"

I coughed and spit to clear my throat of the last pieces of my Caesar salad dinner before pushing open the stall door. "I'm going home."

"Your shift isn't over until two."

I hugged my bare arms, still shivering. "You want me retching on people?" That was enough to make him leave.

When I walked to my car in the November chill, I wondered if I left a trail of that little girl's blood on the pavement, the girl I raped tonight, the one I couldn't surgically remove. Her death was no more than a fantasy. I was stuck with her. As soon as I shut the driver's door, she took control. She cried hot, enraged tears. Tears of confusion. Tears of betrayal.

I couldn't contain them as they carried dark trails of makeup down my cheeks. That kid wasn't supposed to cry. She wasn't allowed to. Jeff didn't like that. The tears had to stop.

They did by the time I pulled into the parking lot at

school. My sleeves were covered in mascara, my cheeks puffy, my green irises surrounded by crimson capillaries. I didn't need to get my key from Cash since my door was already cracked open. It was only 12:30. Everyone was still awake. If Jo or Nicole was in my room, I didn't know. Getting my towel and shower caddy was all I could focus on.

The shower burned. Scalding droplets pelted me as I scrubbed every inch of reddening skin. I slipped my fingers into my vagina, cringing as I scrubbed it over and over until it was dry and raw. I even brushed my teeth in the hot water, the cool mint stinging my throat where the vomit had chafed it.

I was as clean as I could get in my blue flannel pajama pants and tank top when I saw Cash sitting against the wall outside his door. His headphones were on, and he seemed engrossed in whatever he was watching on his laptop. I snuck in front of him to my door. I jiggled the handle. Locked.

"Need this?" Cash asked, holding out my gold key in his palm.

"Yes, thank you." I tried to force a smile, but only half of my mouth cooperated. I reached for it, but his fingers closed over it.

"You okay?" He tilted his head and narrowed his eyes, ready to disbelieve whatever I said.

"Yeah," I sighed, "just a long night."

"Aren't you home early? A couple of hours early?"

"I threw up at work." Code for *give me my key now.*

"That's no fun." He furrowed his eyebrows as he inspected me. "Come here." I leaned toward his outreaching hand to let him brush the damp hair from my forehead and press his palm against it. He turned his hand over and ran the backs of his cool fingers down my pink cheek. My eyes closed at his touch. "You feel pretty warm, but I don't think it's quite to a fever."

I nodded. "Yeah, it's nothing." I reached for the key again. Instead, Cash picked a book up from the floor beside him and put it in my hand. Seriously, this guy could not take a hint. "What's this?"

"Jo said you wanted me to buy you something pretty." He smiled.

"So you got me a book about a woman who carves words into her skin and tries to solve the murder of two little girls?"

"I did?" He took *Sharp Objects* from me and flipped it over to find the synopsis. "Jo said you liked Gillian Flynn." Right, that did come up in a late-night slumber-party-esque conversation.

"Oh, I love her. She's the Ernest Hemingway of the twenty-first century."

"Who says that?"

"Uh, I do," I said with unquestioning confidence.

He gave me a wary look.

"I mean, they're different writers, for sure, but they're both stylistic renegades. There's Flynn, whose prose bites you so you're bleeding out and begging for more. And Hemingway, who gave the literary world the finger by creating beautiful works with simple words and run-on sentences glued together with a hundred *and*s. They're both honest in that sharp way that makes you feel what you'd rather not. You know what I mean?"

Cash smirked as he analyzed me. From his puzzled expression, I could tell he was coming up short.

"I don't expect you to understand. You're an engineer."

"And what are you?"

Alone. Damned. Whore. Hunted. "Undeclared."

He took another second to scrutinize me—me and the truth of my statement. Then he pushed the book back toward me and said, "Look inside." I moved my finger under the cover and flipped it open. The inside was signed by Gillian Flynn herself.

"No!" I collapsed to sit on the floor next to him, careful not to put weight on any sore spots, and pushed his shoulder. "How did you... Where did you get this?"

"A little bookstore in Santa Monica."

"I feel like I shouldn't touch it." I set it carefully in my lap. "I don't want to depreciate the value. How much did this cost you?"

"Not that much." He shrugged. "It's not like it's *Jane Eyre*. We're not *that* close." His lips curved.

"I can't accept this. It's way too—"

"Think of it as a 'thank you' for bunking with my baby sister for three days."

"You didn't need to do that. Jo's actually pretty great."

"I told you she was."

I stared at the book, the dark cover with the razor image. After tonight, I needed a little more of what I didn't deserve. So I stalled to keep Cash in the hall a bit longer. Okay, a lot longer. "What are you watching?" I nodded toward the screen before recognizing it. "*Moneyball*?"

"Yeah, I've never seen it, but Jo said it was written by some great screenwriter and I needed to watch it."

"Aaron Sorkin." I shifted my back against the wall.

"That sounds right."

"It's one of my favorites. 'How can you not be

romantic about baseball?'"

"You like baseball?"

"No, that's a quote from the movie. And sort of. It's my dad's sport, and I love my dad so I tolerate it."

He raised an eyebrow.

"Yes," I relented. "I have a dad. Anyway, the movie is about math, too. Wait," I said as I placed my hand on his forearm and gave him the most intense look I could muster. "Are you sure you can follow along?" He elbowed my ribs before unplugging his headphones and pressing play.

I felt myself flirting with sleep even before my shift had been due to end. Call it an exhausting night. Or maybe I actually was sick. At some point, my temple slumped into Cash's shoulder, firm and comfortable. I perked up enough to mutter, "He gets on base," every time Brad Pitt cued Jonah Hill to. Cash's shoulder bounced beneath me whenever I did.

My eyes flicked open to Cash's neck, the tip of my nose brushing against it, breathing in the subtle scent of his cologne. I felt his arms cradle my back and legs. The movie must have been over, but I couldn't remember the last half of it. He unlocked my door, striding over to lay me down on my bed. That instinctive fear pricked every inch of my skin when he didn't leave right away. He moved toward the foot of my bed, took off my sandals, and then dropped them to the floor. The hair on my arms raised. What was he going to do to me? I couldn't fight anymore, not tonight. I felt him lift my back slightly to pull the covers down under me, then back up to my chin. His palm checked my forehead for fever one last time before brushing my hair away from my ear. "Good night,

Sawyer," he whispered.

The anxiety dissolved, and an ache replaced it. It was this dull pain chipping away within my chest when he touched me. "Good night, Cash," I mumbled and rolled toward his retreating warmth. I didn't care that it hurt. I wanted that ache back. Wanted him here beside me to keep me safe as I slept, to push away everything that happened that night, everything that had happened the last seven months. But he closed the door, shutting me into the darkness behind him.

My eyes stared wide at the grey shapes in the room. Sleep wouldn't return. I was alone. And they knew how to find me.

December 2017

*I*T WAS NEVER A GOOD IDEA TO PARTICIPATE IN AN optional six-hour math competition between stripping shifts, even if told it was impossible to score so much as a point because the questions were unworkable and the graders are over scrupulous to the point of sadism. Trust me, giving into the temptation to say *fuck you* to those who assured my failure by sitting for the exam wouldn't be worth it.

Even if I did score in the top three-hundred in the nation.

I was already seated in the fluorescent-lit classroom with my foot-tall caramel macchiato that Saturday morning when Cash walked in. He paused to stare when he saw me, like it was weird *I* was there. He started down my aisle. "What are you doing here?" he asked.

"Me? Are you sure you're not lost? This is a *math* competition." I smirked.

"You're taking the Putnam Exam?"

"Am I not allowed?"

"No, it's just," he paused to keep from saying

131

something regrettable, "why weren't you at the practice sessions?"

"Cash..." I whispered and leaned against my elbows on the desk. "I have a certain reputation to uphold."

"One that doesn't involve being smart?"

"Not at math."

"Is that why you're in disguise?" He suppressed a smile.

I glanced down at my frumpy Southern Oregon outfit: ripped jeans, high top Converse, a cream thermal shirt under my dad's flannel. My hair was up in a bun with a thick headband to hide that scar on my scalp. My thick-rimmed glasses focused my eyes instead of my usual contacts. And my few freckles and flaws were on full display without any makeup to cover them. Fine, so I was trying to hide in plain sight. "Shut up," I murmured with a laugh.

He crossed his arms and cocked his head to the side. "What's your major again?"

I narrowed my eyes on him. "Undeclared."

"Liar." He smiled as he slid in the desk behind me. "Whose shirt is that? Does he know you love math?"

"First," I slapped my pencil on the desk and turned around, "I do not *love* math." A big fat lie. I was in awe of math, like cavemen were with fire or ancient Egyptians with the Nile. It was the only constant in my eighteen years. The only concrete thing in the universe: rules that couldn't be bent, truth that couldn't be manipulated. It was the only exact science, a stillness in the middle of any chaos, and everything in my life was chaos. So, yes, I fucking *loved* math.

"Then why are you spending six hours on a Saturday

in a math contest?"

"Second, if you want to know if I'm sleeping with someone, just ask."

"Are you?"

"No." I tugged at the flannel. "And he died before I figured out I 'love' math."

His smile fell. "Sawyer, I'm sorry. I didn't—"

"—didn't know. It's fine." I shifted to face my desk again. Cash's silence was thick from behind me. I shouldn't have made him feel so bad, but he just asked way too many questions. All. The. Time. I was getting sick of it.

I CURLED UP IN BED after the test, hoping to catch the sleep that had eluded me the past three weeks. Each time I closed my eyes, I saw Simone and that groomsmen. I saw that video Travis blackmailed us with. I saw Jeff. So I made a habit of staring at the wall, hoping sleep would close my eyes. The result—I fell off the pole last night. I wasn't totally sure what happened. My arms started shaking and then my hands slipped. Muscular fatigue, I guessed. No bruising, just full-body flushed embarrassment and a loss of about one fifty in tips. Tonight was my last shift of the week and my highest-paying one. I *had* to sleep.

But I didn't. Two hours of dreading my shift passed before I finally convinced myself not to call in sick. I needed the money after a month of refusing illegal VIP room favors, so I forced myself out of bed and into the shower to shave and slather with body oil. The hot water did little to help the exhaustion headache that spread over my entire face and down my shoulders. In front of the mirror, I blew out my hair, lined my bloodshot eyes black, and painted my pale lips red.

"Hey," Cash said as I shut my door to leave. "How'd you feel about the test?"

"Killed it." I forced a smile. "You?"

"No idea. Are you free tonight, or do you have work?"

I sighed out, "Work."

He studied my face. "You feeling okay?"

After a long stare between us, I said, "I don't know."

I CAUGHT A SECOND WIND at the club, the pounding music, slimy gazes, and wandering hands keeping me on edge. Two hours into my shift, I was strutting past the bar when a leathery hand shoved a wad of cash into mine, pulling me back so I tripped in my heels. I spun around to see Allen Buchanan, an old regular I hadn't seen in two months. It had been so long I was hoping he had died or slipped into a coma or something less dramatic but equally permanent, so I wouldn't have to deal with him anymore. Because, here was the thing about regulars—they thought I should be so grateful for their constant contribution to my salary that they try to pull shit like paying five hundred for a full fuck because "that's all the ATM would let me take out." But they knew it was what they wanted when they walked in, and I had seen them stuff twenties in my coworker's panties earlier in the night and pay cash at the bar. They had the money. And an expensive watch. And, of course, I couldn't report that I was getting stiffed because prostitution was not only illegal but also a fireable offense. So, I chose my battles and my clients and my clients' watches carefully.

And of all my regulars, Allen was the worst. He was an old perv, in his fifties if I had to guess. He actually bragged to me that I was younger than his youngest daughter when I was unzipping his slacks. I wondered what those poor girls endured at his hand. There was no way in hell I'd ever want to have sex with him. So I hadn't. Sure, I stomached hand jobs every time, a blowjob once when I had a few drinks before work, but never sex.

I led him through the thick curtain into the dim VIP room and pushed him onto the couch, trying to ignore the sight of his white dress shirt struggling to stretch over his round gut. Straight from the office, I assumed. I was sure he or the assistant he was screwing informed his wife he was *working late*. I straddled his lap and whispered heavily in his ear, "It's been ages, Allen," as I undid the buttons under his collar. He smelled old, like heavy cologne and sun-scorched skin. I just had to get through twenty minutes. God knew I had endured worse for twenty minutes.

Allen pushed his hand into his pants pocket and took out a handful of bills. I saw the purple, shimmering stripe on each hundred. Underneath them was a condom. His thick fingers moved under my straps as he pressed the bills into my bra with one hand and the condom in between my fingers with the other. I took a deep breath, pulled the money out of my bra, and returned it and the condom. "I don't do that anymore. You want me to get Sapphire?"

"Come on, baby." His hands slid over my hips until he groped my ass. "Delilah never said no, did she?"

Delilah.

I was right. They *all* knew where to find me.

But still, what was with these pedophiles? I wasn't a little girl anymore. Hadn't I grown too curvy and athletic for their taste? Why were they all trying to fuck me?

Allen's fingers moved under the lace of my panties. It was when I reminded him that he was wrong. Delilah said "no" all the time. That was why they all liked Simone better than her.

Allen's hands on my butt was the last coherent memory I had. Whatever happened next was like watching a horror movie on a vintage projector, except several of the slides were missing. Everything came at me in flashes, like I was outside of my body one second, then in it the next, then not even in the VIP room for the third. So flashes—vibrant, searing, incohesive flashes—across a screen were all I got. My back against the sticky couch. A deep pain in my wrists. A sharp pinch in my thighs. The thing I remember most was beating the shit out of Jeff, which, even in the moment, I knew didn't make sense. Why would Jeff be there? Had he found me? If he had, I wouldn't be safe until he was dead. So I kept slamming the head between my hands against the wall until the drywall crumbled to expose the stud beneath.

Then a thick arm around my waist knocked the wind out of me. Ivan tore me backward, my fingers still digging into Allen's skull as he dragged me away. I crumpled on the ground where I heaved and coughed. There I saw the last slide in the projector: Allen unconscious, his head bleeding, his nose gushing, too, and Ivan pressing two fingers to his neck.

Shit.

Had I just *murdered* someone? Shit. Shit. Shit! I tore

through those slides in my mind, hoping to find a way to erase the last two minutes. I should have just said, *Yes, Delilah would love to fuck you.* He was just one client. I'd survive. I had so many times before. Why did I suddenly have to have principles?

"Is he alive?" I breathed, my lungs barely filling.

Ivan answered after what felt like an hour. "Yeah, you lucky bitch." He pulled his cell from his pocket, I assumed to call an ambulance. My cue to leave.

I didn't realize until then that my panties were around my ankles. I pulled them up with my shaking hands. My hands that were splattered with blood. My forearms were, too. And my chest. I hugged the edge of the club as I made my way to the locker room, trying to hide the evidence of attempted homicide covering my body. I unsnapped my bra and slipped down my underwear, splashing water and soap over my bare skin as I scrubbed away the drying blood. Scarlet swirls pooled in the white sink, and pink puddles collected on the counter.

"Fuck, fuck, fuck!" I hissed as I tried to wipe the counter down with paper towels. Now I had bloodstained towels. I slammed open a stall door and flushed them. All right, the sink looked okay. It was going to be okay. I was going to be okay.

All right, next—the lingerie. His blood was on there, too. I'd have to toss it in a dumpster somewhere. Not here.

I slapped on a different bra, a tank top that hardly covered it, and jeans. Shoving the remaining evidence in my purse, I forced myself to tread an inconspicuous pace to my car. There were blue and red lights at the front of the club. I was in the back parking lot. I could escape. I had time.

I made it into my car and turned over the ignition. As I slammed the car into reverse, a yellow glare blinded me through my window. "Put your hands on the steering wheel," the officer demanded. I clutched the wheel at the midnight position and pressed my forehead into my knuckles. So close.

I shivered outside my car as the young, sun-spotted cop questioned me. "Did you assault Congressman Buchanan?" Oh, I'd forgotten Allen was our congressman. Eh, it wasn't like he showed up to work much.

"Buchanan?" I smacked my lips and scrunched my nose. "I'm not familiar—"

"First name Allen."

"Doesn't ring a bell," I said as I shook my head and hugged my bare arms.

He scanned my body with his flashlight. "What happened to your arms?"

I glanced down at my swollen, red wrists. "I fell off the pole yesterday."

He shone the light into my car through the open driver's door, over my bulky purse in the passenger seat. "Can you open your bag, miss?"

"Do you have a warrant to search my stuff?"

"Would you rather I arrest you and obtain the warrant while you wait in jail?"

I drew a deep breath and rolled my eyes before reaching over the driver's seat to grab the damning evidence. "Knock yourself out," I said as I handed it to him.

He slid on a glove before reaching in to pull out my

blood-splattered bra. "Is this yours?"

"Pretty, isn't it? It looks even better on."

He took my bruised wrist in his hand and snapped a cuff on it, twisting my arm behind my back as he pressed my chest against my car. "You're under arrest for the assault of Allen Buchanan. You have the right to remain silent. Anything you say..." He rambled as he dragged me by the arm to the patrol car.

We drove past the paramedics loading Allen into an ambulance. He was so messed up. Even from a distance, I could tell. It seemed like he still hadn't regained consciousness. That couldn't be good.

What was the protocol for this sort of thing? Should I send flowers to his hospital room? Maybe with a note?

Sorry I bashed your head in. I thought you were my abusive stepfather. No hard feelings?

XOXO Emerald

Ps. Burn in hell, baby fucker.

I was thinking lilies. Yeah, everyone liked lilies.

At the station, a different cop plopped me in a cold interrogation room after what felt like hours of processing: mugshots, photographs of my injuries, fingerprint scans, mouth swabbing, knuckle swabbing, swabbing of whatever they wanted. There I waited, freezing, for my next line of questioning.

A female officer finally bounced in with a file. Her body was in uniform, her dark hair pulled back in a tight bun. "Ms. de la Cruz," she started and reached out to shake my hand. I shot her a suspicious expression as I accepted her weirdly polite gesture. "I'm Officer Kelly. I'm terribly sorry it's taken so long to get to you. It's been a busy night." She sat down in front of me, spreading her elbows laterally and intertwining her fingers. "Do you need anything to drink?" Wow, she took good cop to a whole new level.

"I'm fine, thanks," I said, even though I was thirsty. I wasn't sure why I did that.

"Okay, so you're a dancer at Sunset Stripped, correct?"
I nodded.

"Did you have a shift tonight?"
I nodded again.

"When was it scheduled to end?"

"Two AM."

"Can you tell me why you were in your car at ten thirty?"

I sighed. "Look, let's not waste each other's time. Obviously, they're going to find Allen's blood on my bra. Ivan'll rat me out for what he saw. But just because Allen's more fucked up than me doesn't mean this was my fault."

Kelly smirked, satisfied. "Okay. Why isn't it your fault?"

I looked up at her through my eyebrows. "He tried to pay me eight-hundred dollars to have sex with him. I believe you all would call that 'soliciting sex?' Last time I checked, that was still illegal in California." She didn't need to know I had broken this law countless times. "I gave him his money back, then he asked again and said, 'Delilah never said no.' I tried to leave, but he pinned me to the couch and tried to rape me."

"When you first struck Buchanan, did he back off?"

"I don't know." And that was the truth. I had no idea what happened to him, only what happened to Jeff...who wasn't there.

She took down a couple of notes, then flipped through the file. "Buchanan's initial medical evaluation shows he has a concussion, brain hemorrhage, broken nose, and blunt force trauma to his penis and testicles. From the size of the wounds, it appears that someone stepped on his groin with a stiletto heel."

With eyes closed, I shook my head and whispered, "*Shit.*" I was sure I'd remember crushing a guy's nuts with my shoe, but I didn't.

"Now, you're saying that, in a club full of people, including an able-bodied bouncer within earshot, you needed to nearly kill this man in order to keep him from raping you?"

"I did! Did you even listen to what I said? He called me Delilah."

"Delilah?"

I glared at her as I took a deep breath. "Forget it."

"Miss de la Cruz—"

"That's a mouthful. Just call me Sawyer."

"Okay, Sawyer. If you are or were in danger, we can help you. But you have to—"

I cackled. "Oh, sweetie, you can't help me."

"Can you tell me why you think we can't?"

"Can we just do bail now? I have class Monday and finals the week after next. I need to get home."

Her eyes ran up and down my scantily clad body. "Are you cold, Sawyer?"

I stared at my arms, inflamed and covered in goose bumps. "This is LA. It's never cold."

There was a knock on the mirror. "I'll be right back." She folded the file and took it with her out the door.

No more than a minute later, the door opened again.

"Here's a coat if you want it." She handed me a baggy LAPD windbreaker. "It's clean, I promise. And your bail is set at twenty thousand. Do you have anyone who can post that for you?"

"Is this when I get my phone call?" As I asked this, I wasn't even sure who I'd call. This was one of those times that having a family would come in handy. Or a boyfriend. But all I had were friends, and only a few at that.

Pressing my ear to my cell phone, I listened as the phone on the other side of the line rang. Once. I tapped my fingers on the back. Twice. I tapped them a little faster. Three times. This was too familiar. I had placed three calls like this in June. Just like then, leaving a message after the beep would be no help. Then, at 1:07 AM, "Hello?" he answered, his accent heavy with fatigue.

"Cash, hey. I'm so sorry for this," I hurried my words. "But I didn't know who else I could call. I have an enormous favor to ask you." There was a long pause. Had he hung up? I checked the screen. Nope. "This is Sawyer by the way."

He let out a soft laugh. "I know." I knew then everything would be okay.

....

THE CLANKING OF THE CELL door startled me to sitting. I lifted my arm from my eyes. "That was fast," I said under my breath.

Cash's usually bouncy curls looked tired through the window of the police station door. He ruffled them and then pushed up the sleeves of his university hoodie.

I took a deep breath. When I glanced down, I realized how slutty I still looked. When the cop opened the door, I felt shame-laden blood rush up my neck and face. Cash's pale lips curled into a sad smile when he saw me.

"I'll pay you back tonight. I'm good for it. I swear," I started.

"Let's just get you home." He stood and led me out the door with his hand between my bare shoulder blades. Once we were out in the cold, he pulled his sweatshirt over his head and handed it to me.

"Thanks," I whispered. I tugged it on and over my bare waist. It was soft and still warm from his body, saturated with his scent: sandy like the beach but fresh like clean laundry.

The adrenaline of the evening wore off as I rested my head against his passenger window. I closed my eyes as if that would make everything go away. Maybe if we kept driving, we could escape this. There had to be someplace in the world, someplace we could go, where this night never happened. A place where none of those men could find me.

"You okay?" Of course that was what he asked, not, *Why the hell did you call me in the middle of the night to bail you out of jail?*

Shaking my head, I felt a tear roll down my cheek. I brushed it away with the sleeve of his sweatshirt. "I'm sorry you had to bail me out. I can write you a check for the two grand as soon as we get to the dorm."

"Two grand?" He glanced over at me. "It was twenty."

"What?" I bolted upright. "You didn't get a bond? You paid it in full?"

"I didn't even think about getting a bond. I just

wanted to get you out of there."

I buried my face in my hands and groaned, "Cash. I can't pay you back. I'm so sorry."

"It's okay. Just show up to court, and I'll get my money back."

"How do you even have that much money?"

"Are you going to be okay, though? Do you need a lawyer or something?"

I shook my head. "Probably. I don't know, Cash. It's bad. Like, *won't get to pee in private for years* bad. And I don't have enough money or any family to help, so I'm going to get stuck with a public defender who gets paid nothing—" I curled into a ball again with my head on my knees.

"Hey, hey, it's okay." His hand landed on my back, rubbing in soothing circles. "We're going to figure this out."

We? How was this his problem?

Before I could point this out, he added, "My uncle, you know, the one Jo was supposed to stay with until they all got the flu? Anyway, he's a defense attorney. He's good, too. We could ask him to take a look at your case."

I popped my head up. Well, that was convenient. "Really?"

"Yeah, I actually go to their house every Sunday after church. You should come with me tomorrow." I should have guessed that Cash went to church.

"Cash, that would be amazing. Where should I meet you? I mean, I'll have to pick up my car from the club—" As the last word slipped through my lips, I realized he and I never talked about what I did.

"Or you could just come to church with me and we

could get your car after lunch."

A reflexive laugh roared from my gut. I stopped when I saw him cut his eyes to me again. "Wait, you're serious?"

"Yeah, why not?" Such an adorable question. Only Cash would ask it.

"You know I'm a stripper, right?"

"I figured." Cue awkward pause. "If you're worried about people judging you, it's not—"

I shook my head. "No, that's not it."

"Then give me one reason you shouldn't go."

"All right." I shifted in my seat. He asked for it. "My Sunday school teacher married my mom, then raped me for two years. He told me if I didn't do what he wanted, I'd go to hell. He'd quote scripture at me about suffering and punishment and all that. You know like that rich man thirsty in hell and Lazarus one? Or the one about the vines getting cut down and thrown in the fire?" I took a deep breath. Letting it go, I said, "So, yeah. I'm not a fan of church."

Cash ran a hand over his face. "Sawyer, that's awful. I can't even..."

"It was a long time ago." I shrugged.

"I'm sorry." His eyes were soft when they met mine, full of a compassion I just couldn't deal with.

"Thanks, but I just don't think about it." Before he could ask anything else, I added, "Or talk about it."

"Okay." Cash drew in a pensive breath. "But here's the thing—my uncle's really busy. This might be the only way you get to talk to him."

I grimaced and studied his profile as he drove. It was lit up blue in the glow from the dash lights. He was cute even as he searched his mind for a way to drag me to church.

"How about this? We go to church, and we can walk out if something's just too much. They have a coffee shop we can sit in. I know you like coffee." He nudged me. "I'll take you to get your car after we see my uncle."

I bit my lower lip, snuggling deeper in his sweatshirt as I thought. Which torture was worse, church or prison? Church was only an hour or so, and prison could be years. Hmm. Church? Prison? Church? "Okay."

It was almost three AM when we found a parking spot at the dorm. The exhaustion weighed me down as we walked the long hall to our rooms. "Hang on." I yawned as I knocked on my door. Hopefully Nicole wasn't in her usual coma-like sleep. "Let me write you a check for what I have." There was no answer at the door, so I pounded louder. "Nicole, it's me. Open up. I don't have my key."

"Don't worry about the money."

I knocked again. "Are you sure?"

"Yeah." He eyed my closed door. "Do you need to stay in my room?"

I sighed and ran my fingers across my forehead. "You don't mind?"

"Not at all." He echoed my words from September as he slid his key in the handle. "And Dylan went home for the weekend, so we don't have to deal with him."

"How are you guys even roommates?"

Cash yawned. "He was my roommate last year. The enemy you know is better than the roommate you don't know with a bunch of other annoying traits that you could never predict." He laughed as he closed the door.

"Hey, I know this is a lot to ask, but I *have* to shower to get the jail and the cop car and the club and the blood from the perv who tried to rape me off my skin. Do you mind if I borrow your shower stuff?"

He dropped his keys on his desk and turned to me. "Hold on. How were you the one who got arrested?"

I yawned again, waving my hand in front of my face. "I'll explain tomorrow."

"Here." He opened his wardrobe. "Take some clothes, too. Oh, and a towel." He pulled out a mostly folded towel, navy tee shirt, and plaid pajama pants. "And, uh, do you want boxers? Or is that weird?"

"Yes, please."

He nodded as he opened a drawer and pulled out boxer briefs to add to the pile, then gave me his shower caddy.

I pulled a blue bottle out of the caddy. "Wow, you have conditioner?" Whatever kind it was, it looked expensive.

"Sulfate-free, so it won't weigh down my curls." He slipped his fingers through his short hair. I smirked, and he pretended to get defensive. "I don't have to explain myself to you." No, he didn't. Whatever he did with his hair was working.

My shower was hot and thorough, but quick. I just wanted to get the night washed off me and go to bed. Cash's clothes were comically long on me. His shirt almost reached my knees, and I had to roll the pants at the waist and the ankles to keep them from dragging on the floor. But at least they were soft and clean and smelled like him.

When I got back to his room, he was lying on his

back on the thin carpet with a pillow under his head. "Um, no, no, no," I said. I set his shower caddy on the floor. "I'm not kicking you out of your bed."

"I'm not letting you sleep on the floor. And you don't want to sleep in Dylan's bed. I don't think he knows how to operate a washing machine." I glanced at the pile of bedding on his mattress. The sheets did look crunchy. Gross. How did he get girls to have sex with him in there?

Cash would never go for this, but... "We could share." I was quick to add, "In a very Christian, leaving-room-for-Jesus kind of way." Not that there would be room for even baby Jesus in that twin bed. Cash was so freaking tall.

He chuckled. "You're okay with that?"

"*You* are?" I raised an eyebrow.

"Sure." He shrugged and tossed his pillow back on the bed.

Cash climbed under the covers first, then I slid in facing him. I rested my arm across him—to get comfortable, not to cuddle, of course. Instead of scooting away from me, he wrapped his arm under the pillow so I could lay my head on his chest. I nuzzled into him, hoping the excuse of the narrowness of the twin bed would disguise any affection I was displaying. This was strictly platonic bed sharing between two people who had made out a couple of times, one of whom had attempted to debauch the other repeatedly for months. Everyone did that, right? Totally normal.

Fatigue closed my eyes. My body felt leaden against the mattress, against Cash. But I knew I wouldn't fall asleep until I asked, "Cash?"

His chest rose and fell when he said, "Mmhmm?"

"Why'd you answer your phone tonight?"

"Because," he yawned again, "it was you. Why wouldn't I?"

I ran my hand to his waist and hugged him a little tighter. His arm tucked me against him, and his lips brushed my forehead. Warm and safe and with Cash, I fell asleep.

THIRD STREET WAS EMPTY. IT always was at the beginning of this nightmare. The hollow sound of my Chuck Taylors stepping onto the pavement echoed off the houses. The first man emerged from the yellow house onto the east sidewalk. He started whistling and shouting. I wanted to tell him to shut up, that the others would come out if he didn't, but no one in this dream could ever hear me. No one but Simone.

I felt her slender fingers slip into my hand, her steel medical ID bracelet cold against my wrist. Her blonde hair was still streaked with the natural chunky highlights of a child. She was just a child, shapeless and small.

The doors of the houses lining the street opened, men filing out to form a crowd on the sidewalks. They reached out for us, but it was as if there was an invisible fence holding them back. But at any moment, that barrier could break and they could spill into the streets and grab us. They had before.

Simone and I took deep breaths and let go of each other. It was impossible to decipher the demands flying at us from either side of the street, but we had to try. We had to obey. I started by shrugging off my flannel, letting it fall to the rough ground below. After I stepped out of

149

my shoes, I slipped off my jeans. Silk and lace covered my ribs, leaving a hollow where my breasts should have been. Simone wore close to the same, her lips coated in red and her eyelashes in black.

The roaring grew louder, the hoards thicker. There weren't enough houses in the neighborhood to have contained these men. They had traveled from somewhere else.

Even over the din, I heard every breath between the two of us, labored and afraid, each one pushing us forward. Jeff was behind us; we didn't have to check over our shoulders to know. Simone stopped, her heart pounding like a bass drum as she stared ahead.

"What?" I whispered. I followed her gaze to Travis and his three friends at the intersection of Ransom Street and Third. I grabbed her hand. "We have to."

She shook her head.

I dragged her along. Her hand relaxed in mine. Acquiescence. Then she slumped to the ground, her breath wheezing. "Hey!" I stooped down to catch her. She lay limp in my arms as her eyes closed. "Help! Someone, help!"

Shh, Sawyer. It's okay.

But no one listened. Or no one could hear. Maybe my screams were too quiet—just puffs of air over loose vocal chords. "Someone, please," I begged when her breathing stopped.

Hey, you're all right. I'm here.

Sprinting steps closed in. Finally. Travis scooped Simone out of my arms and laid her on the pavement. I waited for him to do something else, something to save her, but he turned back to me and unzipped his pants.

When I went to punch Travis, I fell off Cash's bed.

Pain spiked into each vertebra as my back hit the floor. "Shit!"

"Hey, you okay?" Cash leaned over the side of the mattress, holding his jaw in one hand. Streaks of light streamed through the blinds over the five o'clock shadow on his face.

I was sweaty and breathless on the floor. "Yeah," I groaned as I rolled to sitting. He sat up, still holding his cheek. "What happened to your face?"

"You punched me." He breathed a sheepish laugh.

"What?"

"Yeah, right before you fell."

"Cash, I'm so sorry."

"No, don't worry about it. You were having a nightmare. But it didn't exactly convince me to sleep with you."

"I wasn't having a nightmare."

"Sure. You just yell for help and throw punches in your sleep for no reason."

"Yeah, I don't remember." I stood. "I am sorry about that, though. So," I sighed, "when is this church thing?"

He grabbed his phone from the desk. "Can you be ready in forty-five minutes?"

"As long as I'm not locked out."

I knocked on my door. Nicole answered, finally. "So..." She eyed me up and down. "Cash finally slept with you?"

I pushed past her into our room. "Yeah, only because you didn't answer the door."

"You're welcome." Her face was so smug I wanted to punch it, but I had already assaulted two people in the last twelve hours, so I should probably give it a rest.

I rolled my eyes. "It wasn't like that." I let his pajama pants fall to the floor, and then stepped out of them on my way to my wardrobe.

"Holy crap! What did he do to your legs? And your arms?"

"Nicole, seriously, we didn't have sex." I ducked behind the wardrobe door to examine the deepening purple and green splotches on the outside of my thighs. My wrists were worse. I brushed my fingertips over them. Even just that touch sliced through to my muscles. Pants and long sleeves then. Whatever. It wouldn't be the first time I had to cover bruises.

CASH AND I WENT TO church. It was this massive auditorium filling with hundreds of people like ants swarming over a cookie. There were more people here than in my whole town. We walked down the left center aisle toward the stage. And kept walking. And walking. We didn't stop until the fourth row from the front. Really? Couldn't we hide in the back? By the door maybe? Or in the lobby?

Cash's cousins saved two seats for us. We slid in front of them. "This is Amber," Cash said, introducing me to the girl his age sitting on the end.

"Hi. Sawyer," I said.

"And Sydney." A girl about my age.

"Hey."

"Noah and Sophie." A little younger.

"Hi." How many were there?

"Andy. And Uncle Stephen and Aunt Becca."

"Hi. Sawyer." I made sure to shake Stephen's and Becca's hands. Especially since Stephen might get me out of jail.

When we sat down, I whispered to Cash, "Holy crap! Five kids?"

He laughed. "I'm number three of seven."

"What? It's not just you and Jo?"

He shook his head. "What about you? Any siblings?"

"Nah. I was a condom accident. My parents were seventeen."

You, of all people, should know better, Sawyer.

I squeezed my eyes shut. "Then my dad passed shortly after my mom finished nursing school, so they didn't have time to have another when they could afford it."

Cash knitted his eyebrows together and stared at me. "What?"

"The shirt you wore yesterday..." His voice lowered as if it hurt to even ask the question, "That was your dad's?"

"Yeah, but it *is* possible I just scarred them so badly they never wanted another."

"You didn't tell me your dad died."

I shrugged. "It was a long time ago."

The worship team started playing. Acoustic guitar strums with the lead singer greeting everyone over it. "How long ago?" Cash asked.

"Twelve years," I said, standing with the rest of the congregation as the music started.

"I'm sorry, Sawyer."

"Stop." I put my hand on his arm. "It's not a big deal."

The room was dim, hiding me in the crowd flanking me on every side. But then the music ended, and everyone sat. The lights flickered on, illuminating a thousand faces behind me. I didn't see them. I only felt them, the way people sensed they were being followed without hearing footsteps. Someone knew Emerald—how thoroughly, I did not know. Someone knew Delilah, knew I was named that for my aim to deceive, my ability to cripple the strong, the contagious nature of my sin. In a congregation this size, someone knew. But I didn't know who.

There were whispers in the row behind me. A head in front of me turned to the side so I could see the white of his eyes. The hairs on my arms stood on end. If I got up to leave, they'd all see me; those ones who already knew could follow me. So I slouched and watched my knees bounce.

Cash rested the back of his hand on my thigh, brushing that clothed injury from hours before: an offer of fingers waiting for mine. I slipped my hand in his and squeezed my eyes shut. It was just me and Cash, his warm palm against my cold skin. No one else was here. No one could see me because I couldn't see them.

I HAD NO EVIDENCE CASH had given Uncle Stephen a head's-up that I was at Sunday lunch for legal counsel. We just sat across from him at the table for lunch and joined in the family conversation. I answered the barrage of questions from his family.

I'm from Oregon.
No, nowhere near Portland.
I haven't decided what I'm studying yet.
Cash and I are neighbors.

No, we're just friends. How was that their business?

An hour passed, but Cash said nothing to Stephen that suggested I went to church for any reason other than masochistic torture. His cousins and aunt scattered from the table, clearing plates and casserole dishes. Stephen lingered over his empty plate, folded his hands below his chin, and asked, "So, Cash, you were arrested?"

I nearly cackled. Cash do anything wrong? Had he just met these people?

"No, Sawyer just had some questions for you."

Stephen waved his hand at me to start.

I cleared my throat. "Well, if someone got arrested for assault when they were defending themselves, um..." I swallowed and glanced over at Cash. "What would you do?"

"Can I have more details?"

"Yeah. A congressman attempted to solicit..." I winced and darted my gaze around. "Ah...*favors*," I inserted air quotes, "from a *dancer*," air quotes again. "When she said no, he attempted to," I whispered the next word, "rape her. She fought him off, but took it a little far. And she just has a few bruises. She got arrested, and he didn't. What are her chances of walking free?"

"How far is a little far?"

"He's lucky to be alive."

Stephen nodded and focused on me intently for a few seconds. "Cash, Sawyer's just about out of tea." He handed Cash my mason jar half-filled with ice. "Would you get her a refill?"

"Yes, sir." Cash brushed his hand over my shoulder as he stood.

When Stephen brought his attention back to me, I

knew what he was going to ask. God bless him for getting rid of Cash before he said, "Had you accepted payment for illegal sexual contact with this congressman before last night?"

I ran my hands over my face and nodded.

"What about with other clients?"

I nodded again before tucking my hands in the crooks of my arms and resting my elbows on the table. "I stopped in November, though." As if that made a difference.

"Can anyone besides those who solicited sex confirm you received payment for sex?"

"I told one of the other dancers a while back. And, Ivan, one of the bouncers..." Ivan. He'd walked in. It was so humiliating. Even more so was giving him half my tips from that blowjob to keep him from telling the manager.

"Okay." He let out a long exhale. That couldn't be good.

Before he bore the bad news that I was going to be wearing orange until I turned twenty-five, I added, "Wait." I glanced over my shoulder. Cash was talking with Sydney. Or Sophie? One of them. I had time. I lowered my voice and leaned over the table to Stephen. "Does it make any difference that he tried to have sex with me because he recognized me from kiddie porn?"

Stephen laced his fingers together on the table and tilted his head back and forth as if bouncing the question around in his brain. "Kind of."

Yep. Going to prison for sure.

"How'd it go?" Cash asked after he closed the driver's

side door.

"He's going to set me up for a psych eval to show I acted under extreme stress or trauma or something."

"That's good, right?" He was optimistic. Always so freaking optimistic.

I sighed. "He doesn't think I'll win if it goes to court."

"What? How? You acted in self-defense."

I stared out the window. "It's his word against mine for the attempted rape, and Stephen doesn't think the jury will sympathize with me."

"Why not?" Cash was incredulous. I wasn't sure what it was about me that made me seem like a lost puppy, but I could assure him that he was alone in his perception.

"Because the jury is going to see a trashy hooker who nearly beat a congressman to death. Who would you believe?"

"Hooker?"

I dropped my head, gazing down at my fingers twisting together in my lap. Out of the corner of my eye, I saw him turn back to the road and nod once. He said nothing. I wished he would just say something, anything. But he said nothing. And never said anything about it after.

Cash took me to get my car as promised. The drive back to the dorm was the first time I had been alone since washing out my bloody bra in the strip club sink. I was surprised how alone I felt. Scared, actually. Small. Sober. Too sober. I needed a drink.

I dropped my keys on my desk, noticing Cash's pajamas folded on top of my bed. I changed back into his tee shirt and boxer briefs before opening the bottom drawer of my desk, also known as my liquor cabinet. It had been a whiskey neat kind of twenty-four hours. I grabbed a bottle and one of the four tumblers I had from my short stint living in a ghetto studio apartment this summer. After I poured two fingers, I swallowed half, relishing the burn all the way down. There was a knock at my door. I opened it with the glass discreetly dangling from my fingertips behind the door.

"Hey." Cash smiled. "What's this?" He pointed to his shirt hanging loosely from my shoulders.

"Don't flatter yourself." I smirked. "I need to do laundry."

"Hmm." He nodded doubtfully.

"Can I help you?" I eased the door closer around me.

"Yeah. Have dinner with me Thursday night."

I squinted at him for what felt like a full minute. "What?"

"Dinner. You know, eating, probably at a restaurant." Cash answered, placing his hand on my doorframe.

"Like a date?"

"Yeah, like a date."

I sighed. "Cash, I might be in jail Thursday. My arraignment is tomorrow."

He waved his hand in front of his chest. "You're not going to jail."

Again with the relentless optimism.

"You really don't have to ask me out if you want sex. We should do it now, just in case—"

"No." He rocked back on his heels and crossed his arms. "Just dinner."

"What if I want dessert?" I shot him a lubricious gaze.

"Literal dessert?"

"Fine." I flicked my fingers.

"You like ice cream?"

"Sure, everyone does."

"Then we'll get ice cream."

"No, I don't eat ice cream."

"Why not?"

I shook my head. "What do you get out of this just-dinner with the prospect of literal dessert?"

"Time with you."

I narrowed my eyes at him. "This is weird."

"I'll pick you up at six. Bring thick socks and a coat." He started to walk away as if I might change my mind if he stayed.

"Wait, why?" I called. I knew he heard, but he shut his door behind him anyway.

....

THE THURSDAY NIGHT AFTER CASH bailed me out of jail, I stood flushed from the hair dryer in my violet bra and jeans searching for something warm to wear. I slid hanger after hanger along the rod: long sleeve tee, sweater, sweatshirt, sweater, leather jacket. I pushed to the next sweater so I wouldn't have to see that jacket from Jake's dad. Jake was gone. I was gone. I'd tell myself a thousand more times if I had to.

Someone knocked on my door. I checked my phone. It was already ten after six. I grabbed the next shirt on the rod and pulled it on before opening the door. Cash was in a sweater, not his usual plaid shirt rolled around his forearms. It must be his version of dressing up. "Hey, what's this?" I pointed to the lilies in his hand.

"I told you that you wouldn't go back to jail."

"Yeah, yeah." I pushed my feet into my boots. "Released on my own recognizance because, according to your uncle, I sacrificed everything to go to school here, I'm an excellent student, and I have no ties anywhere else to anyone so I'm not a flight risk. Oh, and I'm too poor to flee." I tiptoed to kiss his cheek and then took the flowers. They were already in a vase and everything. "Thank you. They're beautiful."

"You like lilies?"

"Everyone likes lilies." Which reminded me, was Allen still breathing through a tube? I hoped not. That'd probably be bad for my case.

"Do you have thick socks?"

I stepped backward toward my wardrobe. "Are you going to abandon me on a mountain or something?" I asked. I shoved a pair of socks into my purse.

"Don't tempt me."

"Well, that might get me out of prison," I suggested as I closed the door behind me.

"You're not going to prison." He took my hand, and we started down the hall.

"You have a lot of faith in your uncle. But I've thought about it, and it might not be so bad."

"You think?"

"First, they have libraries, or I'd at least have the right to access one, so I could read all I want."

"You do like books."

"Second, no men could find me there."

"Except correctional officers."

"Damn."

"Who are you running from anyway?"

"Third, I actually look phenomenal in orange."

"I'm sure you do, but none of that matters because you aren't going to prison."

"Where are we going?"

"You're impatient, you know that?"

"You make me wait a lot." I winked.

"Get used to it."

He opened the passenger door of his silver Audi for me. "I've been meaning to ask," I said as I slid into shotgun, "shouldn't you have a truck?"

He leaned a forearm on the top of the door and the other on the top of the car. "Why?"

"'Cause you're from the South. Your life's like a country song, right?"

He smirked at me. "Shouldn't you know how to milk a cow since you're from Oregon?"

"I do. And how to castrate a bull."

"Are you serious?"

"I never lie about my emasculating abilities."

"Hang on." He shut my door, walked around the car, and scooted into the driver's seat. "What?"

"Yeah, there are a few different ways, but on my friend's ranch, we just cut the balls off with, well, basically bolt cutters."

Cash's face went ashen. Nothing made a man sympathize with an animal like emasculation. Sure, men could hunt, shoot, and slaughter them, but snipping off their manhoods crossed a line.

"Those new steers were *pissed*."

"Ya think?"

"Sorry. We don't have to talk about this. I'm not exactly good at...conversations."

He laughed. "You've been able to skate by on your

good looks so far?"

"Pretty much." I shot him a wink. "You're welcome to bring up any equally sexy topics tonight. For instance, flesh-eating bacteria, whether peeing on jellyfish stings is effective, politics—"

"I feel like I'm playing *Cards Against Humanity*."

"Cash, my life is *Cards Against Humanity*."

His smile fell. Time to change the subject.

"Are we in Brentwood?"

"Yeah, I think so."

"Didn't OJ kill those people out here?" Murder. That was a step in the right direction. "Are you going to kill me, too?"

"Nah, I don't have enough money or fame to get away with that." He half-smiled and cut his eyes over to me.

"But you do have twenty grand to spare for the stripper next door?"

"Sure."

"How?"

"I have a job."

"As a drug dealer?"

"As a freelance hacker."

I had never liked Cash more. He was dirty, too, in his own geeky way. "So people pay you to hack into other people's systems or something?" I wasn't really a computer person, clearly.

He looked amused. "No, into their own systems. To improve their security."

"Ah." I nodded, slightly disappointed. "How'd you get into that?"

He turned a corner onto a coastal highway, the dark ocean glowing in the moonlight. "I started the summer before my senior year in high school by hacking our family bank's online customer interface. You know, for fun."

"Wow. You were out of control."

"Right? No, actually I got this nasty flu for a couple of weeks, so I was home sick and bored."

"And that's what we all do when we're bored."

"Anyway," he continued, pretending to be annoyed. "I was able to break into my parents' account without their login information and set up bill pay to myself. So, I told the bank—"

"That was your mistake."

"—and they paid me to fix it."

"Seriously? You know how to do that?"

He nodded.

"Then why are you majoring in Engineering?"

"Because I already know how to program. I'm not going to pay someone six figures to teach me."

"Makes sense. Although, I wish you would've told me this back in September."

"Why?"

"Because I'm in this programming class, and it's killing me. I'd drop it, but it's required for my major."

"Really? I didn't know *undeclared* had any required classes." I avoided his gaze as he turned his head to me, eyebrow raised, the heel of his hand resting on the top of the steering wheel.

Touché. "Mathematics with a minor in American Literature and Culture."

"American Lit," he repeated under his breath.

"Any excuse to read and talk about Hemingway."

"The Gillian Flynn of the twentieth century."

"Right!" I grinned like an idiot. "I have an incurable crush on him."

Cash snorted. "Isn't he old? And dead?"

"He wasn't always old. And you know what I mean."

"I can't even begin to understand what you mean."

"Like I'd be his girl if I was born a century earlier. Well, not his girl really. You know how good girls always fall for the bad boy and are all like," cue mocking voice, "'Oh, he'll change for me. He loves me.' Hemingway was *the* bad boy of twentieth century American literature. Philandering, alcoholic, tortured writer haunted by the image of his father's suicide. Mmm..."

"You think that's sexy? Promiscuity and childhood trauma?"

"Don't you?" I raised my eyebrow.

"Okay, just so I understand..." Cash glanced at me with those island-blue eyes when he stopped at a red light. "Your fantasy is to have been born at the turn of the century and be the good girl Hemingway changed for?"

"No, that's ridiculous. I'm not stupid."

Cash chuckled as if I had said something silly.

"No, I want to be the bad girl *he* thinks will change for *him*. I imagined we'd meet in Cuba, you know? I catch his eye on the beach after he's had a rough day fishing. We run into each other again at a bar off the shore. He buys me a whiskey neat. I drink one. Then another. He out-drinks me. Then he wakes up after our moonlit night together, and I've fled to America. He never hears from me again. I'm the ultimate girl who got away. He'd sit outside at a cafe and see a dark-haired woman pass by on the street, and his heart would jump because he'd think it was me, but it's just another dark-haired woman because, you know, there are a lot of them in Cuba. And so he'd take me to his grave."

Cash was pressing his lips into a hard line, his cheeks tight to keep from laughing.

"Maybe I'd be his muse for a character. I don't know. I haven't really thought all that much about it."

Cash glanced at me before pulling into parking garage. "Wow, I'm not your type at all."

I nodded and pursed my lips. "We should probably just go back to the dorm, huh?"

"Nah, I think I'm just going to abandon you on a mountain like I originally planned."

"Aren't we in Santa Monica?" There was no mountain in sight.

He flicked his fingers through the air to brush me off, then opened his door. I pulled the handle on mine, then heard, "Stop," as I cracked it open. I rolled my eyes, but let him open it for me. Must be a southern gentleman thing. I wasn't sure a guy ever opened a door for me unless I was too drunk to. "So, do you want to skate or eat first?"

Ah. Socks. "Eat. I at least don't want to be hangry when I fall on my ass."

WE SAT DOWN AT A table for two in this seafood restaurant on the pier. I flipped open the menu. Nothing was under fifteen dollars. There was no way I would be able to afford dinner here. "Do you want to split something?"

Confusion crossed his face. "Why?"

Oh, right. Cash had money. I shook my head. "Never mind." I scanned the appetizer page and picked out a starter salad I could afford.

The waitress stopped at our table. "Can I get you anything to drink?"

"Water's fine, thanks."

"Coke for me," Cash ordered.

"Separate tickets, please."

Cash shook his head. "Just one." He smiled at the waitress. After she left, he turned to me. "Get whatever you want."

I leaned my head toward him and whispered. "But I'm not putting out, right?"

He ran his hands down his face, his fingers lingering over his lips. Had I said something wrong? "Sawyer, what do you want to drink?"

Beer. "Ice tea." I scrunched my face as I relented. "Sorry. I've never been on a first date before."

He studied me a moment. "How is that possible?"

"Unless holding my friend's hair while she puked up rum at a party, then having my date drive me and her home counts."

"When was that?"

"Like three years ago. She puked in his car, too."

"Nice."

"Actually, it was his mom's car. We spent the rest of the night cleaning it up. And I felt awful because he was trying to ask me out, and I'd dragged him to that party even after he said he didn't like people or drinking."

"He doesn't sound like your type either."

"We actually dated for a couple years after that." *Ah! Shut up!* "But, that's not what you're supposed to talk about on a first date, right?"

He shook his head and half-grinned. "It's better than

castration."

I took a sip of my water. "All right, then I'll keep going, you know, since I'm on a roll."

"Might as well."

"What's your deal with sex? Are you like an after-the-third-date kind of guy, or only with your girlfriend, or fiancée, or—"

"Wife."

"Ah." I sat back and scanned him. "Wait, you're a virgin?"

The waitress set our drinks on the table. "Could we have an ice tea, too, please?" Cash requested.

She nodded and walked away.

"Yes."

My eyes widened. "What? So you've never had like a girlfriend or—"

"Had a girlfriend for two years. We broke up this summer."

"And you didn't—"

"No."

"Not even—"

"No."

"How?"

"We were almost never alone behind a closed door. And our families and friends held us accountable because they knew it was important to us."

My eyebrows stitched together. "Wow, so you're like a good guy."

He lifted a shoulder. "I guess."

"Or secretly gay."

"I don't think that's it."

"So why are you slumming it with a hooker?" The

waitress set the tea in front of me with a variety of sweeteners. I picked out a raw sugar and started shaking the packet.

"*I* am on a date with an inexplicably gorgeous girl who is stronger and brighter than anyone I've ever met, who, yes, did some illegal things to get by for a few months."

"That's precious."

"You never did tell me why you needed to get by on your own, though."

I smiled and combed my fingers through my hair to distract him from my abrupt subject change. "What's your family like?"

"Well, like you said, there are a lot of us."

"Do you have a picture?"

He reached for his phone on the seat next to him and swiped until he found a group photo from a wedding. The first thing I noticed was they were all model tall and stunning like Cash. "That's my older brother Johnny's wedding in June." He pointed to the bride. "That's his wife, obviously, Caroline, and that's my older sister June and her fiancé Armi."

"How old are they?"

"June's twenty-two and Johnny's twenty-three. You know Jo, and there are the twins, Jackson and Carter. They're fifteen. And that tiny thing is Sue." I took the phone and pulled it close to my face to see the sweet little blonde with sapphire-blue eyes. "She's five."

"Whoops."

"Yeah, vasectomies are not one-hundred percent effective."

"Good to know." I inspected the girl a little closer.

"She's so freaking adorable."

"I know. We're all wrapped around her finger."

I sat back and tapped my fingers on the table. Something about those names. They weren't just southern... "Hold on. Johnny, Cash? June, Carter?"

"Yeah, I was hoping you wouldn't notice that."

"Jolene's the only one who got out unscathed."

"Well, not really."

"Oh, no!" I cupped my hands over my mouth. "I did ask her if she was named after that song."

"Yeah." Cash grimaced.

I looked at his phone again and started singing, *"But I shot a man in Reno..."*

"Nope." He shook his head. "Date over."

"Just to watch him die."

Cash shuddered like a chill went through him. "That's even creepier when you sing it."

"Excuse me?"

"No, your voice is just so haunting." He pulled up the sleeve of his sweater. "See, goose bumps."

"It's pretty cold in here, but nice try." I scanned the screen again. "Is that your ex?" I pointed to the slender blonde his arm was around.

"Charlotte." He nodded and took his phone back.

"Sorry."

"No, it's fine. We only broke up because she couldn't handle long distance. Didn't want to stay together when she went to college this fall. I guess a year of that was enough for her."

"So, she made you stay loyal to her for your first year of college, when you were meeting all these new people, but she didn't want to do the same for you?"

"Huh." He sat back, his eyes considering. "I never thought of it like that."

"That's pretty fucked up, Cash."

He burst into laughter. "Yeah, I guess it is."

"Your family—are they all perfect and moral like you?"

"They're Christians if that's what you're asking." He took a drink, then asked, "You were raised in a Christian home, right? I mean, besides your stepdad."

"Right. Went to church and Christian school through eighth grade, then my mom let me go to the public high school and decide if I wanted to keep going to church."

"Is that when you stopped?"

"Yeah, I figured there was no point, you know? Because I'm eternally damned and all. I might as well get to have *some* fun."

"I'm sorry." He shook his head. "Damned? What is that supposed to mean?"

"You know, not chosen. Not elect. Not died for."

"Hopelessly hell bound?"

I swallowed a drink of my tea and nodded. "Exactly."

"Sawyer, that's *not*—" He shook his head again.

"What don't you understand?"

"Okay, so, you believe in God, Jesus, the Bible—"

"All of it," I confirmed. "I mean, I've done so much research over the years, especially about the historical evidence of the resurrection. It's impossible to deny. Those Jews wouldn't have ditched so much of their religion and died at the hands of their own for a lie. And if the resurrection is true..." I sipped my tea again before adding, "It's all gotta be true."

"Okay. So what's the problem?"

"My name's not in that book, babe."

Cash refuted with an emphatic, "That's not how it works."

"Lots of people believe that's how it works."

"Hmm." Cash narrowed his eyes on me. "You don't seem like the type to give up that easily."

"Don't I? Two weeks without a job in Los Angeles and I resorted to stripping." I pointed at him and said, "That's the attitude of a quitter."

"No, a quitter would have gone home."

I glanced up at the ceiling and muttered, "Lesser of the two evils."

"You don't have to be hell bound."

Reaching for his hand, I quirked a sardonic smile at him. "That's cute, and you're wrong."

He pulled his hand back and crossed his arms. "Prove it."

"How?"

Cash leaned his elbows on the table and folded his hands at his chin. "You're going to hell, yes?"

I mimicked his posture and affirmed, "Yep."

"Then you should be afraid of dying."

Holy shit, where was this going? "Are you going to point a gun to my head?"

"No! Sawyer, what's wrong with you?"

"It'd be faster to list what's right with me."

"But you should be afraid to walk on the pier railing, right?"

I stared at him. "And if I'm not scared?"

His eyes shot wide open. "You're going to do it?"

Ah, I called his bluff. "Why not?"

"You might die."

"Isn't that the point?"

"I only said it because I was sure you'd say no."

"Then you don't know me very well, do you?"

After dinner, we walked out into the brisk December air. I ran my hand over the cold metal railing, the pale blue paint bumpy under my skin. Cash's anxiety was thick as we reached the end of the pier. "Let's go skate before the ice rink closes," he suggested. I shook my head.

Even with my gymnastics training, I couldn't balance atop the narrow cylindrical bar. So I stepped on the bottom bar, then the next, before swinging my leg over the railing. An onshore breeze picked up, whipping a few strands of hair into my eyes. I pressed the back edge of my left heel and then my right into the inch overhang on the boardwalk. My heart pounded as I stared at the glistening black water below my feet. My fingers gripped the top rail as I smoothly extended my arms until my elbows locked. My chest and neck hung over the ocean, my sweater flapping like a ship's sail.

Cash's warm hands slid over mine. He leaned over, his face against my neck. "Come back," he whispered.

"You were wrong." I felt my arteries swell with each vigorous pump of my heart. I could barely breathe, but not from fear. It was exciting, flirting with death and feeling safe. "I'm not scared of hell," I announced. Hell held no terror worse than Third Street. "I'm more afraid of here." Cash's fingers slid up, tightening around my bruised wrists. I squeezed my eyes shut against the pain.

"Sawyer, come back here," he said a little louder.

I gazed out at the silvery horizon meeting the ocean miles away in a dark line. Maybe I'd be safe somewhere out there. Alone. Off the grid where no one could find me. But that wasn't real, was it? They'd always find me. Unless there was no one to find. I relaxed my fingers and let them slip over the paint of the bar, which was now warm from my skin. I imagined how quickly that railing would cool if I let go of it, how fast the ocean spray would erase the evidence of my life here.

Cash moved a hand around my waist. "Now, Sawyer."

I eyed the water. It was too close. I wouldn't die. I'd drown or get hypothermia, but the impact of the fall wouldn't do it. It'd be slow agony drifting toward that horizon I'd never reach. All the exhilaration of the fall drained out through my toes. That familiar fear, so comfortable under my skin that I didn't notice it until it was gone, sank back through me. It couldn't be now. Hell would have to wait.

I turned toward the rail. When I started to pull my body into it, Cash helped me climb back over. He stroked my arms, and I tried to smile up at him.

He pulled me into him and pressed his lips into my hair. "You're brave, Sawyer," he whispered, and I knew he meant for not letting go.

I buried my face in his chest and let the tears fall, soaking through his sweater to the tee shirt below. Time stopped. I was warm surrounded by him, protected from the biting ocean air swirling around us. He pulled back and wiped the tears away with his thumbs. "I want to show you something."

His fingers laced between mine as he led me down to the sand. He took his shoes off a few yards onto the shore, once we passed most of the cigarette butts and litter. I did the same with my knee-high boots and socks. I hadn't felt chilly sand between my toes since I fled

Oregon. It reminded me of home, in the best and worst ways. We made it back to the pier, though under it this time. All the trips I took to the beach during the summer, I had never done this. The waves echoed under here, making the rest of the world a silent memory. I leaned back against a splintering wood pillar, my hands in Cash's swinging back and forth like pendulums. I closed my eyes as I listened to the ocean's symphony with the sand. In that moment, it was enough to pretend that this strip of shore was all that existed, that Cash and I were the only people who existed.

"Can I kiss you?" I asked. He studied me for a moment. "I won't try to unbutton your pants, I prom—" Cash bent, smoothing my hair from my temples to the nape of my neck, stealing my words with his lips and tongue. My hands skimmed his chest, his neck, until my fingers reached his hair. He had the *best* hair. He inched closer until his body pressed mine into the pillar, cascading hot chills down my neck and thighs. His lips moved along my jaw and down my throat, his hands to my waist and hips. "Cash?" I breathed, trying to focus.

His murmur was hot in my ear, "Sawyer?"

I pushed my hands gently on his chest. "You should stop unless—"

He pulled away. Scanning my face as if trying to convince himself of something, he sighed and nodded.

Resting my forehead on his chest, I closed my eyes so I could listen to his lungs and heart calm, quieting until the ocean drowned them out.

We sank into the sand a few yards away to watch the steady repetition of the waves. I sat with my back against his chest, feeling it rise and fall. His legs bent on either side of me, and his arms wrapped around my waist. He rested his cheek on my head and said, "Can I ask you something? You don't have to answer."

"Sure."

"What was your dad like?"

I relaxed my head against his shoulder, feeling my face come alive at his question. No one but Jake had ever asked about my dad, not in a way that let me talk about him like he was alive. "He was very...Cuban. Intense and careful and frugal. Worked harder than anyone I've ever met. He was a wet-foot-dry-foot immigrant, and his family got sent back on their first attempt. Because of that, he took being American really serious. Always voted, was involved in local politics, all that. And he was obsessed with American literature. We lived half a mile from the beach. When the weather was decent enough, we'd walk down there after he got home from work and sit in the sand against this fallen tree. He'd read Hemingway, Twain, or Faulkner aloud. He'd wrap his arm around me, and I'd snuggle up to him even though he smelled grimy because it was his smell, and I loved it. I was just a kid so I didn't really understand the stories, but I loved his voice and when he laughed at Twain's jokes that I didn't get. His sound was sweet and deep, and his accent was rich like espresso. It was one of the few times I'd hear him speak English."

Cash leaned to the side to see my face. "You speak Spanish?"

"Sí, mi papá sólo me hablaba español."

"What did he do for a living?"

"He was a mechanic. But he was only doing that because he knocked my mom up, and one of them had

175

to work while she went to school. His parents were so pissed."

"About him getting your mom pregnant?"

"No," I answered immediately. But then I realized, "Well, probably. They were mad because they nearly died getting into the United States and my dad had been accepted to Stanford, but he turned it down to work so my mom could get her degree first. Then they were really mad when he died without ever getting to go to college."

Cash's fingertips traced along my neck to sweep my hair behind my shoulder. "Sawyer, I'm so sorry you lost him," he said into my neck as he pressed his lips there.

I rested my head back, relaxed into his warmth, and sighed. "Me, too."

Every single day, I thought about what my life would be like if he hadn't died. His death was the defining moment of my life—I guess that was what someone could call it. The shitty thing about defining moments was that they weren't the big ones we celebrated or prepared for: the first day of school or graduation, a first date, or a wedding day. They were ambushes, shooting from their hiding spots in mundane trenches of everyday moments.

And that was life, wasn't it? A battlefield each person had to walk through, terrified and shaking, looking over their shoulder, glancing right and left while wondering who would die next. The battlefield itself wasn't scary. It was nothing out of the ordinary. Just grass or shrubs or buildings or streets. It was those defining moments lurking in the darkness waiting to strike, waiting to fuck people over—that was what made it war.

....

I WOKE UP IN A panic after my first deep sleep in a month. It was bright outside, midday bright. "Shit," I hissed. I leaned up on my side from Cash's chest. "What time is it?"

Cash patted the desk for his phone, picked it up, and squinted at the screen. "10:03," he mumbled in his thick, sleepy accent. We must have fallen asleep watching *Sherlock*. He had never seen it. I made him watch it with me after our date so he could see his celebrity hair doppelganger. He hadn't even known who Benedict Cumberbatch was. What kind of guy was I falling for?

"Oh, no, no, no! I have that appointment at 10:30!" I climbed over Cash, knees and hands straddling him, and gave him a quick kiss. "I gotta go. Stop by later?" I slid off the bed. When my feet hit the floor, I bolted toward the door.

"Can't wait," he called.

I managed to brush my teeth and change before getting in the car. At a stoplight, I corralled my hair into a matted ponytail. I made it to the cozy waiting room at 10:34. Thankfully, the psychologist was running late, too. He was tall, Cash tall, with broad shoulders and a sturdy torso. Despite his bull-sized frame, his face was gentle and kind.

"Sawyer," he greeted me with a handshake. "It's great to meet you. I'm Dr. Pewter."

Nodding, I took his hand. I followed him through the door to his office, a comfy chair across from a couch with the middle cushion disproportionately broken in. "Go ahead and have a seat," he said, picking up a clipboard from the end table by his chair. "How are you doing today?"

"I'm all right. You?"

"Great, thanks. Okay, so let's get this out of the way." He handed me the clipboard. "These are confidentiality forms that basically say anything we discuss stays within these four walls with three exceptions: if you are a threat to yourself or someone else, if you mention ongoing elder abuse, or ongoing child abuse."

I scribbled my signature.

"Now, of course, since this is for legal proceedings, it is in your best interest to release this information to your lawyer. For that reason, this session will be recorded. If you sign that second form there," he pointed to the next page on the clipboard, "I will be able to share what we discuss as well as any diagnosis I may make with Attorney Colburn."

I scribbled my signature—what the hell—then handed him the clipboard.

"Thanks," he said under his breath. He set the clipboard down on the side table and pressed a button on the recorder. "Okay." He pulled his ankle up onto his opposite knee. "What brings you here?"

"Well..." I crossed my legs. "Wait, what if I told you I did something illegal? Are you going to report it?"

"Are you abusing anyone?"

Not currently. "No."

"Then I'm not telling anyone."

"Okay, well, I'm a stripper. Or I was. I kinda got fired last weekend because I assaulted a client, though he tried to rape me first, so...basically, Colburn wants your help showing I took my self-defense too far because I was traumatized or something."

"Do *you* think this assault was trauma-induced?"

I shrugged.

"Can you tell me everything you remember from that night?"

I told him everything I could. I told him I snapped, that I thought Jeff had found me and was trying to rape me. And I told him about Jeff, that he raped me in front of the camera and posted it on the darknet, that Buchanan wanted to pay me for sex with that little girl. I was honest because my freedom was on the line. I had to be.

"All right, this thinking someone was your stepfather or someone else from your past, has that ever happened to you before?"

I shook my head.

"Do you ever feel separate from your body? Or like you're in a dream when you're not?"

"Sure."

"When has that happened?"

"During sex."

"Every time?"

"Not with Jake."

"And who is Jake?"

I waved my hand as if to push him on to the next subject. "He's not part of my life anymore."

"Okay..." He dragged out the word as if to say, *okay, we'll come back to him.* Not a chance. "Did you feel separate from your body when Allen attacked you?"

"Sort of. I can't remember much of that part."

Face neutral, he continued. "Did you have anything stressful happen earlier that day?"

"Nope."

He nodded. "Other than Saturday night, do you ever see or hear things that other people don't?"

"No."

"Have thoughts of hurting yourself or others?"

My body hanging out over the ocean last night came to mind. "No."

"How's your appetite?"

"Normal."

"How's your sleep?"

"Fine."

"Do you have trouble falling asleep, staying asleep, or waking up?"

"No."

"Nightmares?"

I sighed. "Sure, everyone has nightmares."

"How often?"

"Recently? Almost every night."

"When did that start?"

"About a month ago."

"Did something happen a month ago?"

I pulled in some air while I decided what to tell him. This could ruin my case, right, if I got paid for sex with a client as Delilah, but then said "no" to another for the same thing? I shook my head and answered, "Nothing in particular."

The questions kept coming. He asked about my recurring nightmare, my family, my community—or lack thereof. If I drank—*yes*. How many drinks a week— *oh, you know, I'm more of a social drinker, so just a drink or two a week*. If I smoked—*no*. Had I ever had a head injury—*kind of*. If I had ever seen a therapist or psychiatrist before—*hell no*. In my church, it was safer to be a witch than a mental health professional. We didn't believe in therapy. If somebody had a problem, their faith would make them well.

"Are you in physical pain?" he continued.

I nodded.

"Where?"

"Besides the bruises on my arms and legs?"

"Mmhmm."

"Pretty much everywhere a thong would cover."

"How bad is the pain?"

"Mostly just an aching, dull pain, if that makes sense."

He repositioned, crossing his opposite ankle over his knee. "Okay. Let me ask you this—whose fault do you think it was that you were abused as a child?"

What did that have to do with anything?

"My stepfather's." Obviously. "And my mom's for not believing me when I told her afterward, and for letting him back home."

"What about Simone, the girl you mentioned from your dream? Whose fault is it that she died?"

I swallowed hard and could barely say, "Mine."

"Why is it your fault?" he asked with a softened voice of false compassion.

Huh. His job was a lot like mine—getting paid to pretend to be something for someone because they couldn't get it in real life. For me, it was sex and lap dances for men who couldn't get a girl or whose wives were prudes. This guy, this therapist, was just giving me sympathy, a listening ear, pretending to care because I paid him enough. We were both just great actors, just good liars. Was he really better than me?

I straightened up to answer with a firm, "I don't talk

about that."

"How'd she die?"

Stubborn silence.

"Did you kill her?" Pewter asked as casually as if he asked if I had taken the bus to his office.

"Define kill."

"Did you inflict bodily injury that caused her heart to stop?"

"No."

"Did you implore someone else to—"

"I don't talk about this."

He nodded as if I had said enough to answer all his questions. "And what about Allen? You tried to kill him because you thought he was Jeff?"

What was he trying to prove? That I was a threat to society? I guessed I was. But society was a threat to me first.

I released my arms to free them up for some angry gestures and rebutted, "I didn't want to kill Allen. I had to. Because in that moment, I was eight years old, in my room, hearing my doorknob turn. Allen was Jeff, and Jeff needed to die. That makes sense to you, yes? Because I'm not safe if Jeff can find me. Turns out I'm not safe now that any of them can."

Dr. Pewter shifted forward, pressing his elbow into the arm of the chair. He stared at me for a few long moments before asking, "Can you tell me more about that little girl?"

I snapped back, "Who? Simone? Of course you want to talk about her! They all liked her better. That blonde-haired, blue-eyed Nazi shit. And something about her being willing or *looking* willing. Apparently, the fantasy is raping kids who want it."

"I meant *you*. The eight-year-old. The one who is scared and alone and has to fight so hard to survive."

Is? How was I the crazy one here? "I don't understand why you're referring to my younger self in the present tense. She's gone. I grew out of her. I'm not her anymore."

"You just told me you were her on Saturday when Allen attacked you. Can we talk about her?"

I rolled my eyes. "Oh, what the fuck is this? There is no little girl anymore. You want to know how I know? Because I'm old enough now to get paid to pretend I like sucking some stranger's dick. No one's making me. No one can anymore."

Dr. Pewter sat back with his hands folded on his clipboard, his body language composed but his face twitching slightly at my outburst.

I leaned forward, elbows to thighs, biceps to breasts, hands clasped between my knees. My voice was just above a whisper, sultry and smooth. "You want to know this little girl so bad, then there are a hundred sites you can find her on. Maybe you've already met her. If you're looking at me hoping for her, you'll be disappointed. I've been told she's more fun to fuck than me." I tilted my head to the side and narrowed my eyes. "That all you need, baby?"

Face tightening ever so slightly, he nodded.

CASH WAS IN CLASS WHEN I got back to the dorm. I put my key in the lock, feeling naked and followed with a prickling, crawling sensation under the skin of my arms. I needed a drink. That would dull it all—all those feelings that shrieked so loud when I was sober.

In my room, I took off my pants, changed back into Cash's sweatshirt, and found the nearly full bottle of tequila in my desk drawer. I curled under the covers with it and Fitzgerald, whom I was reading for class.

I didn't wake up when Cash knocked the first time. Or the second. I didn't hear his text alert, either, but I saw it after I vomited into the trash, which I barely found in the now-dark room. I was thirsty and had no water. At least I remembered to put pants on before I went into the hall to fill my bottle.

"Sawyer," Cash called through his open door. I held up a finger as I passed, trying to walk straight as I hunched over to keep from puking again. Of course he didn't leave me alone. "Are you okay?"

I nodded and ducked into the bathroom, making it to the toilet just in time to puke again. I came out to fill my water.

Cash took the empty bottle from my hand. "Go lay down." But he didn't sound compassionate like usual. He was pissed, or Cash's polite version of pissed. So I obeyed. He handed me my water half a minute after I got back in bed. He flipped through my covers until he found the bottle and what was left in it. "Where's the rest?" he demanded as he held it up.

"Rest?"

"You can tell me, or I'll just start going through your stuff."

"Knock yourself out." I pulled the covers over my face, groaning when he flicked the light on. He wasn't exactly subtle when he tore through my wardrobe and searched under my bed. "I don't know what the big deal is. Am I not allowed to drink if we're dating?"

He stood up and crossed his arms. "Sawyer, this is not normal drinking. This is self-medicating."

"You say that like it's a bad thing."

I peeked over the edge of my comforter as he neared my liquor drawer. He pressed his hand on my desk and pulled open the top drawer. "You need better ways to cope. Here we go," he said as he opened the drawer with my stash and started collecting the bottles in his arms, the glass clinking together.

"What are you going to do with those?" I asked, struggling to sit up.

"I'm going to dump them out."

"No, no, no, no. Cash! Stop!" I grabbed his arm.

"Why? You don't need it to get through the day, do you?" He raised his eyebrow in a challenge.

"You don't understand. Faulkner said, 'Pouring out liquor is like burning books.'"

"Has a book ever made you this sick?" he asked, unzipping my backpack and placing the bottles inside.

"Yes! *Wuthering Heights*." Cue high-pitched, girly voice, "'Oh, Heathcliff, you and I are one because we are both the most intolerably obnoxious people in the world. I can't live without you, but I'm going to marry some pathetic, pale little guy anyway because I'm an idiot.' Gag me. Bitch, just die already."

Cash's eyebrows wrinkled together as he stared at me. "What?"

"Please, just leave them alone! I had to do unspeakable things to pay for them." Crap. Still drunk. Shouldn't have said that.

"That's a terrible defense," Cash muttered before

taking off down the hall with my backpack slung over one shoulder. I could almost hear the *clug-clug-clug* of them draining helplessly into the sewer where they never belonged. I didn't even get the chance to say goodbye. I should have fought harder for them. I should have blocked the door, punched Cash, locked him out, anything. But I felt too crappy to even get up.

Cash walked in all friendly, acting as if he hadn't just stolen and destroyed my property. "So, how'd the psych eval go?" he asked in that sarcastic way like he already knew the answer.

I flipped him off.

"Aw, you're such a sweet drunk," he said, plopping on the edge of my bed.

"Dr. Pewter said I'm normal and healthy and allowed to drink whenever I want."

"That sounds like most psychologists I know."

I sighed. "It wasn't the most pleasant two hours of my life."

"I'm sorry." He forced a sad smile and tucked some hair behind my ear. "Did you get a diagnosis?"

"Post-Traumatic Stress Disorder." I didn't add that he said it was as if the initial trauma happened ten days ago, not ten years. Not that any of this was real. It was just to get me out of going to prison. Colburn said the diagnosis was excellent for my case. *Hooray.*

"I'm sorry, Sawyer."

"For pouring out my booze? I'll try to forgive you."

He moved his hand from my hair to my back. "Break's coming up. What are you doing for Christmas?"

"Let's see..." I squinted and clicked my lips. "I'll probably go for a run, then pick up some Starbucks for breakfast, and watch *Miracle on 34th Street* while I drink the rest of the day."

"Yeah, you're not doing that." He reached into his sweatshirt pocket and pulled out a folded printer paper. "Here's your plane ticket. We're going to Atlanta in a week."

"What? That's a terrible idea."

"Why?"

"Didn't you describe me as quote 'a loose cannon capable of destroying an entire fleet?'"

"Did I say that? Wow, I'm pretty clever."

"Please don't bring me around your perfect family."

"Too late." Cash patted my thigh through the comforter. "Get some rest." He stood up and left.

....

"Cash, this is a bad idea. I can feel it." I took his hand while we waited for our suitcases at baggage claim in Atlanta International Airport. It was decorated for Christmas, which just made me more anxious. My heart was racing, my empty stomach stirring up the nothingness inside it.

He pressed his lips into my forehead. "Relax. You've been driving me crazy for the last five hours. I was this close," he held his thumb and index finger an inch from each other, "to switching seats on the plane."

"It's not too late to get me a ticket back to LAX."

Cash gestured toward the conveyor belt where our bags were. He reached for both suitcases. "They're going to love you. I don't know why." After an exaggerated eye roll, he headed for the door. "But people do."

"Cash," I pushed out through clenched teeth as I strode to keep up with him. I spotted the sparkling red Mustang at the curb with Jolene climbing out of it. My lungs deflated with relief. Just Jo.

"Cash, are you kidding me?" she yelled as she punched his arm, pretty hard actually. Jake would have been impressed. "What's this?" She pointed at me before giving me a hug.

Cash! I could just kill him. "You didn't tell them I was coming?"

"Relax. I just didn't tell Jo because she's been nagging me to ask you out since November."

"Really?" I tilted my head in confusion to stare at the innocent teenager as she opened the trunk of her car. She remembered I was a stripper, right?

"Yeah, he was so obviously in love with you. I mean, I get why he chickened out so many times. You are *way* out of his league." Sure...the sweet, rich, hot guy wasn't good enough for the ex-hooker, soon-to-be-inmate. That made sense.

I squashed my smile and side-eyed Cash. "She knows you can hear her, yeah?"

He lifted the second bag into the back and shrugged.

Jo's constant talking and Taylor Swift blasting lulled me into a false calm on the twenty-minute drive to the Colburn's. But then she turned into a wealthy neighborhood, before turning another corner into an even richer one. The houses grew grander as we drove until we pulled into the semi-circle driveway of a towering brick mansion. The size alone was ridiculous: three times my childhood home, if not larger, and infinitely more gorgeous. I would taint the air inside just by breathing. "Uh, what do your parents do?"

Cash answered, "They own fourteen Chick-fil-A franchises. Why?"

"Fifteen," Jo corrected.

"Oh, right, the new one opens in January."

I buried my face in my hands. His parents couldn't be grown, spoiled, trust-fund kids? They were decent *and* rich? Though I hadn't yet ruled out money laundering. Maybe there was still hope to find a flaw.

"Sawyer, calm down."

Calm down: two words a man should never say to a woman. That sounded sexist. Two words no one should say to anyone.

"What's wrong?" Jo asked.

"She thinks they're not going to like her."

Jo cackled and opened her door. "Sweetie, that should be the least of your worries."

"Wait, what?"

She shut the door.

"Jo!" I called. I turned back to Cash, but he was already out of the car.

We didn't go through the front doors, instead entering the kitchen through the garage. Everything about the kitchen was light except the dark wood floors, the air inside stuffy with the scent of sugar cookies. A few kids were at the bar glopping icing and sprinkles onto baked cutouts of stars and Christmas trees, and a couple of women were talking at the dining table behind them. The kid with chunky blond highlights shouted, "Cash!" before she hopped down from her bar stool to run toward us. Cash scooped her up in his arms and kissed her cheek. "I made you a snowflake!"

"You did? Thank you!" Cash feigned excitement the way people did with kids. "Sue, this is Sawyer."

She blinked twice as she stared at me with her giant blue eyes. Something about her face made me sick to my stomach, and not because she was scrutinizing me for several long, uncomfortable seconds. She finally asked, "Are you Pocahontas?"

My eyebrows scrunched together as I shot a questioning look at Cash. I didn't have a chance to answer—not that I knew how to—before her little hands were in my long, dark hair.

I tried to understand her mix up. My hair wasn't quite as long as the cartoon character's, but it was almost as dark. I wore it mostly straight today, the humidity here bringing out some of the waves. My skin was tan, but not *that* tan. I *was* busty like the girl in the Disney movie—

"Sue!" Jo pushed Sue's tiny wrists down, out of my hair. "You need to ask before you start playing with people's hair." Jo turned to me to say, "Sorry. We're super into nineties Disney around here. She idolizes Pocahontas."

I nodded as if this cleared everything up. For the record, it did not.

Sue continued to stare at me, apparently waiting for an answer. From the corner of my mouth, I whispered to Cash, "Has she never seen brown people before?"

Cash suppressed a laugh before pointing at my face. "Sawyer's got green eyes, see, Sue? What color are Pocahontas's?"

"Brown." Sue's little head bounced with her decisive nod.

"Right." He kissed her cheek again. Cash neglected to tell her that Pocahontas had been rotting in the ground for four hundred years, but I imagined those were the kinds of things kids were kept in the dark about, along with the truth about Santa Claus, the Tooth Fairy, and probably sex. Though once kids learned the truth about that last one, all hope in anything greater than the norm was crushed. It was hard to believe some red-suited stranger was going to give out presents without demanding something in return.

"Now, go get me my cookie," Cash said as he set her feet on the ground. "And one for Sawyer."

Sue skipped away, the dining table behind her now empty. The next thing I knew, I was being pulled into the embrace of a petite blonde who introduced herself simply as Cash's mama. "We're so glad you're here, Sawyer!" Her accent was thicker than Cash's, more like warm, sticky caramel than brown sugar.

"Thanks for letting me invade your space. Cash bought me a ticket before I could even—"

She clicked her tongue, almost aghast. "Honey, don't even think about it. You're always welcome."

Wow, Cash must have told some fat lies about me, including omitting the fact I was on trial for assaulting a congressman in a strip club. Those were the kinds of things kids kept parents in the dark about, apparently.

June, the other person from the dining table, shook my hand and hugged Cash. "Y'all better go upstairs before Mama starts her inquisition," June suggested.

Great idea. The fewer questions asked, the better.

Cash and Jo led me through the breakfast nook, which I had mistakenly thought was the dining room.

Apparently, there was also a formal dining room. We entered a living room that had the same dark floors and light walls but with an added fireplace. It was also *not* the living room, but the family room. We passed it into the front room, what they called the living room, which housed another light couch, comfy chairs, and a baby grand piano. A staircase climbed opposite of the front door. We lugged our suitcases to the top onto the balcony lined with open doors to bedrooms and bathrooms. The hallway ended into a loft with slanted ceilings, the walls of which were lined with easily a thousand books. The loft had *another* fireplace. "Are there any more living rooms?"

"Just the basement." Cash pointed to the closed door at the opposite side of the loft. "That's my room, and that's a bathroom," he added as he pointed to the door cater-corner to his. "But there are two others in the hall if you'd rather share with the twins or Sue."

"And two downstairs besides our parents'," Jo chimed in. Six freaking bathrooms! I didn't know houses existed with more than two and a half. "You're bunking with me," she said, opening the door just to the right of the loft.

Right. I couldn't share a bed with Cash here, even though he was obstinately chaste. I'd given up trying to get him to give it up.

I'd known I liked Jo. After seeing her room, I loved her. First, it was spotless, uncluttered, and didn't smell, nothing like Nicole's side of our dorm. The walls were such a pale blue they were almost white, all except one that was painted with chalkboard paint and covered in movie quotes. White floating shelves boasted three antique cameras that once shot films, but were benign and unusable now. A bunk bed was pushed against one wall: a twin bed above and full-sized one below. Both were covered in down comforters and black-and-white decorative pillows.

I folded my suitcase open and rifled through the quarter of it that was full of books, my spoils from my pre-vacation library raid. Reading was a great way to hide in plain sight, to eavesdrop. Yes, it sounds creepy. But, hey, I didn't know these people, and it was now a medically documented fact that I was paranoid.

Book in hand, I wandered into the loft. Wandered was the word for what I wanted to look like I was doing. I was sucked in there like it was a black hole and I was space dust. There were just so many books. What was I supposed to do? My fingers traced over the book spines and then the thin covers of the vinyl record collection. I wanted to flip through them, but I had just gotten here. I should probably wait to play with the antiques.

Some thumping sounded from inside the door Cash said was his. It was closed. I knocked.

He cracked it open so I could see his face. "Hey."

"Can I come in?"

"Um..." He glanced back in his room and shook his head. "Nah."

"What? Why not?" It wasn't like he was naked or something. I could see his whole body blocking the entrance to his room.

"I'll be out in a second."

I tipped my chin toward him. "You got a girl in there?" I snickered.

He winced.

I glowered at him and shoved the door open. My

eyes bounced around the room and into the open closet, which was full of plaid shirts and flannels. Then scanned the walls.

There were vinyl records in here, too, but displayed in places of honor up on shelves. Each case was signed. His wall had three framed posters with ticket stubs inside. The posters were also autographed. All by the same artist. And, most damning, on the shelf next to a record was a framed photograph of Cash with his arm around the waist of the leggy blonde musician.

I raised an eyebrow at Cash, who was studiously avoiding me with his arms crossed. "Cash, this is embarrassing."

He lifted his right hand as if he were going to defend himself before letting it clap against his flannel-clad bicep. "Yeah," he sighed. He finally looked at me, and we both laughed.

"Oh...*this* is why you won't let me see you naked."

"What?"

"You're not chaste! You have a tattoo of her face somewhere."

He chuckled and covered his mouth.

"Where is it? On your thigh? Your ass?"

"No!"

"Which cheek? Left or right?"

He kept laughing. "Sawyer, no."

"I won't believe you until I have proof." I shook my head. "And you teased me *so* much about crushing on Hemingway."

"Yeah, but he's dead. And I don't have elaborate fantasies about having a one-night stand with Taylor and then deserting her like you do with Hemingway."

"Oh, 'Taylor?' You're on a first-name basis with Taylor Swift?"

"I've been to her Nashville house," he said with a little too much pride.

"Sure, but is that proof you're friends or that she should get a restraining order? I mean, Cash," I pointed at the shelves, "this is a freaking shrine."

"She invited me as part of her *Reputation* private preview she did for five hundred fans at her houses."

Suppressing another smile, I nodded. I picked up the framed picture of him and Taylor. "I'm really not your type, am I?"

He shrugged. "What're you going to do?"

"Play your favorite." I tipped my chin toward the records.

"Really?"

"Sure," I said. I sat on the floor with my ankles crossed in front of me, my weight reclined on my hands. "I've never heard her on vinyl."

Cash drummed his fingers over his lips and scanned the albums before picking *Red*.

I heard someone in the loft. Cash must have, too, because he yelled, "Jo! What's more embarrassing? Having a crush on Hemingway or Taylor Swift?"

I thought that question would give anyone pause, but not Jo. She shot back, "Taylor Swift. Clean-cut military Hemingway was downright sexy."

"Told ya." I laced my fingers behind my neck and laid back on the carpet.

He stretched out, too, his head on my abdomen. "Jo's a writer. She's partial."

I rested my palm on his chest, drawing invisible

shapes on his shirt with my fingers. "*You* asked her."

He yawned. "I don't know why flying makes me so tired."

"I blame finals," I breathed as I closed my eyes. I also blamed the fact we woke up at five-freaking-AM to catch our flight. "Cash?" I asked. I looped a couple of his curls through two of my fingers before letting the silk strands slip between them.

"Mmhmm." He nuzzled against me.

"Are you going to name all your kids Taylor-themed names? Taylor? Abigail? Stephen? John?"

"Not John. Really, Sawyer?" He let out a soft laugh.

I giggled. "I think you have a problem."

"Just the one?"

"That's the only one I've found so far."

He took in a deep breath and let out, "Then you're not looking very hard."

I wasn't sure what time it was when we fell asleep, but it was dark out when we woke up to Jo yelling through the loft that it was time for dinner. Both of us were groggy and adjusting to the time change when we plodded down the stairs.

Cash and I sat at the kitchen table. Carter and Jackson burst through the French doors from the backyard. The twins were pink-cheeked and musty, their short espresso hair damp with sweat. One of them dropped a basketball on the floor by the bar stools. They brushed past us into the kitchen. When the refrigerator door opened, Mama Colburn shouted, "Get out of there! Dinner will be here any minute."

The refrigerator door slammed, and Jack or Carter returned with a mouthful of cookies. He swallowed before reaching his clammy hand out to mine. "I'm Jack. You are?"

Cash punched his arm before admonishing, "She just got here. Quit it!"

"That's the best time to do it!"

"That's Carter," Cash said with endearing exasperation.

"And you are?" Carter repeated.

"Sawyer," I said as I shook his hand.

"That's a beautiful name." His lips curved into a crooked smile, his hand still holding mine. "It'd sound even better with my last name after it."

Damn, this kid had game. I pulled in my breath slowly to buy time to respond. "Yeah, you know, it might sound nice. You'll be the first to know if your brother ever proposes."

He dropped my hand, letting it thump against my leg.

"Him?" He raised an eyebrow and jutted his thumb toward Cash. "He's kind of nerdy, don't you think? I mean, he does a math competition every year. And he likes programming."

I raised my shoulder toward my ear. "I'm just in it for his money." I winked. "Oh, and the fact that he can legally drive me."

Carter pointed at me as he made his way to the stairs. "I'll call you in five months."

I pointed back. "I wouldn't expect anything less."

Before I could even see Cash's reaction, Carter's twin emerged from the kitchen, also having absconded with a few cookies. He stopped when I caught his eye. He shook my hand, voice barely audible when he introduced himself. "I'm Jack."

"Sawyer." I smirked, waiting for his pickup line.

But he just blushed and broke eye contact as he said, "Nice to meet you," before turning in the direction his brother had.

Cash's hands slapped the table as he stood. "And those are the twins. I'm going to help bring in dinner."

SUE INSISTED ON SITTING NEXT to me at dinner that night. In fact, she insisted every time we had to sit for a meal or game or project for June's wedding, which was the weekend after Christmas. Sue was this shadow I couldn't dodge, haunting me wherever I went. And I knew it shouldn't have, but it made me uneasy, nauseous even. It was ridiculous. She was just a kid. I should have been annoyed, not nervous.

I was sure she was just enamored with me because I resembled her favorite Native American. Positive, actually, because one night, Cash, Jo, and I were watching a movie in the basement when Sue decided to join us. She stood on the couch next to me and asked if she could braid my hair like Pocahontas. Before I could answer, she climbed to the back of the couch and draped her legs over my shoulders.

Cash flashed a sweet smile our way as his sister pulled on my hair.

"Sawyer, what's this?" Sue asked, her tiny fingertip poking at the fleshy seven on the side of my head.

"It's a scar."

"What's that mean?"

"It means I got a bad cut, and it didn't heal quite

right."

"How'd you get cut?"

"Car accident."

"Car accident? Did it hurt really bad?"

I felt Cash's gaze, his listening ear. Keeping my glossy eyes on the TV, I answered, "Yeah, sweetie. It hurt really bad."

I snapped my eyes to Cash's. He knew, I could tell, that I had watched my dad die. Face sad, he flickered a sympathetic smile my way. I shrugged.

I did adapt to Sue following me around, and I even started to miss her when she wasn't two steps behind me. So, it was half my fault that she crossed a line the fifth night I was there.

Jo's bedroom door creaked open in the middle of the night, flooding the room with light from the hallway. I squinted my eyes open against the glare to see the silhouette of Sue in her fleece footie pajamas walking toward me, a stuffed animal tucked under her arm. She put her hand on my cheek and whispered in that loud way kids do, "Sawyer, I had a bad dream."

Yeah, kid, they happen. What did she want me to do about it? She just kept staring at me with those haunting blue eyes, waiting for me to fix it for her. I asked the only thing I could think of, "What was it about?"

"I lost Bunny at the park, and Daddy wouldn't take me back to find her." Bunny, I assumed, was the tattered stuffed animal she was now cuddling to her cheek. Ah, these were the real tragedies.

I whispered, "I'm sorry," because, really, what else was I supposed to say?

"Can I sleep in your bed?"

Um, what? No. Absolutely not. What would her parents or Cash think if they found their precious Sue sleeping in bed with a whore? They would think the worst. Abused people abused people, right? Not that I ever would. It was just that I already had.

How had I not figured this out sooner?

There were a dozen reasons this girl shouldn't be around me, but the one that was scratching at me for days, the one that made my muscles rigid whenever Sue touched me, finally hit—she looked just like Simone. Not high-school Simone, but grade-school Simone, the one who Jeff invited to our home to "play with me," the one I watched get raped over and over.

And this little girl—Sue—was just going to climb in bed with me, a total stranger. Had her parents not taught her anything? Sue was a perfect target, and she was going to be dead in a decade just like Simone, dead because of someone like me.

I opened my mouth to tell her to go back to bed or find someone else, but she was already lifting the covers and crawling between the sheets. She snuggled her back into my chest and closed her eyes against the pillow, her arms clutching Bunny tight to her body. Her tiny frame was so close to mine that my arm had nowhere to go except over her.

Once Sue's breathing evened and slowed, I rolled away from her, scooting toward the wall until my back pressed against it. My eyes stayed wide open, focusing on the lit hallway through the ajar door. I couldn't fall asleep in here with Sue, not after what I did to Simone. I needed to find a way to get this girl the hell away from me.

But I did drift off after an hour or so. When I awoke, Sue was gone, the bedroom door wide open, and the sun fully up. And the house was loud. Voices were chattering downstairs, June and Jo's among them.

I plodded down the stairs in the flannel pajamas Cash had loaned me, folded around my hips with a navy cheer tee over them. Ducking into the kitchen, I hoped to avoid the attention of the gabbing women around the table. Had Sue told them she slept in my bed last night? Had Jo noticed? Maybe they thought nothing of it. Maybe they were all just as naive as her. Maybe that was worse.

June had transformed the breakfast nook into her wedding workstation. Her hair was spilling out of a messy bun as she leaned over a pile of a hundred place cards and her mug of coffee.

"Have the McCains RSVPed yet?" June asked with her forehead on her palm and elbow on the table.

Some bridesmaid bouncing a tiny baby against her chest skimmed her finger over a list. "No," she answered.

"Okay. Jo, can you be in charge of calling them? Like now, please?"

Jo pulled out her phone. "On it!"

Just beyond them, Sue and a boy her age were playing in a massive pile of Legos on the family room floor. Bunny was spectating from against the couch. One of those pseudo-news morning shows was playing on the television.

"Aunt Autumn," Sue called, unalarmed and focused on her Legos. "Tommy's nose is bleeding." The four of us in the kitchen turned our attention to the little curly-haired boy sitting on the beige rug. Just as Sue said, blood was dripping from his nose, not that this seemed to bother him. He was still fitting Legos into the plane he was building.

"Okay!" the bridesmaid yelled before starting a frantic search of the room for something to stop the bleeding. I'd panic, too. A bloodstain wouldn't come out of that light carpet easily. "Tommy, don't move." This order he followed perfectly. He never even glanced up from his project.

I was pulling a banana from the bunch on the counter when Autumn swept past me to get to the paper towels by the sink. The sleeper-clad infant in her arms started wailing as she ripped a towel from the roll. It was just the worst sound. Screaming for no reason. And how was she so loud? She was like ten pounds. "Shoot!" Autumn sent me a pleading look. "Can you take her?"

What? No! Was everyone in this family so trusting? "Uh, I don't—" Before I could say, *think that's a good idea*, she thrust the red-faced thing at me and bolted toward Tommy. My arms were tense around the baby, which made the shrieking louder, a feat I thought impossible. I pulled her against my chest, her head resting against my shoulder. I bounced and swayed her like I saw her mom do in the forty-five seconds I got to observe them. Jo struggled to collect the RSVP over the noise, so I slipped out of the kitchen to the deserted living room, now adding a back pat to the soothing routine.

Did people actually try to make these things? Jake wanted this? Really? The whole time I tried in vain to comfort her, I thought, *I can't do this. I could never do this. How could Jake have thought I could do this? I was right. I was right. I was—*

There was a gurgle from the baby's mouth, then a warm gush of something sticky and sour on my shoulder. Spit up, right? Was that what people called it? Whatever it was, it made the crying stop. I switched the kid to my other arm, so her cheek could rest on my dry shoulder. I kept rocking from one foot to the other, when I noticed her once well-controlled head was now jiggling with each bounce. I slid my hand up to cup the back of her neck, holding her against my chest as we swayed. Her gaze softened, and her eyelids drooped. Within another minute, her dark eyelashes were flush against her fat cheeks, and her pink lips puckered open.

I made my way back into the family room and eased into the squishy recliner, careful not to wake her. The baby's soft hairs tickled my cheek as she slept against me. I watched her rounded back rise and fall with each calm breath. It was relaxing somehow, even to me. Maybe because it felt like I had something to do with it—her feeling so safe against me that she could shut her eyes and doze off. She didn't know me very well.

All I kept thinking was, *Shit. Jake was right. He was right. How could I have—*

"Hey, thank you so much," Autumn blurted out in front of me. "Oh my gosh, you got her to sleep?"

I nodded.

"Thank God," she sighed. "I'm Autumn. You must be Cash's girlfriend. Sawyer, right?"

I nodded and gave her a polite smile. "Does she need a blanket or anything?" I whispered.

"You really don't mind holding her?" Autumn asked before rummaging through her diaper bag on the floor.

"Not at all."

"Oh no! Did she spit up on you? You'll need to use baking soda to get the smell out. It's worse than poop."

"It's fine," I mouthed. "What's her name?"

"Grace."

Of course it was. *Christians.* "How old is she?"

"Six weeks," Autumn answered as she returned to the table.

I did some quick math. How old would my baby be? No, I'd still be pregnant. Seven months, about. It seemed so impossible, that alternate reality where I was in maternity clothes and counting down to a due date. Would I have been one of those people who found out the sex of the baby? Or would that have made it hurt worse to give it away?

My chest ached as I stared at Grace, warm and alive in my arms. I wanted to give her back to Autumn and never feel this again. At the same time, I wanted to bolt out the door with her. My eyes started to sting. No. This was ridiculous. I didn't have Grace; I had something entirely different. This was not what I lost. And I would tell myself that as many times as I needed to.

Cash's voice made me jump. "How long were you awake before they roped you into babysitting?"

"Um..." I stared up at him, also still in his pajamas. "It's fine."

He patted my waist to scoot me over so he could sit next to me in the recliner. His arm wrapped behind my shoulder when he asked, "Are you sure? Because you don't seem fine."

I just shook my head.

He glanced at Grace. "She's so cute, huh?"

"Adorable," I murmured.

Cash turned his gaze to the TV. "Any word from Stephen?" he whispered.

"Plea bargain is still in the works, I guess. Prison time isn't off the table yet, but it won't be more than a year. And it won't be a felony charge at least."

"Sawyer, I'm so sorry. I'm sure he's going to get you out of this."

I shrugged.

"When will you find out?"

"Got an email last night that my court date has been set for January second."

That date loomed over me every hour the rest of the trip, winding me tighter as the days dragged on. Christmas Eve was when the weight of it sank in—would I be in prison for Christmas next year? What would happen with Cash and me? There was no way he'd stay with me while I served a year sentence for assault.

Even worse, we had to go to church on Christmas Eve. I went voluntarily with Cash a second time back in LA because no one bothered me there and it felt nothing like Jeff's church. But this one in Atlanta—something about it made me itch under my skin, itch that part of my flesh I couldn't reach with my nails. Two of the Christmas songs were ones my childhood church always played, both of which I tuned out by drifting away from my body like I did during sex. Then the pastor introduced himself as Pastor Mike, the same name as the lead pastor at Jeff's church. Unbelievably, that pastor dismissed the children after worship, just sent them away. The adults sat down at the end of the song, while at least a hundred kids remained on their feet. A few adults with matching tee shirts and lanyards herded them toward the doors at the back of the sanctuary, like sheep being led to the slaughter.

Sue skipped in front of us to join the droves.

"Where are they going?" I whispered in Cash's ear.

"Sunday school."

I knew what that meant. It was a casting call. An audition. And Sue would get the part.

I marched toward the back exit and into the lobby. I didn't make it in time to find Sue's bouncing blonde ponytail in the mob of children disappearing down the halls on my left and right. She was so tiny; how was I supposed to find her? One by one, the classroom doors closed. I started toward the left. Some of the younger kids went that way. Maybe I'd find her room.

Large fingers wrapped around my arm. "Sawyer—"

I spun around and clutched Cash's wrists in both my hands. "Sunday school? Are you fucking kidding me, Cash?" I whisper-screeched, trying to keep my volume down. After all, this was church where we were supposed to pretend we didn't know such vile words.

"What's wrong with—"

"Where do you think they groom kids? And she's the perfect victim: beautiful, trusting, compliant." She really was just like Simone. "Her life will be over."

"Not everyone is your stepdad."

"Yeah, and not everyone is perfect like you. What happens when they molest her, huh? And film it and post it online? What happens when men recognize her when she's in high school or college and try to rape her again? I swear, it's like your family lives in this bubble where everyone has the best intentions and is honest and trustworthy. Did you know Sue got in my bed the other night? Why didn't you guys teach her it isn't safe to do that?"

"Can you let go of me, please?" Cash asked, his tone even and patient.

I looked down at my fingertips digging into his wrists. Embarrassed, I let them go. "Sorry."

He put his hands on either side of my face, his fingers in my hair. "Take a breath."

I obeyed, drawing a shallow, quivering inhale.

"Is that what happened to you?"

I watched his island eyes for a minute before I finally nodded.

Cash pulled me into his chest, wrapping his arms around me. I shut my eyes against his sweater, pushing out a frustrated tear. "She's okay. June teaches in her class most weeks. She'd tell us if there was something off. Does that make you feel any better?"

I nodded against him, more tears falling over my cheeks.

My phone buzzed in my pocket. Then a second time. And a third. "Hello?"

"It's Colburn. I need to meet with you Thursday." Why was Stephen working on Christmas Eve? I mentally crossed *attorney* off my list of potential future careers.

"Uh, yeah. Is everything okay?"

"Not the best. They haven't found evidence that Buchanan downloaded your images."

Shit. "But he did."

"I know. But right now, it's your word against his." He didn't even take a breath when he continued, "Your sentence is down to six months. And there's a great psychiatric facility I can get you in if they'll agree to that over prison time."

I swallowed hard. I wouldn't put "great" and "psychiatric facility" together in the same sentence. I wasn't sure how that'd be better than prison. "Okay."

"See you Thursday at eleven."

"Yeah."

He hung up.

"Everything okay?" Cash asked, his hands still on my arms.

I sighed. "You'll need to find another date to June's wedding."

I FLEW BACK WEDNESDAY FOR my Thursday meeting with Colburn. He told me they finally agreed to no prison time, no parole, just six months mandatory inpatient psychiatric treatment.

I had five days before my hearing, five days of freedom, of which Cash would be gone for the first half. So, I did what any reasonable person in my situation would do—I replenished my stash of alcohol, logged into Netflix, and drank with my hand down my panties. Might as well relish in a pain-free fog before I had to face six sober months. *Sober*. Didn't the word itself seem to protract time?

January 2018

I WOKE UP PARCHED, MY HEAD THROBBING, TO bright sunlight and a wintry breeze compliments of my now-open window. The trash can was empty with a new liner, and there was an unopened water bottle on my desk. The bottles—empty, full, in between—were all gone, as was my comforter, which Cash had replaced with his own.

Crap. Cash was here. What day was it? Had I missed my hearing? What state was I in when he found me? This was bad, or at least, not cute.

"Hey, I'm glad you're alive." Cash's voice was flat, irritated.

"Cash, I'm—"

His tone had a muted fury to it when he interrupted me, "I almost called an ambulance when I found you. You didn't wake up when I shook you. You had a pulse, though, which I figured was a good sign. Anyway, I was about to dial 9-1-1 when you mumbled something in Spanish, so I decided to let you sleep it off." He gazed up at the ceiling and added matter-of-factly, "That was yesterday around noon.

I closed my eyes and asked hoarsely, "What time is it?"

"Nine AM. How many days did it take you to go through those bottles?"

I shook my aching head.

He raised his voice. "Sawyer, what happened?"

I covered my ears, not just because he was loud and I was hungover, but because I was sober and sober meant I could hear every sound in a five-mile radius: those damn birds squawking outside, a sprinkler flicking water, the wind smacking a living leaf against its dying neighbor. Sober meant life in high-definition—too noisy, too crisp to tolerate. That was it, the difference between Cash and me. His vision was always softly lit, fuzzy around the edges like a lip-locking scene in a black-and-white movie. His world wasn't a deluge of noises and sights and crawling sensations beneath his skin, like the muscles had torn from the bones and were scrambling to get free. It wasn't fair he was always drunk without alcohol, that he thought I had some *problem* just because he'd never have the imagination it took to see that the world was actually glaring and shrieking with bright colors and dark screams and a constant creeping fear that could only be softened with drink. And it wasn't fair that he took away my ability to live in his world of dampened senses when he dumped out my booze.

"The trash can was half full of just vomit," Cash continued. "And you puked on the bed and carpet, too. I could smell your room all the way down the hall."

"Cash..." I ran my hand over my face. "I'm sorry."

He sat on the bed next to me and ran his hand over

my hair. "Sawyer, this isn't—" He took a shaky breath. "I can't do this if this is what it's going to be like."

I studied him a while, wondering why he had cleaned up my barf if he was planning to break up with me. "What were you expecting it to be like?"

"Not this. I dumped out all those bott—"

"Yeah, and took me to church a few times and brought me home to your family. Was that supposed to transform me into someone who was suddenly worthy of you?"

"That's not what I'm saying. Sawyer—"

"You can't save me from whatever you think I need saving from."

"I know."

"So stop trying."

He sighed and swung his gaze out the window. "Your comforter is in the dryer. I'll drop it off when it's done," he said as he stood.

"Thanks," I whispered.

"Try to take care of yourself, okay?"

I nodded and watched him leave, unsure if he'd ever talk to me again. I was sure, though, that no one wanted me now. I was alone. And I had only myself to blame.

THE NEXT MORNING, CASH WAS already in the courtroom when I arrived for my hearing.

I turned to him from my seat at the defense table. "I thought you were going to stop trying."

"Annoying, isn't it?" He tried to smirk.

I shook my head as tears filled my eyes.

"I'll visit you every week, okay?"

"You don't have—"

"I'm going to. Even if you don't want me there."

I laughed, the movement making my tears spill over. He'd be there. I was sure of it.

....

AFTER SURVIVING MY FIRST FULL therapy session with Dr. Harper, I shuffled down the long hall to the next in my flip-flops, my silent rebellion against the no-laces rule. I brushed passed the sedated pacers on the way to my room, the last on the right. Still, from the end of the hall, I could see them make their U-turns to start their new laps. It unnerved me when they glanced at me sitting on my bed. This went on for hours each day. I would have shut the door, but Cash was on his way.

From the foot of my bed, I scanned the stack of books in the cubby across from me to make sure I had read them all. Five library books atop two of my own. Stories, stories, more stories—anything to send me somewhere beyond the doors with the *High AWOL Risk* signs.

Those doors opened and shut now, with cheerful greetings dripping in among hushed gossip and the occasional borderline-personality-disorder outburst. That always involved a string of curses at a parent or boyfriend and a stomping out into the hall. Oh, and booty juice when they threw stuff, apparently.

"You attacked a patient?" Cash asked. He stood outside my door with four books cradled in his bare forearm, the long sleeves of his flannel shirt rolled to his elbows.

"Let's not be dramatic. I missed."

"Oh." He glared at me, sarcastically adding, "That's better then."

"He called me Delilah."

Cash cringed.

"Don't worry. Next time, I'll aim better."

"Next time? Where is he?"

"They moved him to another wing." I straightened up from my bed, reaching to take the books he brought to replenish my supply. He jerked them away.

"Are you taking your meds?"

I narrowed my eyes and smiled. "How do I take you off my 'extended treatment team'?"

"So, that's a no." He pulled the books behind him again. "Sawyer, can you at least pretend to try?"

"Oh! Speaking of bullshitting," I said as I dug through my patient assignment folder. "I need a 'loved one' to write me a letter about the stuff they love and appreciate about me, blah, blah, blah. Interested in making up some good qualities about me?"

Cash's face softened playfully, and he snatched the paper from my hand. "Happy to." He added, "As long as you stop picking fights."

"You're no fun."

February 2018

M Y PILLOW WAS COVERED IN SWEAT WHEN I woke to screaming. It took me a full two seconds to realize it was coming from my lungs. My heavily sedated roommate didn't flinch, but Nurse Trevor was at my side by the time my throat was hoarse.

Full disclosure, I had a girlish crush on Nurse Trevor. He had a gentle demeanor and phone-book-tearing arms. I was a sucker for that kind of thing. The night-shift nurses were in amazing shape. And tan. Apparently, that was what happened when they worked only three to four shifts a week and had the sun and gym all to themselves during business hours. Even so, the last thing I wanted to see was someone with a penis. I grunted I was fine and pushed past him to the bathroom.

I stripped off my cheer tee shirt and slouched to sit on the linoleum with my dewy back against the chilled wall, the only barrier between it and my skin being my soggy sports bra. The darkness made the tiny room feel unending. I flicked the light on to try to stay awake and off Third Street. To say I was fucking tired of that Third Street dream was a disgusting understatement. I'd even broken my own rule and tried to take medication to sleep the other night. The trazodone just made the colors brighter, Simone's cries higher, and escape impossible— like I was paralyzed but awake while undergoing some kind of gruesome surgery.

So, I played a game in the bathroom to stay awake: what in here could be used to kill myself? It was an exceptional challenge and against our contracts as patients. Yes, I actually had to sign a contract to stay alive. The way they violence-proofed this place, my word clearly meant nothing. It did, however, make this game extra fun.

I started with the shower curtain, wondering if someone had ever tried to hang themselves from it. It was suspended from flimsy metal clips that wouldn't hold any significant amount of weight, so I figured anyone who attempted was unsuccessful. If the clips could be unfastened, they could be sharpened. Even so, I doubted they could do much damage. The cutters would have some ideas. They were the most creative here. And resourceful. One girl actually used her teeth and fingernails on herself.

There was no shampoo or body wash in the shower or toothpaste by the sink. They rationed these to us in travel-size containers each day. My bet was that someone swallowed too much once.

Hygienic blades were out. Dark hairs still clung to the shower from yesterday. That was the first time I shaved since I was admitted. A CNA handed me a cheap razor and watched the entire time I used it. It was why

I'd waited until my legs and armpits were covered in soft fur to shave. Eh, it was February, not exactly shorts weather. Besides that CNA and the nurses who did the strip search, excuse me, *skin check*, on my first day, no one saw me naked.

I bet my navel ring could have done something if I had been able to sharpen it, but the nurses made me pull it out during the nude inspection. It was currently in safekeeping with Cash.

The underwire in my bras would have provided a warm, easy death, if the staff hadn't taken those away at the door. "I can remove the metal if you want to have them here," the orderly said while holding my favorite violet, black-laced push-up. The horrific image of her with a murderous grin as she sliced away at my lingerie made my stomach flip. I ripped it from her hand as if she had threatened to cut open my child. Then I frantically dug through my bag for the rest of them, as if the hospital staff had plans to slowly torture all my expensive bras. Cash had those stashed away for me, too.

I ran out of trouble to look for. *Congrats, hospital designers. You did a thorough job.* I woke up with my cheek pressed against the linoleum, opening my eyes to my roommate peeing in front of me.

"Good morning!" Tori smiled as she wadded toilet paper around her hand. After living with this crazy-eyed middle-aged woman for five weeks, I still didn't know what she was in for. All she said in group was, "I didn't refill my medication. I guess that was important." I propped myself up on my hand, feeling the rippling aches over my ribs and hips as I rolled upright. Tori flushed the toilet, and then did a cursory rinse of her hands without soap. Gross. "See you in group?" she asked before drying off on my paper-thin towel.

Really?

I nodded.

March 2018

I WISH I HAD AN EATING DISORDER.

Off the common area, there were two locked pantries: one for us addicts, maniacs, and the generally crazy to have a post-dinner snack and one labeled "E.D. Pantry." I wanted to know what was in there so bad! Did they have Swiss Rolls? Or Fruit Rollups—not just the cheap red kind, but the multi-flavored ones? If they had dark chocolate-covered pretzels, I'd purge loud and clear whenever my roommate got her daily butt shot so the nurses would overhear. I'd get my diagnosis. Then the snacks would be mine.

"Are you eating?" With my ear pressed to the patient pay phone, I could hear Cash crunching over the line.

"Chick-fil-A," he confirmed before slurping back what had to be sweet tea.

"I'd kill three people for sweet tea and a chicken sandwich."

"Three?"

"No fewer. You having fun at home?" Cash was on spring break back in Atlanta. He made sure to bring me a dozen books and a stack of impossible math problems to keep me out of trouble until he could see me next.

"Yeah. Sue asked about you."

I sucked in my breath. "What'd you tell her?"

"That you were home, sick."

"Thanks."

"And I said 'hi' to Jackson for you, but not Carter."

"Did it piss Carter off?"

"And made Jackson blush."

"Love it."

"Oh." *Crunch, crunch, swallow.* "June's pregnant."

"What? Already? How?"

"Well, when a mommy and daddy—"

"Yeah, I think I know about that." Better than he did, that was for sure. "Your family mates like bunnies."

"Right?"

"Not that I know from experience."

He sighed, letting us both hang in silence. "I never said never."

I laughed. "Sometimes I really hate you."

....

"I BROUGHT YOU SOMETHING," CASH announced as he tucked my hair behind my ear. We sat facing each other on a blanket on the non-smoker lawn of the hospital, feeling the cool Los Angeles breeze that carried the tobacco stink from one building away out of our courtyard.

I felt my eyes brighten with false hope. "Did you sneak Chick-fil-A past them somehow?"

"Sorry." He scrunched his nose in contrition before handing me a thick white envelope. "I finished your letter."

I felt the weight of it in my hands. It had to have been as heavy as some of the novels he brought me. Seriously, what had he written? "Thanks," I whispered.

"You gonna read it?" His accent was thicker today. It always was when he was tired. I wondered if he stayed up late last night writing this. But, no, I didn't want to read it. If it was kind and thoughtful like Cash, it would break the last intact piece of me.

"I'd rather not cry in front of you."

His hands trailed down to mine. "That's right." He suppressed a smile. "You don't like crying."

I SLEPT IN CASH'S SWEATSHIRT that night at the hospital. His letter was tucked under my arm, the letter I couldn't bring myself to read. I held it like a kid held a blankie. I'd keep it safe; it'd keep me safe. And when I dreamt of Third Street, it would be there when I woke up. It would be my proof that the dream wasn't real. Well, that it wasn't real anymore.

It was three AM when my eyes shot open to the dark hospital room. My clammy hands left damp marks on the envelope, smearing my name on the front. I took it and a pillow into the bathroom, then flipped the lights on bright. I pulled the letter out and started.

Dear Sawyer...

April 2018

$\mathcal{W}$AS IT POSSIBLE TO GO THROUGH withdrawal from a person? I couldn't believe I just said that. Not only because it was cheesy, but because it wasn't fair to the people going through actual withdrawal. The recovering addicts here looked equally like they were going to die and kill anyone watching them die. So, I shouldn't have said I was going through withdrawal. Because, technically, I didn't feel like I was dying.

I just wanted to die.

Maybe I had more in common with the addicts than I gave myself credit for. I was in pain all over, and I had tried to kill someone—no offense to the nonviolent junkies. Maybe I'd been going through withdrawal since May. Maybe this was how my body responded to the absence of Jake.

I flexed and extended my feet in my seat in group to keep the cramping at bay. Then I tucked my foot under the opposite thigh, letting my foot swing like a pendulum, ticking away the seconds I had to be stuck here listening to other people's problems.

It was no surprise I wasn't a fan of group processing, except for the kindergarten elements like the play dough and caramel apple pops. The first time our peppy Jamaican therapist, Mae, added those lollipops to the candy box, I slipped two up each sleeve and then worked them down into the abdomen pocket of Cash's hoodie while my recovering addict friend, Sam, was processing. I paid extra special attention to what she said in case I got caught. I still remember she talked about how her mother claimed to be emotionally triggered by Sam's Seroquel-induced weight gain. What a bitch. And moms wondered why their daughters ended up in places like this. Not my mom, of course. I was dead for all she knew.

Five of us sat in that circle with our shared therapist for an hour every Tuesday, Wednesday, and Thursday. Emotional check-in was mandatory. We passed around a laminated Feelings Wheel with synonyms for angry, scared, joyful, and a few dozen others spinning out from the center of the circle like a pinwheel of DSM symptoms. Then we decided if we wanted to process. After we all checked in, we volunteered to talk one at a time.

My check-in always went something like this: "I feel tired," the most benign emotion on the wheel, "and I do not want to process." Then I got to suck on my caramel apple pop, testing the sour and sweet on different parts of my tongue. I couldn't tell the difference between the tip, which supposedly tasted sweet, and the sides that were allegedly sensitive to salty and sour. I was pretty sure that diagram they showed us in grade school was crap.

But this Tuesday, I stared at the feelings wheel when

Sam handed it to me. I blurted out, "I feel lonely. And confused. And like drinking and lying in bed all day. I don't see that on the wheel." I turned the paper circle around. "That really should be on the wheel. Anyway, I should probably process." I popped the sucker back in my mouth and passed the wheel left. There was a pause as everyone's gaze lingered on me.

April made me think about Jake. No, made me crave him. Made me ache and feel so hollow in his absence I thought I'd cave in. Collapse. Total structural failure. Maybe that was what I hungered for now. Feeling nothing so I couldn't feel him gone.

Everyone was quiet after the last patient checked-in, apparently waiting for me to start. They did this usually when someone who never talked finally grew a pair. It was my turn to lose Talk Chicken. I didn't have some planned fragment to process so I just started talking about Jake, listing off memories as if they could be conjured up and relived, as if talking about him could bring him back.

I signaled I was done talking by unwrapping a second caramel apple sucker and popping it in my mouth. This one I unabashedly pulled from Cash's sweatshirt pocket. The strength sufficient to hide my klepto tendencies escaped me today.

"He sounds like a great guy," Sam said.

"What happened to him? Are you guys still together?" a newer addition to our circle chimed in. Her name was Elisa, or maybe Alicia. She had only been here two weeks.

I felt my skin flush from scalp to the soles of my feet. My eyes burned, and my throat was so full I could hardly speak. I whispered to keep my voice from breaking.

"Could I use the bathroom?" I asked Mae like a seven-year-old in school.

"Of course." She smiled sympathetically.

I dashed out the door, down one long hall to the next, feeling the tears fall past my cheeks to Cash's sweatshirt as I raced to my room. I still ached as I crawled in bed. Burying my face under the thin covers, I wept.

....

I STAYED IN BED FOR the next three days, getting up only to use the bathroom, grab the occasional bland bite, or get a new book to read. I ditched therapy, group and individual, and class. I had a "cold." *Cough, cough. See, you don't want this. I better stay in bed. You know how fast germs spread in a hospital.*

Friday arrived as it always did, and with it came Cash. I only knew it was Friday because I heard a knock on my open door when I was curled under the covers. "Come in," I groaned. Okay, I still didn't realize it was Friday until I felt the mattress dip under me and that familiar hand in my matted hair.

"You know I'm not supposed to be in here." I could hear a smile in Cash's words. I rolled over to look at him. "I hear you're 'sick.'" He put air quotes around *sick*. Jerk.

"I *am* sick."

"Didn't you once tell me that you were immune to all the diseases in North America from working in a strip club?

"What am I? An epidemiologist?"

"And didn't you also say if you ever did get an infection, you fought it with alcohol, the ultimate germ killer?"

"Well, there's no hooch here. So I got sick."

He shot me a doubtful look.

"I don't need to prove anything to you." I rolled back over.

"Come on. Let's get you some fresh air." He rested his hand palm up on my hip.

I rolled my eyes and put my hand in his.

After days inside the unnecessarily frigid hospital, the grey air felt thick, muggy. I shed my long sleeves and sat on the bench with Cash, my head on his shoulder and his arm behind me. He ran his fingertips up and down my arm.

"You want to talk about it?"

I shook my head and relaxed against him. I was safe with him, safe enough to tell him more in the last four months than I had ever told Jake, safe enough to be in pain, safe enough to just be silent. I'd grown too used to that security. Maybe that was why I didn't see the threat walking toward me.

"Hey, Sawyer?" Cash nudged me on the bench in the hospital courtyard. "Do you know those people?"

I glanced up to see a man and a woman walking straight toward us. As they closed in, it was clear they weren't hospital staff. They were dressed more professionally than the therapists and psychiatrists. The man was wearing a tie. No one wore a tie in a psych hospital. That was just asking for trouble. I shook my head.

But my skin crawled with that feeling of being found when I wanted to be lost.

The female of that out-of-place pair walking toward

Cash and me in the courtyard introduced herself. "Sawyer de la Cruz?" she asked as she pulled a bronze badge from her blazer.

"Who's asking?"

"I'm Agent Holt," she announced with her badge and ID bifold extended toward my face. "This is Agent Espinoza," she gestured toward the swarthy guy next to her, "with the FBI."

"Yeah, I'm Sawyer." What'd I do this time?

"We need to speak with you in private." When Cash stood with me, she repeated, "In private." I took Cash's hand and shook my head. "Okay, but you can change your mind at—"

"I won't."

Cash took my hand as we followed the agents into an empty therapy room a nurse unlocked for us. "Have a seat, Sawyer," Holt said and pointed to the couch. I sat down, still holding Cash's hand. "You were arrested in December for assaulting Congressman Allen Buchanan, correct?"

"Well," my forehead crinkled, "yeah, but I'm doing my time right now." Were they trying to get me on prostitution charges, too? Busting a first-offense hooker seemed like awfully small potatoes for the FBI.

"Did you tell your lawyer that Buchanan attempted to rape you because he recognized you from child pornography?"

"Yeah, I did."

"What name did he call you?"

"Delilah."

Holt nodded and opened a briefcase. She pulled out a folder and spread three glossy photographs on the coffee table between us.

"Sawyer..." Holt's voice was gentle when she asked, "Are you the girl in these photos?"

All but the faces had been blurred, like a fog had rolled through my Third Street nightmare. The first was just me, naked, scared, but pretending not to be. The second was Jeff and me. The third was Jeff, Simone, and me. Jeff's face was conveniently cropped out. Son of a bitch.

Jeremy had sent Simone and me a video, just the one. But never photographs. I hadn't seen these. I had no idea how many more there were, what they were of, or who had seen them. Or who would.

I nodded and swallowed over the lump in my throat. Cash squeezed my hand.

Holt asked, "I know this must be difficult for you—"
No shit.

"—but can you tell me about how old you were at the time these were taken?"

"That one," I pointed to the first photograph, "I was eight." I remember because it was one of the first he took. I remember because I was a virgin in the photo. I remember because I wasn't right after. I ignored the rising memories from the other two. "I think I was nine in these."

She pointed to the second and third photos. "Can you tell us who this man is?"

I nodded. "Jeff Lindley."

"Okay, thank you, Sawyer." She scribbled on a pad of paper. "Lindley is spelled?"

"L-I-N-D-L-E-Y. You'll find him easy. He's on the sex offenders registry."

She inclined her head. "And do you recognize this girl?" Holt pointed to the third picture.

Simone's body was intentionally distorted, but those shattered-glass irises still reflected me when I picked up the photograph. Not the brunette child in the picture, but me, fully grown, staring at the fear in the fragmented blue. I nodded.

"Do you remember her name?" I closed my eyes and took a deep inhale.

"Simone," I whispered. "Simone Carson. She was in my grade. Jeff picked her up with me after school most days because her parents worked."

Holt gave another brusque nod. "Thank you, Sawyer. Is there anything you can tell me about her?"

I swallowed back the sour acid in my throat. "Like what?"

"Do you have any idea where she is now?"

Yeah. I did. And my stomach rejected that fact. My eyes darted around the room for a trash can. I spotted one under the desk by the door, flung the office chair out of my way, and vomited into the plastic bag inside.

Cash pulled my hair back at my neck as I heaved mostly nothing into the garbage bin. I hadn't eaten much in days. "Are y'all about done?" he barked.

"Just about," Agent Espinoza, that quiet guy with her, finally spoke up.

"She's dead." I collapsed to sit on the floor before answering with my voice husky from the bile burns.

"Do you know when—" Holt started.

"Four years ago."

Holt left it at that and collected the pictures. "They found evidence Buchanan downloaded your images."

"They did? When? They didn't have that before my trial. Does that mean I get to get out of here?"

She shook her head. "No, I'm sorry. It doesn't change anything about your plea bargain." Of course not.

Espinoza chimed in, "You'll be receiving an official notice of his conviction in the mail, along with notices of all other convictions where the perpetrator downloaded your images."

"Why? Why would I want to know?"

He cracked a smile. "So you can sue their asses."

"What would I get out of that?"

"Talk to your lawyer," Holt said. "By law, you're eligible for a certain amount of restitution."

"You mean like money?"

"Yes." Espinoza shot me a satisfied grin. "Hopefully a lot of money."

"Yours and Simone's are the most downloaded child pornography images out there," Holt added as she snapped the briefcase shut. "We've been searching for you for years. So have authorities in England, France, and Australia."

I buried my face in my hands. "Glad to hear I'm so popular."

"Thank you for your help, Sawyer." Holt reached her hand out to shake mine.

I took it. "Fuck him." Then I reached for Espinoza's hand. "Please, I mean."

"That's the goal," Espinoza said through that same smile.

"Thank you."

I started to follow them out when Cash caught my hand. "Hey," he whispered. "You gonna be okay?"

229

I turned to him and scoffed. "Yeah, it's nothing new."

"Sawyer, you should talk to someone about this."

"Yeah, I'll get right on that." I glared before flouncing toward the door.

"Sawyer—"

Spinning on my heel, I barked, "Talk, right? Because that'll help. That'll erase all those photos. That'll stop those men from jacking off to Simone even though she's been dead for four years."

He ran his hands up and down my arms. "What can I do?"

I shook my head and sighed. "I think visiting hours are over."

"We have a few minutes."

I couldn't look at him. And I couldn't stand him looking at me, not after he saw those pictures. "No, we don't. I'll see you next week."

He gave in, his face crestfallen. I closed my eyes to feel his lips against my forehead, but even that didn't slow the disgust and rage pumping through my arteries.

I was helpless to change anything. And I always would be.

May 2018

---

*T*HE DAYS AFTER THE FEDS LEFT, I FOUND myself lingering on those images of self-annihilation that popped in my mind.

When my arms would itch with that creeping under my skin, I'd search for anything to scratch it. I knew I'd only find relief by slitting deep beneath to the fat and fascia to let the sensation drain out with my blood. My bare legs would swish under the cool sheets as I lay awake at three AM craving the taste of steel in my mouth, colder and harder than a cock, with rougher edges. Would I wait to warm it with my tongue before revving up the nerve to pull the trigger, or would I barely think before closing my lips around it and painting the room behind me red? Now that I had time to think, jumping didn't sound like my style. Something about the uncertainty of the fall. What if I survived? What would my quality of life be with my body paralyzed and mental capacities diminished? How would I finish the job then? Hanging sounded awful. Not that any of the above would work here. Well, maybe I could drown: stop up the sink in our bathroom, hold my breath in the shallow water, then inhale it when I blacked out. Unless I fell backward and not into the water once I was unconscious. Shit.

I'd keep these images of my death alive in my head when I needed comfort. I fantasized about them when I tried to sleep at night, the way I thought of Jake between my legs instead of my hands when I needed a breathless orgasm. Then I started to rely on this reel of violence to get through each day, not just as a warm blanket to cuddle up to in bed. Thinking that a day was my last made me almost giddy, fearless. The world was painless and pretty because all the hurt and ugly would end soon. Then I'd remember I was here, kept so cruelly safe. No guns, no blades, no tubs. Just endless fucking life.

It made me hate Simone, that delicate little bitch. Suicide in a mental hospital would have been a breeze for her. She could take a bite of yogurt at breakfast, and her dairy allergy would do the rest. That was how she did it, by the way. Her brother found her slumped on her bed with a pint of Ben and Jerry's melting into the carpet below, her silver medical ID bracelet sticky from the poison. She always wished she could have eaten ice cream. I guessed she took her only chance. Good for her.

After one particularly sleepless night in May when all I could think about were those men all over the world still commenting and downloading and watching, watching, watching Jeff rape and choke me with his dick while they had their hands wrapped around their own, I decided to try Simone's way. She had it right all those years back. They were still using her, but she didn't have to feel it anymore. I wanted that. And I was smart. I was inventive. I'd figure it out, even in this place. At breakfast,

I skipped my strawberry yogurt and slipped the plastic spoon on my tray up the sleeve of Cash's sweatshirt.

That afternoon in the hospital courtyard, I laid on my stomach on the lawn with *As I Lay Dying* propped on the edge of the sidewalk. Underneath the back cover, I sharpened the curve of the plastic spoon against the cement before working on the handle.

....

It was cloudy and misty and cold. I stood resolute in the middle of Third Street, unafraid of the dream this time. I had a plan. Turning to my right, to Simone, I ran my hands over her arms, her goose bumps rising under my fingers. "I'm sorry, Simone," I whispered. I pulled her into my chest, her face against my shoulder. She was always more petite than I was. "I'm so sorry. I'm going to make this right," I breathed into her hair.

I woke up. It was three AM. My hands searched in the dark in the underside of my pillowcase for the altered spoon and the folded lined paper. I left the yellow notes on my pillow and pulled the covers up neatly.

The bathroom was cold, and the water would be at first, too. I turned the shower on as hot as it could go and listened at the door for Tori. Nothing. I rolled my leggings down to my feet, stripped off my panties, then, once the bathroom was steaming, I took off Cash's sweatshirt and dropped it on the floor before slipping behind the shower curtain. I turned the water temperature down as it scalded my feet, letting it flush my skin without burning me.

I took the sharpened spoon to the swollen blue veins

of my left wrist, but I could barely scratch the first layer of skin. It wasn't the insufficiency of my tool. It was my damn drive to self-preserve. I'd have to be stronger, push harder, slice quicker. I pressed the back of my forearm against the chilled shower wall, using it as a chopping block. I closed my eyes.

This is the worst. This is the worst. Just do it, and the rest will be easy.

I raised my right arm and slammed the spoon against my flesh, scraping and carving down my wrist, nearly biting a hole in my lip to silence the pain. Sawing, that was the best way to describe what I had to do. It was a weak object, that plastic spoon. I had to keep at it to dig deeper and deeper. Then that white plastic broke in my clenched fist, and my fingers surrendered the two pieces to the shower floor. I finally exhaled and opened my eyes to see if I had done enough. The jagged cut wasn't as deep as it felt, but blood gushed from it as the hot water ran over it. The white floor below turned pink, then translucent scarlet, as the drops of red bounced with the water from the faucet. I used my finger and thumb to pull the wound apart, to keep the blood flowing.

The pain was good. More like a bruise than a sting; I hadn't expected that. And the itching was gone. I smiled. I'd done it. I got rid of that damn crawling, skittering feeling under my skin. I'd never have to pretend I didn't feel it again.

I laid on my back in the stall shower, my head on the lip by the curtain, my legs perpendicular to the floor, ankles crossed up the corner of the wall. The bloody water pooled around me as I blocked the drain with my back. Then it overflowed onto the bathroom floor. My fingers kept prying my skin apart in the puddle, letting the water run it clean.

As I felt the dark headache sink in, I thought of Jake. Had I written enough to him in my note? I wrote enough to my mom and Jeff. I tried to explain what I could to Simone's family. I tried to apologize. Of course, I could never write enough to Cash, but this, right here, was the best I could offer him. He would be relieved, I knew, that I wasn't his burden anymore. And he knew how I felt, how I'd always feel about him. But Jake's...the words weren't even my own. I stole them. And what if Jake wasn't at his same address anymore? How would my note even get to him? What if he never knew he was all I could think about as my life drained from me?

What if he didn't care?

I closed my eyes when I couldn't endure the dizziness anymore, when I couldn't see the ceiling because it was covered in purple and grey splotches. I wish I was relieved, but I was terrified when I realized I was slipping away and couldn't turn back. In a vain grasp at life, I tried to open my panicking eyes one last time just to see if my numb legs had folded on top of me. Even that simple motion was impossible.

It must have been then that my consciousness surrendered.

....

"I NEED ANOTHER UNIT OF A-negative," a foreign voice commanded in the darkness. Beside his words, I heard fast beeps pacing with quick breaths. No, not just with quick breaths, with pain—a stabbing ache shooting down my sternum and out over my chest, like my ribs were a spider someone had stomped on.

Shit. Those breaths were mine. I was breathing.

I'd survived.

I lifted my heavy eyelids to the spinning sight of scrubs and fluorescent lights and medical equipment. My eyes shut in protest. It was too dizzy in here—too bright and noisy and alive. I forced them open again to see the thick needle in the crook of my right arm. I reached to pull it out, but my arm didn't move. Again, I reached. Nothing. My gaze rolled to my left forearm. It was strapped down above the bandaged wound, cuffed to the hospital bed with a padded restraint. My legs couldn't move either. I couldn't see why, but I assumed it was for the same reason.

I sank my spine against the mattress, resigned. That hurt, too. And I was sure a vice was squeezing my skull. There was no saliva in my mouth or throat. My left wrist ached with a pain deep between the bones. And I was cold—cold past goose bumps and shivering, that motionless cold of the dead. But I wasn't that lucky.

"How are you feeling?" that same voice from before asked.

Eyes still closed, I barely shook my head.

"Are you in pain?"

I nodded down once.

"On a scale of one to ten, how bad is it?"

I spread out seven fingers, hoping he'd see. "Water," was the only hoarse word I could manage.

"Sure, we'll get you some water. Did you take any drugs? Even over the counter? Aspirin? Ibuprofen? Anything?"

I denied with a weak head shake. Maybe I should have. Maybe that would have gotten the job done. I couldn't even begin to figure out how to sneak those, though.

I looked at the bag above me as a nurse replaced it—full, bulging with someone else's blood, blood that another person had sacrificed to save someone's life, someone who was actually sick or hurt, someone who deserved to live. That made me want to puke.

The doctor was about to leave when I breathed out a husky, "How close was I?"

He stared at me for a second with his hand on the door handle, rolling his lips inside over his tongue. "Are you feeling well enough to speak to a psychiatrist or do you want to wait another hour or so?"

My eyelids slammed shut at the idea. No. I didn't want to talk. I didn't want to be here. In the hospital, fine, but not in this room. In a colder, more final one. And if they wanted words, they could just read my letters.

I must have drifted off. When I opened my eyes again, that annoyingly hopeful light of dawn—dawn I didn't want to make it to—was forcing itself through the window, and the donor blood had been replaced with saline. I felt warm again, except for where the fluids were flowing into my arm. My headache was nearly gone, too, and I couldn't feel much more than soreness in my chest. I lifted my left arm so I could see the bandage. Hey, the restraint was gone. I carefully swished my freed feet under the blankets before turning to see if the cuff around my right wrist was gone. It was, but a large hand replaced it. It was attached to a rigid, seething Cash sitting beside my bed.

Terror froze me. Jake had a temper. *He* was the one who yelled and fought dirty like me. Cash's fuse was long. Whatever I did was bad enough to burn it all up and detonate him. And I had yet to see the explosion.

He held the yellow lined paper I had addressed to him clutched in his other hand and started, "You wrote me, and I quote..." His voice sharpened with rage. "'I love you. I am so grateful for you and all you've been to me. I've never deserved so much. And I can't begin to express how *sorry*,'" his emphasis, not mine, "'I am that I met you and spent the last several months hurting you. I hope you are relieved by my decision and can have an incredible life now that I can no longer interfere with it.'" His fingers slid to my hand, which was colder than I thought now that I felt the heat of his, and squeezed it tight. Then he pierced me with his gaze, his blue eyes burning with rage like a driftwood flame. "Don't you *ever* apologize for being in my life. You are not allowed to destroy something beautiful that I love."

I turned my face back toward the window to wipe away the tears gathering in my lower lids, but he cupped my chin to force me to look at him.

"Do you hear me? You cannot take you away from me like this."

That lump in my throat rose, and my hot tears poured over his fingers and thumb. There was nothing I could do to stop them. "I'm sorry," I choked out. And I was, because I shouldn't have invited him to study that day. I should have left him in the hall. I'd always feel bad for what I had become to him.

"No, Sawyer." He shook his head. "That's not good enough. You're never going to do something like this again, understand?"

I nodded.

His hand moved to brush over my tangled hair. He whispered, "Why would you do this?"

But I just wept. He should have asked why I didn't do this years ago. Maybe Simone would still be alive. Jake would have been spared from loving me. So would Cash.

Cash kept stroking my hair and holding my hand until my crying broke up just enough for me to say, "Simone."

"Okay?" Cash dipped his chin, trying to track with me.

"It's my fault."

"No, no," he said, his voice gentle. "It's not. How can you—"

"No." I sniffed. Cash handed me a few tissues. I wiped my face with them. "I'm why she killed herself."

"Sawyer," he said softly, tilting his face and running his thumb over my hand. "You can't blame yourself for that."

I jerked my head up and down. "I can, Cash." I took a deep breath to calm the shaking in my chest. "We didn't know about the videos and pictures. I mean, not how it really worked. Like, we knew Jeff filmed everything and that we'd do weird stuff like hold notes up to people while naked, but we didn't know it was going anywhere outside our room. I didn't figure out until later that we were probably taking requests most of the time.

"Anyway, Jeff went to prison when I was ten for lewd conduct with this seven-year-old girl in our Sunday school, this girl he was grooming to replace me since I was hitting puberty fast and awkward. Apparently, pedophiles don't like that so much. Simone and I thought it was over once he was in prison.

"We were in ninth grade when this asshole basketball player, Jeremy, found one of the videos online and showed it to three of his friends, also jocks, real big guys, you know? They told us they wouldn't show anyone if we did what they wanted."

Cash pulled in his breath, eyes darkening with fury. "So they blackmailed you into sex?"

I squeezed my eyes shut. "Simone said no, that we should tell our parents. She was a really good Christian girl." She'd kept going to church after Jeff's arrest. Although, he'd always told her how much Jesus loved her and how pure and sinless she was and how she'd go to heaven. Unlike me, of course.

"What did you say?"

The tears started falling again as I stared out the window. I couldn't face Cash when I said, "I told her she needed to grow a pair and just deal with it, that she could fuck up her life but not mine." I took a deep inhale and shuddered out, "The four of them took turns raping us the night Jeremy showed us the video." I closed my eyes and shook my head. "It was so much worse than I thought it was going to be. I could hear Simone crying and begging them to stop, but I did nothing." I settle my tortured gaze on Cash. "It was like *I* raped her.

"When it was over, I thought we were done with them. But they kept texting us and cornering us at school. So we were on call. But Simone wasn't the same after that night. She shut down and wouldn't talk to me or anyone else. And a week after that, she killed herself."

Cash just stared at me and held my hand. "What

happened to you after that?"

I narrowed my eyes and cried, "What?"

"Did they keep raping you?"

I threw my hands half in the air. "Why does that matter? Did you listen to anything I just told you?"

"But don't you feel bad for her?"

"Yes! Cash, that's what I'm—"

"Not for Simone. For you—four years ago, ten years ago."

I rolled my eyes. Shrink talk. Everyone wanted to talk about *that little girl.* "No. Why would I?"

Cash pressed his fingers into his eyebrows, trying to summon some patience or think of a different angle. It was hard to tell. "Sawyer, could you trust your mom when you were a kid?"

"What does this have—"

"Just answer."

"No."

"Would she have listened to you?"

I let out a shaky sigh. "No."

After Jeff went to jail, I tried to tell her what he did with me, but her response was always—*I'm sure that's not what happened, sweetie.* Or—*Did a cop tell you to say that?* Or—*That's a lie. Don't bring this up again with anyone. Do you hear me?* God forbid Jeff spent any more time in prison.

"You were both in an impossible situation. And probably mortified. I mean, *that's* how you found out that, what, hundreds of thousands of people saw you get molested? And now these guys at school found out. You had to have been terrified."

Cash's view of me was wearing on my patience.

"Right?" he pressed.

I nodded, but only to end this conversation as fast as I could.

"Simone made a choice. She could have told her parents. You didn't point a gun to her head to stop her."

"But I bullied her into it." *Bully*: that magic word. Anyone could be absolved of their actions if they were *bullied* into them. Using, drinking, sex—slap *bully* before that and the perp became the victim, and the bully the villain. *Come on, Cash, see me as the villain.*

"You did. And that was wrong," he agreed. "But you didn't kill her."

"That's debatable."

He spoke over me, "And killing yourself won't bring her back. Right?"

I started searching for the give-me-more-morphine remote—anything to get me out of this conversation—but I couldn't find it.

"What are you doing?"

"I need more drugs. Where's the button?"

Cash pointed to the wall behind me. I craned my neck to see a clear plastic box with the drug drip locked inside.

"I don't get a button?"

"No! You just tried to off yourself. You're lucky I got them to remove your restraints." He grabbed the remote with the button to call the nurse and held it out of my reach. "Answer my question, and I'll get you more morphine."

I glowered at him and grumbled. "No. It won't bring her back."

"Good." He called the nurse, and then dropped a note on my lap. I leaned forward to see it was written for

242

Simone's parents. "Two down," he mumbled. What did that mean?

After I got another dose of opioids, Cash reached into his pocket and took out another yellow paper. The letter was Jake's. My stomach tightened as Cash read, "'Jake, I love you and I always will and I am sorry. What a useless word.'" He folded the note, rested his elbows on his knees, and regarded me thoughtfully. "You've lectured me enough about Hemingway and his famous use of 'and' that I suspected this was either inspired by him or plagiarized. Turns out, it was plagiarized."

"You know..." I smirked, my eyes still swollen and teary. "It's not polite to read other people's mail."

"You never told me why you guys broke up."

"Actually, I think it's illegal—"

"Yeah, well, you had no pulse. And I wanted to know why."

Damn. I *was* close.

"Really?" I asked a little too enthusiastically.

"I guess, technically, you had a pulse, but they couldn't find it. And your breathing was so weak the nursing student who found you panicked and started CPR." Ah, that explained why my ribs were cracked. "If this," he held the paper in front of me, "has anything to do with last night, you need to talk about it."

Again with the talking. "Cash—"

"I'm not saying it has to be with me. Just someone. You're supposed to see a psychiatrist here, right?"

"I don't want to talk to anyone else." *Please don't leave. Don't leave. Don't.*

He took my hand. "Okay. Can you tell me what happened?"

I did. I told him Jeff raped me and that I left Jake so

I could kill my baby. I told him Jake wouldn't take me back even though I begged. I told him I started stripping when I couldn't find work.

He leaned toward me and took my hand. "You went through all that alone?" he asked with that classic Cash compassion.

"Cash, I deserved—"

"Shut up." He stood over me and pressed his lips into my forehead. Then he stared in my eyes and swept his fingers over my bandage. "Stop punishing yourself." He hugged me carefully to avoid pressing his weight into my battered sternum. I buried my face in his chest, lifting my hands to his waist.

He straightened up and let my letter to Jake fall to the covers. Cash's hand reached into his pants pocket again to retrieve my final letter. The one to Jeff and my mom. They lived in the same place, and theirs were each short and sweet enough to fit on one page.

Cash read, "'Jeff, fuck you, you vindictive son of a bitch. The only reason I'm going to hell is so I can watch you burn in agony for eternity.'"

Whoa. Never heard Cash swear before. It was shockingly sexy—that sugary Georgia inflection over my bitter words. Damn. I could listen to him curse all day. Too bad I couldn't provoke him to do it on his own.

"'Mom, you should have listened. I hope the images of your precious husband raping your only child haunt you until you die, hopefully longer. Dad wouldn't have let that happen.'"

Cash swung his eyes to me, his lips curving into a smirk. "Sawyer, you moron."

July 2018

I THOUGHT I'D FEEL LIKE A BADASS WALKING through those doors with the "High AWOL Risk" signs tacked to them, like one of those moments when someone quits a job where they hated all their coworkers and leaves telling their boss where to shove it as they flip the bird high and proud.

But it wasn't like that at all.

I stepped out into the stuffy July sunlight shaken and scared with a new puffy scar on my wrist, as well as a half-dozen bottles of pills for anxiety and Major Depressive Disorder, Single Episode, which was what I got for hacking away at myself with a plastic spoon. Released back into a world that was still too big and too bright and too sharp to handle. It wasn't the same few faces anymore: therapists, patients, nurses, doctors. There were millions again, any of whom could have known my face, my body, and I couldn't tell. As much as it irked me to admit, that hospital was the safest place I'd been since Jeff was released from prison.

But now Jeff was going back behind bars, and I was

supposedly getting a say in how long. The FBI got their arrest, and Simone and I got our conviction. Jeff's trial had been going on in Oregon while I finished serving the rest of my sentence in LA.

Three days after Agent Holt told me they had Jeff in custody, I worked up the nerve to call my mom. Cash held my hand while I listened to her phone ring through the free patient pay phone. With each ring, I prayed she would see the unfamiliar California number and ignore the call. My heart stopped when her weary voice answered, "Hello?"

I swallowed hard and forced out, "Mom?"

Weeping broke out on the other side of the line. "Sawyer?"

I sighed. "Yeah, it's me."

But she didn't say anything. I sat there watching the phone timer tick away three whole minutes as she sobbed. What was she crying about? Maybe she saw the pictures the feds showed me and felt guilty. No, that was far too optimistic. It was probably because her lovey-dovey was in jail again.

Mom only saw Jeff as the carefree, kid at heart. The acoustic-guitar-playing Sunday school teacher with those cute thick-rimmed glasses. He was just too darn gentle and charming and kind to be capable of harming anyone, let alone a child. How could anyone even imagine he'd hurt a kid? The police *had* to have been wrong that first arrest. She was convinced the mom of that little girl had some vendetta against him. Maybe that mom tried to get Jeff into bed, and he resisted so she set him up. I guessed denial was that form of delusion people didn't get locked up for.

My mom wasn't alone, though. He did seem sweet, benign. Plus, he was cool and charismatic, so people were eager to please him, to be part of his inner circle. Even Simone was. Her parents hadn't had any problem leaving her with him every day after school. Of course, Simone kept her mouth shut when Jeff raped her repeatedly. Because even in the horror and the disgusting pain, she was in his world. He made her feel special. He made her feel saved.

Apparently, I was the only one who never wanted any part of him. I wanted *my* dad back, not this slimy replacement. So, while Simone was his pretty little pet, Jeff convinced me that he was holding me by the collar as I hung over the precipice of hell. If only he had let me fall.

I had no idea what my mom had to cry about. I waited for her to blubber an explanation, impatiently tapping my big toe against the sole of my flip-flop.

"Sweetie," she sniffed. "I'm so sorry. I can't even—" More crying. Huh. Maybe she did feel bad. She finally choked out, "Where are you, honey? Please, come home."

"Um..." I raised a brow at Cash before answering, "I can't until July." And even then, I didn't want to.

But I did, the morning I was discharged. Cash and I went straight from the hospital to LAX. We flew into the hardly functioning airport in the prison town thirty miles south of my shit town.

My mom picked us up at the deserted curb, suffocating me with her hug, crying into my untamed hair. I patted her back. "It's fine, it's fine," I muttered the lie. What was I supposed to say? Was it really *my* job to comfort *her* for her husband raping me repeatedly and posting it online? How was that my role?

She blabbed the whole ride home on the narrow highway darkened by ominous redwoods, through rolling green farmland, into our beach town with scattered squat buildings and poorly planned neighborhoods. It seemed like she was trying to keep the conversation light by sputtering out questions as fast as she could: *How was college? What are you studying? Have you heard from Jake? Did you know his sister's getting married? I heard Tatum got pregnant. Do you talk to her anymore? Cash, what do you study? How do you two know each other?* This last question was accompanied by a sideways glance, code for, *He's cute. What's wrong with him?*

Ah! *Shut up!* I pressed my fingers into my temples and leaned my aching head, eyes closed, against the passenger window. "Mom, could we just listen to music?"

She muttered a passive-aggressive, "Sure, sweetie," and stopped talking.

We passed over the bridge with the river on the east and harbor on the west, stopping at the three traffic lights of our town, turning right at the last light. A few more turns and we were on Third Street, driving onto the pavement where my demons clawed and scratched and waited for my return. I stared the street down, ignoring the nightmares flashing across it. None of the men were on the sidewalks. Simone wasn't here. Jeff wasn't either. Travis and his friends weren't at the intersection at the end of the street. And Cash was here. I had Cash. I would be okay.

"Do you want me to order pizza for dinner? Or do you want to go out?" my mom asked as we pulled into the driveway of the little blue house.

Out? No. Jeff was on trial. Our whole town knew by now that he raped me, that I was all over the web. There was no way in hell I was leaving the house. "Could we order in?"

"Yep. Do you want to have any friends over? I heard—"

"No," I answered too quickly as I climbed out of the car.

I led Cash inside through the living room into my room. After I flicked the light on, I scanned the white dresser, my made bed with the purple down comforter, the window by it. I stepped back at the memories of Jake's skin in the moonlight, the taste of his sweat, his warmth against me under those sheets. Shut my eyes when I pictured waking up naked, half under the covers, sore and sick after Kyle's party. I turned around to bolt out when I felt the thick fear in the room from a decade ago, bumping into Cash's chest. "Uh..." I stuttered as my anxious eyes stared up at him. "You should take my room. I'll, um..." I glanced past him to the living room. "I'll sleep on the couch."

"Sawyer, no, you just got out of the hospital. You should—"

"I can't sleep in here."

He nodded. "Yeah, okay."

After I wheeled my suitcase into the bathroom, I sorted through my belongings. I had everything now, including triple-blade razors that didn't scrape my skin with the added bonus of no CNAs to supervise me using them, a hair straightener, and all my yummy hair and skin products. I turned the shower on hot and stripped down, then scanned my body in the glaring bathroom lights. It was emaciated and unshaved. The mirror showed my pale skin and hair left natural and wavy, dull from crappy conditioner.

After I showered and shaved all those gross hairs into oblivion, I put on and fastened my favorite violet bra I'd saved from mutilation. It didn't fit. Was I not a D-cup anymore? Was I a sad little C? I hadn't been a C since I was fourteen. I tightened every strap and made the best of it. My jeans were a little loose, and my shirt hung shapeless from my shoulders. Hospital food hadn't kept me curvy, and sulking in bed for months wasted away my athletic shape.

I blow-dried my hair and smoothed it with the flat iron, so I wouldn't have to deal with it in the morning. I already had plenty to deal with.

I picked at my pizza at the kitchen bar, my mom on my left and Cash on my right. "You ready for tomorrow, Sawyer?" my mom asked. "You know you don't have to do this. Maybe I could read it for you? Or the lawyer?"

"I got it," I muttered. I took a bite of pepperoni and cheese just to have an excuse not to talk.

There was a chance Jeff would only spend a lousy fifteen years in prison, pay some fines, and be out by the age of fifty-three. The maximum was life. I was here to convince the judge that Jeff needed to die in prison. I knew this was the only way I could do right by Simone, do right by me.

That didn't make it easy to sleep that night, especially on the living room couch with Third Street watching me through the sheer curtains of the front door. I even tried Jake's TV-to-sleep method, letting my eyes glaze over and dry out to reruns of *Friends*. I was still awake when Cash got up to pee at one AM. Did he have the tiniest bladder in the world?

He saw me on the couch, the muted blue light flashing over my face. "Can't sleep?" he asked as he pushed his hand through his hair.

I shook my head. After he went to the bathroom, he sat down on the floor, his back against the couch in front of my chest. "I love this one," he said about the episode of *Friends* now on.

My fingers wandered to his curls, looping through a few of them, pulling them straight, then letting them bounce back. "I'm scared," I whispered.

He rotated toward me, sweeping the backs of his fingers across my forehead to return a few flyaways where they belonged. "I know." His lips curved into that sad, compassionate way he smiled and ran his hand down my back. "Do you want to pray about it?"

Oh, funny story. That morning in the hospital after I put myself into hemorrhagic shock, Cash told me that watching Jeff burn in hell wasn't a legitimate reason to go there, that believing I was damned because my pedophile stepfather/Sunday school pastor told me so was illogical. He'd said, *Aren't you a math major? Don't you like logic?*

When I told him I was having too much fun to deal with Jesus and all his rules, he did the highest eyebrow-raise I had ever seen before pointedly staring at my taped-up arm. He'd said, *This is fun? And rules? You don't get it, do you?* Then he told me he loved me, that he had been and would always be there for me no matter what I did even when it hurt him. *Oh, and, by the way, Sawyer, this is excruciating.* That was how God wanted me. Only he had endured more pain than Cash ever could for me.

And so I gave in, swollen eyelids, dry throat, and sliced wrist, to Cash and his God.

I know. I was shocked, too.

And I knew Cash said I just needed a friend for now, but after that day, there was a shift between us, like the timer started ticking down until we got back together. It was in the way his eyes flickered when he saw me, how his hands lingered in mine, the speed at which his heart beat when my ear pressed against it. But since he broke it off, he would have to ask me out again. I had been brave enough lately.

Cash fell asleep on the couch behind me, my back against his chest, his arm over my waist. With him so close, I was able to get a few hours of sleep, too.

THE COURT WAS SMALL AND sparse and had a chilled scent of mold. I barely smelled it because I couldn't breathe. That eight-year-old I couldn't exorcise was squeezing my lungs and kicking at my heart in protest. I could almost hear her screaming, *What the hell are we doing here?*

Jeff's mom and dad were seated in the benches on the left, Simone's exhausted and anxious parents and brother on the right. I nodded down toward them, sick with the knowledge I was about to confess to killing their daughter.

I kept on, passing through the hip-high door to the table where the prosecutor sat. He was a thin old man with deep wrinkles engraved in olive skin. He looked into my eyes with his gentle ones when he shook my hand. "It's an honor to finally meet you, Ms. de la Cruz."

An honor. It didn't make sense to me. Still, the words stung my eyes as I let go of his hand.

"Thank you," I whispered as I sat in the chair he motioned toward. I couldn't speak any louder. I was terrified. How was I going to read this letter? I shifted in my seat to see Cash and my mom seated in the bench behind me. Cash placed his hand palm-up on the bar between us, like he had on my thigh that morning in church—an offering. I placed my hand in his, the warmth sending a calm up my arm that spread through my chest where the nerves threatened to strangle me.

"You've got this." He smiled. For a second, I believed I did.

A door opened at the front of the court. I snapped my head forward to see a petite woman decked in charcoal grey from shoulders to ankles, her hair curled and teased in excess, as if this was the 1980s. Her heels click-clacked over the wood floors as she approached the defense's table. Her client was behind her, ushered by the bailiff.

The familiar stomp of Jeff's feet I had heard approaching my room a hundred times stopped my heart. I thought for sure that eight-year-old inside had punctured my ventricles, letting the blood spill out while the cardiac muscle spasmed in vain, because my vision started clouding at the sight of Jeff's pale blue eyes, his blond hair starting to thin, and his sturdy, tall frame that had crushed me too many times. Those pasty eyes met mine, and he suddenly appeared small, inconsequential. This time, *his* fate was in *my* hands. I felt peace, strong like I never had before. I took a deep breath, more exhilarated than scared.

"You okay?"

I glanced back at Cash and nodded.

Past his shoulder, the courtroom door opened and another body slipped in. *Oh, shit. Oh, shit.* I was *not* okay. What the hell was Jake doing here? *I can't do this. I can't do this. I can't say any of this in front of him.*

Jake caught my eye. For a moment, my whole body hurt. He watched me as he sat down on the bench along the back wall. No smiles, no nods, no mouthed words exchanged between us. Just an unbreaking stare. I had to wonder if his heart stopped like mine did. Of course not. He knew I'd be here. But why was he here?

"Really?" Cash interrupted my gaze. I jerked, staring at his tilted head as he squeezed my hand. "Because you look like you're going to pass out."

"Just nerves." I fought through a shaky smile before turning forward.

We all stood for the judge like we were supposed to. After we sat, that big-haired attorney started her statement about why the judge should go easy on Jeff.

"He was let out of prison six months early for good behavior, hasn't violated his parole, and is in excellent standing with his parole officer...

"Furthermore, he has committed no such illicit acts since his release last year and shows deep remorse for his crime."

It was so hard not to cackle at this. I started to, but then covered it with a cough when the prosecutor shot me a cutting glance and put his hand over mine.

"Since this reincarceration of my client is interrupting his successful reentry into society, we ask that you allow him to serve the sentences for production of child pornography and the two counts of first degree sexual abuse concurrently, giving him the minimum of fifteen years. We also ask for the possibility of parole after eight, since he has already served seven years."

What? I leaned to the prosecutor's ear. "Can they do that?"

"It's not going to happen," he said. He pointed subtly with his hand on the table toward the judge, whose face was twisted in an *Are you fucking kidding me?* expression.

I sighed in relief. Not that the feeling lasted long. It was my turn.

The prosecutor stood. "Your Honor, this is Sawyer de la Cruz, whom you may recognize as the *surviving victim* of Mr. Lindley's abuse. She has prepared a statement."

"Proceed, Ms. de la Cruz."

I pushed off the table with my hands, and then picked up the typed letter. It shook between my fingers.

"I'm eight," I started softly, stopping to clear my throat, "in my bed, hearing footsteps approach my door. I know they're not my mom's. By now, I know what's going to happen next. I know if I say 'no' when he takes off my clothes and sets up his camera, Jeff will tell me the Jesus I love, the God who comforted me when my dad died, will send me to hell. I know that it will hurt. I know that I have to pretend with noises and words that I don't understand. And I know I can't tell anyone.

"I'm nine, and I can't tell my friend that she shouldn't come over to play after school, that when Jeff says he wants us to play 'dress-up' and 'models' with him, it's not as fun as it sounds. Now she's crying and scared and hurts, too.

"I'm fifteen, and so is my friend, when four junior boys at school start to flirt with us. And we're flattered because they're popular and play basketball and we're just freshman. But now we're afraid again, because they have a video of our least favorite game with Jeff. Now we're humiliated because if they have it, who else does? And now four juniors are gang-raping us, and we're doing our best to comply so no one in school will see the video. Simone is broken from the silence I've bullied her into. Now Simone is dead.

"I'm eighteen, dizzy and drunk after a party in the front seat of Jeff's car. Now I'm in my bed, and my pants are gone. I feel the shooting, tearing pain as Jeff tells me who is really in control.

"I'm eighteen and pregnant, terrified that I might have Jeff's baby. And with my choice to abort, I lose my fiancé and my future."

My vision glazed over the paper twitching in my hands. That was the end of the story as far as Jake knew. My eyes wandered up to the judge, down my right arm to the prosecutor with anxious eyes imploring me to continue. My voice was paralyzed in that moment with Jake's listening ears pressed against me. I couldn't go on. I slipped my index finger in the crease, and I let the paper fold over it.

A hand caught my arm, gentle but firm. The prosecutor's voice in my ear was the same. "This is your chance. Take it."

My gaze met his before continuing over my right shoulder to Jake. His elbows were on his knees, his fingers intertwined at his chin, his attention wrapped around me. Then he nodded, one careful movement of his head that loosened a ribbon of hair from where he had combed it back—a nod that I should go on.

I had nothing to lose. Jake and I had closed the door of our relationship over a year ago. Might as well lock it, deadbolt it, and weld it shut. I returned to the paper and unfolded it. "I'm eighteen," I swallowed, though my throat was dry, "working as a stripper when a man offers me cash to 'fuck Delilah.' And I take it, because I always do, because that's what I'm best at.

"I'm eighteen, when a client at the strip club pays for sex with Delilah. I tell him 'no,' because I can't. I can't do it anymore. He tries to rape me, and I'm arrested for smashing his head in because my mind has disconnected and I'm terrified he's Jeff.

"I'm nineteen, in mandatory psychiatric treatment for severe PTSD and attempted suicide. My nights are filled with dreams where I'm chased and hunted, and I scream but no one hears me. My days are filled with fear and guilt for what I've done to my child and my ex-fiancé and Simone.

"Your Honor, please, I entreat you to give this man the maximum sentence of life. His abuse cost Simone her life. It will haunt me for all of mine."

I looked at the next line of my letter. It was for Jeff. I folded it up and dropped it on the table. "Jeff…" I sighed. "Honestly, I'd love to stand here and say, 'Fuck you, I hope you get raped every day in prison and then burn in hell.' But, I think they'd hold me in contempt of court." I glanced over at the judge. "Right?"

Cash let out a soft exhale behind me, and I knew he was rubbing the embarrassment I should have felt from his forehead. Then I heard a snicker from the back of the room. Jake. Closing my eyes, I bit my bottom lip to hold in a smile.

The judge gave me a wary look and nodded.

"Okay, so, I'll just say this—Jeff, I haven't forgiven you. But I'm going to, and not just because God forgave me, but because you don't get to have that power over me anymore. You don't have any power over me anymore."

Raising my head toward the judge, I said, "Thank you, Your Honor."

After I sat down and the prosecutor said his short piece, which I didn't hear a word of, the judge announced, "In light of the severity of the abuse, the prevalence of the images, and the protracted consequences for the victims, I am sentencing Jeff Lindley to fifty years in Oregon State Penitentiary."

Yeah, I'd call that a win.

I bolted up and turned to Cash, who was already on his feet. His hands out, he asked, "You okay with that?"

"Hell yeah!" I hugged him tight, feeling him press his lips against the top of my head.

When Cash let go, I caught a glimpse of the doors at the back open and Jake leave with his leather jacket over his shoulder. My lungs deflated with relief, but that pain in every inch of me remained. Of course he would leave. I knew he would. It was over. It had to be.

"Sawyer?" I snapped out of my stare at the closed double doors to follow the shaky feminine voice. It was Simone's mom.

I nodded, speechless.

Before I knew what was happening, I was in her arms with her wet face against my shoulder. "Thank you," she sobbed. "It's okay, sweetie. It's okay."

"Thank you," I whispered. I wished that meant more to me, but it didn't. She wasn't Simone. That was who

I wanted to apologize to. But her mom's words stabbed deep, then made me feel lighter, like they'd cut into a bag of sand sitting inside me and now that sand was spilling out. Maybe I wouldn't have to feel the full weight of it anymore.

"SAWYER, ARE YOU SURE YOU don't want to stay a few extra days?" my mom asked while I collected my clothes and pushed them into my suitcase. "You don't have to leave tonight."

"I can't, Mom." What was I going to do here? Stay locked inside while everyone gossiped about the cheerleader who went to LA to whore her way through college?

"You haven't even been to the beach yet. You don't have to leave for four more hours. At least take a quick walk down there, like you and your dad used to."

"Fine." Anything to not hear her voice anymore. I grabbed *A Farewell to Arms*, the book I was reading on the plane, and searched the house for Cash. I spotted him through the window on the phone, so I poked my head through the back door. "Want to walk to the beach?"

"Hang on," he said as he covered the phone. "It's Jo. She's having boy problems and freaking out because June's having pregnancy issues and is on bedrest. I gotta call her next."

"Tell her hi. I'll be back in a bit, okay?"

He nodded and smiled. I heard him say, "Sawyer says hi," as I closed the door.

I took the walk down the street to the beach, finding that massive fallen tree that my dad and I used to sit against on the shore. I balanced heel-to-toe across it until it met the mountainous rock at its end.

It was bright and overcast and cool like most summer days here. I took off my flip-flops and buried my feet in the warm sand, keeping them sheltered from the breeze. Snuggled in my navy Bruins hoodie with my knees to my chest, I leaned my back against the smooth wood. When I flipped open my book, a page of Cash's letter fell into my lap. I had been using pages of it as bookmarks so I could have it handy all the time. After unfolding the lined notebook page, one from the middle of the letter, I started reading the black script at the first complete sentence.

I want you to know that this break in our relationship is not because I love you less because you are in pain. I don't love you less. Nothing could make me love you less. We met at probably the most desperate time of your life, and I want you to be a little more whole, feel a little safer, before we move forward. I think all the time about our first date—how you didn't want me to pay for your meal because you weren't "putting out." I want you to have me, just me without fear of obligation or owing me. If you can get to that point and find that you love me, too, I'm yours.

"I knew you wouldn't leave town without saying goodbye to your dad."

My heart tripped and then thumped in my ears when I heard his voice behind me. I held my breath and not on purpose. He wasn't really here. I turned around to make sure I was just hallucinating, maybe a post-traumatic stress delusion. That was a thing, right?

I wasn't.

Jake was standing on the fallen tree. Now that he

was three feet from me, I recognized his shirt as the grey thermal I wore the morning after Jeff assaulted me. His leather jacket was draped over his arm. I stared at him a moment to remember what he had just said. "Am I that predictable?"

He let a soft laugh escape his nose as he dropped his feet to the sand to sit beside me. "I wish." He reached into his jacket pocket. "Swiss Roll?"

It startled a smile from me. "Please." I folded the letter and closed it in my book. "I've barely eaten anything the past three days."

He tore through the plastic and handed me a pastry. "Can I take you to get some real food?"

Why would he want to do that? Did he not listen to anything I said an hour ago?

I shook my head. "I'm fine. I was just nervous about today."

"You did great." His smile was tilted and sad and made me hurt.

"You don't have to say that."

His gaze fell to my book. "'What do you want to do? Ruin me?'"

"What?"

"*Farewell to Arms*," he said as he tapped the cover. "That's a line from it."

"Yeah, but how did you know?"

"I read it." He gazed out at the water as if it were normal for him to voluntarily pick up Hemingway. But I didn't ask why he read it; I just studied him. His profile was just as I remembered it, maybe slimmer in the slightest, with a new scar cutting through the outer edge of his right eyebrow. I smoothed over it with my thumb.

The feel of his skin made my breath stop. It was cozy and hot, the same as before, except I wasn't allowed to touch it like I wanted. That made me hurt, made me hate myself. "How'd you get this?"

"Fight." He glanced down at my left wrist and took it in his hand. His rough thumb drew a line over my scar. My heart drummed faster. "How'd you get this?"

I wanted to feel him, really feel his hand against my skin, but it would just make leaving harder. I pulled my sleeve down to my palm.

"Sounds like you had a crummy year," he said as he let go of my arm.

"And you?"

In a matter-of-fact tone, he answered, "Well, my pregnant fiancée dumped me with a note and then aborted the baby, so..."

"Wow," I breathed.

"How old would it be now?"

"That's not even a little fair."

"Why?"

"Because you know it wasn't yours."

"You found out for sure?"

I shut my eyes and lowered my face.

"Didn't think so."

"God, Jake! I regret it, okay? Every single day. Does that help? Will it make you happier to know that I feel like shit?"

"Come on, Sawyer, that doesn't make me happy." He took a deep breath. "Can you just tell me why you left?"

I cackled. "You're serious?"

"Yeah."

"Jake, this..." I pointed between him and me. "This

judgmental crap is why I had to leave. There's no way I could have just come home after that and expected you to accept it. You were so adamant—"

"How do you know I wouldn't have accepted it?"

"Because you still haven't!"

He threw his hands up. "I'm here, aren't I?"

"Yeah, but where were you last summer, huh? You couldn't even make the effort to call me back."

"You told me not to!"

"What? I specifically told you to call me if you wanted me to come home."

He let out a defeated exhale as he brushed his hand up his face and through his hair. "I didn't get your messages in time," he admitted with his eyes closed.

"In time?" My whole face scrunched with confusion. "What do you mean by in—'" *Oh.* The look of sorrow he gave me was all the reminder I needed. I gave him a deadline. And he didn't know about it until it had passed.

"My phone broke the day you left." He paused before confessing, "Okay, I threw it."

"There it is."

"I got all three of your messages the week after you left them." He gazed out at the waves before squeezing his eyes shut. "Sawyer, I'm sorry. I should have called or looked for you or..."

The heartache in my chest spread through my whole body until it covered every inch of me. I whispered, "You wanted me back?"

His eyes met mine. "I've always wanted you, Sawyer."

I turned away. I couldn't stand whatever was swirling in the depth of his brown eyes.

Sighing, he continued, "It physically hurts me when

I think about that baby, even if it wasn't mine. I wish with everything in me you hadn't aborted. But after the trial..." I finally met his eyes. "Sawyer, I'm sorry I made things so hard for you last year."

I cringed. "You went to Jeff's whole trial?"

"As much of it as I could."

I squeezed my eyes shut. "Did you see—"

"Yeah," he exhaled. I buried my face in my hands. "The prosecutor put hundreds of 'sanitized' photos of you and Simone on a few of those huge bulletin boards." His swallow was so labored I heard it. "There was a whole wall of them. I—I couldn't—" He paused for a shaky breath. "I made myself look because I owed you that much. I needed to understand what he did to you— what they all did."

My fingers raked through my hair and strangled the strands between them. I didn't want to imagine him seeing that.

"Then someone read off chat room requests and matched them up to the images. I'm sorry. I couldn't handle it. I tried, Sawyer. But I had to leave. How did you survive—"

"Please, shut up."

"Sawyer..." His hand was sliding across my back now. "I'm sor—"

I scooted away. "Please!"

"Okay," he surrendered.

We sat in silence for a long moment. "You shouldn't have looked."

His words were gentle when he argued, "You should have told me."

I scoffed. "Why? What difference would it have

made?"

"Because...why did you tell me you were raped when you were shattered? Repeatedly? Why didn't you tell me you were scared even when we were together?"

"Please, I was fine."

"Right," he snickered, "because people who are fine whore themselves out."

I glared at him. "I'm surprised it took you this long to bring it up."

"I mean, not to be 'judgmental,' but what the hell were you thinking? You could have been raped or gotten HIV or—"

"I always made them use condoms." As soon as I said the words, I wished I hadn't. He winced like I had just slapped him.

"That's what you chose over me," he muttered.

"You weren't an option anymore! And I had to pay rent."

"Bullshit."

"*Excuse me?*"

"You don't want me to treat you like you're broken? Fine! I'm calling bullshit. You could have done any other job."

"You don't think I tried those first?"

"I didn't think you'd just up and leave me, so what do I know?"

"Well, I didn't think my fiancé would refuse to return my calls and leave me desperate enough to do that."

"*You* left! *You* told me not to call!"

I raised an eyebrow. "Bullshit."

"Fine! I was pissed, okay? You took off! *You* should have been the one to grow a pair and come home if you wanted to. Part of me was just waiting for you to show up at my door, mad as hell, ready to fight like we always did. *You* could have done more to fix this than leave a few drunken voicemails. You could have tried harder."

"You could have tried at all."

"Well…" He shrugged. "It looks like you're in a better relationship now."

"What are you talking about?"

"I'm talking about tall, plaid, and handsome all over you this morning."

"Cash? He was not all over me. And it's not really—" I tilted my head back and forth. "We're not really together."

"Not really?" He lifted one shoulder and added a flippant, "So it's like a sex-only thing?"

"Jake, come on—"

"Do you charge him per hour or per favor?"

"Oh, fuck you!" I stormed off, the sand making my stomping less dramatic than I had hoped.

"I don't know that I could afford for you to do that."

Okay, I set him up for that one. Still.

I didn't make it too far before he called, "Sawyer, wait!" I successfully ignored him until he grabbed my arm. "I'm sorry."

"Let me go!" I wriggled to get loose.

"No. Not again." He spun me around and held both my arms.

"You know, Jake, I don't remember you being such an asshole."

"Really?" He smiled that damn crooked smile that made me melt and laugh when I just wanted to be furious. "I'm sorry. I shouldn't have said that." He sighed. "It just pisses me off that you were with me three years and then could go screw a bunch of other guys as if we meant nothing—like it was so easy for you to move on."

"Easy? Jake, nothing about it was easy. And it wasn't 'moving on.' It was making a living."

"Did you think for one second about me, though? Ever?"

"I thought about you every day!"

"Really? You thought about me when some stranger was stuffing cash in your bra before shoving himself into you? Because that to me sounds like moving on."

"Jake—" I hissed through gritted teeth.

"And I was here, up at night like an *idiot*, thinking 'Is Sawyer okay? Where is she? Is she ever coming home?'"

"Jake!" I screamed. "You know how you could have answered those questions? You could have *called*."

"You told me not to!"

"I swear I'm going to punch you if you say that again."

"Okay, fine," he said as he threw his hands in the air. "I should have called you. But it would have been too late, and you know it."

"Seems like you dodged a bullet then. So leave me the hell alone." I turned to leave again, but he caught my hand.

"No."

"No? So there's more you want to berate me about?"

"Sawyer—"

"If you want to lecture me about the things I can't undo—like the abortion or all the things I did in that club—you can't because I'm not your girlfriend anymore. I'm not your fiancée. I'm not your anything. You can be mad at me, you can hate me, but I don't have to listen to this." I flicked my wrist out of his grasp and took off through the sand.

"If you're not my anything, why does it feel like my everything is walking away from me right now?"

My feet planted in the sand, unable to continue, but I couldn't face him.

"Pretending like you're nothing to me makes this easier for you. I don't care. I'm not going to make it easy."

I spun around. "What do you want from me?"

"The rest of your life."

What? He'd just said it was too late. I shook my head. "No. I don't believe you."

"Let me prove it then." Jake ran to me, stopping when his face was just inches from mine. Drawing in his breath, he traced his hands down my arms. He reached into his pocket and pulled out my engagement ring, that emerald surrounded by diamonds, then dropped to one knee.

No, no, no. What was happening?

"Sawyer, we can go our separate ways like before, or we can fight about this. I don't know what you want, but I want to fight. I don't care if we yell about it every day, forever. I don't care if all our fights are like: 'Jake, why are there washcloths in the sink?' And I say, 'Well, why did you whore around?' And you say, 'Why didn't you call me back?'"

I couldn't stand that he just made me laugh.

"I'd rather waste the rest of our lives arguing about this one stupid year than spend another day without you."

"You're insane. We can't just pick up—"

His eyes were wide, his breath wisping around the words, "Why not?"

Cash. Cash was why not.

In that second, Cash was all I could think about. Running my hand over the edge of my book, I felt the folded page of his letter poking out of it. I pictured his blue eyes and perfect curls. Felt the warmth of his arms around me. I thought of all those days he was at the hospital, bringing me books and nagging me about therapy and getting forehead-vein-bursting infuriated with me for trying to kill myself even after we broke up. Those times he knew what I did, what I had done, and loved me anyway. How he never made me feel guilty or less than. How he would do anything, how he did do anything, for me, even answering my call at 1:07 AM.

And Jake hadn't even called me back.

But all that didn't make me want to say no. Maybe that was it. I loved Jake how Cash loved me—that unquestioning, irrational, excruciating kind of love. I loved him when I shouldn't, when I didn't want to. Of course I loved Cash. It was just a different texture of love. Loving Jake was like drinking whiskey neat. It stung and warmed and made me do stupid things. Cash's love was sweet, like his brown-sugar voice. Nothing about it hurt, but I didn't crave it the same way. I didn't think I ever could. And Cash was the kind of guy a girl could crave. It just wouldn't be me.

Jake raised the ring between his finger and thumb. "Do you still want this?"

Swallowing over the lump in my throat, I reached my left hand out to Jake. I made sure to glare through the tears gathering in my lower lids. "Yeah," I whispered. "I want to fight with you."

Jake slipped the ring on my finger and kissed me, his rough fingers digging into my hair, then running along my jaw like they always did, ear to chin and back again. He tasted and felt better than I remembered, like I'd been starving this past year and finally had what I'd been hungering for.

I pulled away to say against his lips, "I'm going to win, you know that?"

His gaze fell from my eyes to my mouth where he breathed, "Not if I get naked." He kissed me again before I could argue.

....

UPON FEELING MY JAGGED RIB cage during our beach make-out session, Jake declared me *malnourished* and insisted on taking me to eat immediately. He ordered our usual at the harbor: a large basket of fish and chips, a bread bowl, and two glass bottles of cane sugar coke.

"I swear, I could put butter on everything," I said as I took a bite of grilled sourdough bread.

"Did they not feed you at the hospital?"

"Nothing good. And LA doesn't use enough butter in general."

"Wait, so why were you hospitalized again?" He lowered his voice, "You tried to kill yourself?"

"Oh." I swallowed. "No, I did that in the hospital. Got pretty close, too." I nodded with pursed lips.

Jake covered my hand with his, staring at me with puppy-eyed sympathy. "Sawyer—"

Please, the last thing Jake should be feeling was sorry for me.

"I got hospitalized," I interrupted, "because I beat a congressman almost to death when he tried to rape me.

So it was that or prison."

He shook his head to process this. "Are you serious?"

"He had to breathe through a tube for a while. And he definitely can't have any more kids."

"Sawyer!" he scolded.

"What? *You* taught me to go for the groin."

He stared at me, the left corner of his lip quivering, fighting a smile.

I nudged his arm with my elbow. "You're kind of proud."

"A little."

"I could have done without the six months of psych incarceration, but it was better than actual prison."

"How'd you score that deal?"

"Good lawyer. There are these restitution laws for victims of child pornography, so that guy I assaulted had to reimburse me for my legal bills and my hospital stay because they finally got proof that he downloaded me."

"Wait, the state didn't pay for your hospital?"

"No, because my lawyer set me up in a really great place. Those state-run places are hell. I mean," I took a bite of a fry, "that's what some of the other crazies told me."

He laughed. "So, are there others?"

"Crazies? Yeah—"

"No, I mean others they know have downloaded..."

"Who've been convicted you mean?"

Jake nodded.

"Yeah, about a dozen that I know of so far. Right now, I'm up to like $160,000 of the $3.7 million I'm eligible for."

"Holy shit! Are you messing with me?"

I tipped my Coke bottle toward him. "The cost of 'never touching a child.'"

"How did they come up with $3.7 million?"

"Something like lost wages, therapy, medication—stuff like that—for my whole life."

"So you're still getting help? Like therapy or whatever?"

I shrugged. "I just got out two days ago."

"Yeah, but you should probably still see someone, right? It's already paid for. And, I mean, you tried to commit suicide. That's a big deal—"

"Et tu, Jake?" I smirked, then changed the subject. "You still live with the guys?"

He nodded as he swallowed his food. "Yeah. But I'm moving out soon."

"Yeah?"

"I got a contract with Golden Boy Promotions, so I'm moving to a city with a real airport."

Translation: Jake was now a professional fighter.

"Jake! Holy crap! Congratulations!"

He smiled before refocusing on his clam chowder. "Thanks."

"Where are you moving?"

"Where do *you* want to live?"

I twisted the ring around my finger. *I got to live with Jake again.* "Well, I'd like to go back to school."

"Yeah? In LA?"

"If you want to. I mean, you can wear your Henleys there."

"I thought you said they don't put enough butter in their food in LA."

"Yeah, but it's not like there's a shortage. It's just my

friends are there, and I like the school. Also," I breathed, "there's this church I like."

Jake stared at me like I was a stranger. "Church?"

"Yeah. It's not so bad, actually." I took a spoonful of chowder.

He smirked, and I wished I could have read his mind. "It must be really great if *you* went."

"It is. You might like it."

"Maybe." He shrugged. "I let my mom drag me to church this year."

"No, you didn't."

"Desperate times. It was right after you left, and I was too depressed to put up a fight. It wasn't as bad as I thought."

I nodded.

He tipped his chin toward me. "How'd you end up there?"

My eyes fell to my fish and chips as I picked up another fry. "Cash." I didn't know what I felt guiltier about: being with Cash this past year or letting Jake put that ring on my finger while the poor guy was still at my house. I was such a bitch. How'd I get either of these guys?

"Sounds like he looked out for you okay."

I agreed. "He's a great guy."

"Were you guys together?"

"For a while." I was quick to add, "We didn't sleep together or anything, though. We broke up before I was hospitalized."

Jake tilted his head slowly, thoughtfully. "Can I meet him?"

My forehead crinkled. In what planet would that be

273

a good idea? *Hey ex-boyfriend who still has feelings for me and stood by me through a ton of shit I threw at you, remember that guy I was totally hung up on? Guess what! We're getting married, and he wants to meet you. Here he is!*

"Why?"

"Because he was there for you when I should have been." He took a sip of his coke. "Because he brought you back to me in one piece."

"Okay, sure...if he'll speak to me after today." My stomach twisted. I wasn't hungry anymore, so I pushed my chair back and stood. "Can you take me home?"

JAKE DROPPED ME OFF AT my mom's. I walked through the front door, keeping my left hand in my sweatshirt pocket. I found Cash in my room, packing up his clothes for our flight out that night.

"Hey." A smile flickered across his face, but then disappeared when he saw my expression, the tension in my jaw, the tears welling in my lower lids. "You okay?"

I shook my head and tried to take a breath, but it was shallow and hopeless. All I could manage to say was, "I can't go to Georgia with you."

He stepped in front of me and tucked my hair behind my ear. "Why not?"

I couldn't say the words. I just froze, standing there staring up at him. Finally, I pulled my left hand from my pocket and held it in front of me. "I'm sorry." The tears fell down my cheeks. "I didn't expect to see him. It just—"

His throat pulsed as he swallowed. "Sawyer, it's okay." But it wasn't. He was choking on his words, running his hand over his flushing face.

"You're not mad?"

He shook his head.

"You should be. I'd really feel better if you yelled at me or something. Please. Tell me how much you hate me and how terrible I am to you—"

He held my arms in his hands. "Stop. You love him, right?"

I agreed without words, my head bobbing, sparing him of just how much I loved Jake.

"Can I see?" His hand slid down to mine, and he examined the ring. "Emerald?"

I nodded at the sound of my old name.

His lips forced a smile. "Your eyes are better."

I laughed and sobbed and buried my face in his chest. "I love you."

"I love you, too," he whispered as his lips brushed my hair.

I didn't let go as I said, "Jake and I are going to move to LA so I can go back to school. So I'm still going to make fun of you for sucking at math, and you're going to force me to listen to Taylor Swift. We'll sit with each other in church and talk about how gross Dylan is. You'll tell me what cute things Sue is doing, and Jo can stay with me anytime. And—"

"You'll invite me to your wedding."

I hugged him tighter. "Please be there."

His head moved against my hair. "You're not going to lose me, Sawyer." But he and I both knew I already had. We could never be the same. I felt it when his arms loosened around me, when I watched him walk back toward his suitcase on the bed. That deepest part of our relationship was in the past. And it had to stay there.

JAKE ANSWERED HIS DOOR WHEN I knocked that night, my suitcase in my hand behind me. "Still want me?"

He smiled. "I guess."

I shoved his chest with both hands, but he grabbed my arms and wrapped himself around me, opening my lips with his, desperate and honest.

When Jake and I took my suitcase up to his room, I froze at the sight behind the door. It was all the same as I had left it that morning: the wrinkled blue comforter on the full-sized bed that jutted into the center of the room, the dresser underneath the cracked-open window, Jake's open gym bag on the floor with boxing gloves and wrist wraps spilling out of it. I burst into tears.

"Hey, hey," Jake whispered as he pulled me close. "What's wrong?" His question, so simple, so sweet and right, was impossible to answer. Maybe it was that the entire last year collided into me that moment. Maybe it was that being here meant Cash was gone, that the parts of our hearts that had been joined were permanently severed. Maybe it was that my last minutes in this room were some of my worst, and I'd never imagined I'd be here again. I hadn't realized how much I missed it.

Jake let me go behind the closed door. He pulled open his dresser drawer. With blurry vision, I saw him take out that army green Henley that somehow had survived so many years of wear. He peeled off my sweatshirt and then unbuttoned my pants, letting me step out of them. Then he handed me that soft shirt, and I pulled it on, sliding my bra out from underneath it.

We curled up together under his covers, my face tight against his chest as I wept. His calloused fingers traced up and down the curve of my back before trailing down my thigh, inching me closer with each touch. I took in the warmth of his hands and the bare skin of his torso, letting him soothe me after I hurt him, protect me after I deserted him. He held me until I was quiet, until I felt safe enough to fall asleep.

....

JAKE AND I MARRIED JULY 28, barefoot on the beach he proposed on. Our newfound faith meant no sex until Jake had a ring. So, three-week engagement it was.

Cash mailed us an early wedding present: a Polaroid camera with a note saying, *Don't let them win, Sawyer.* I relented and hired a photographer for the wedding who agreed to leave all her fancy equipment at home.

Cash flew out for the wedding with Charlotte, his ex, in tow as his plus-one. She did what I should have done with Jake: showed up at Cash's door, confessed she was still in love with him after their year apart, and told him that no one even compared to him.

No shit, idiot.

And Cash, being Cash, took her back. When I met her, saw them together, his arm around her, his lips on her cheek, it was weird, and not because I felt a twinge of jealousy. Envy, rather. He wasn't mine to be jealous over anymore. He didn't look at her the way he looked at me. She made him happy, but that was all she made him. I was his whiskey neat. I wasn't sure Charlotte ever would be. But maybe that was okay. He deserved someone perfect, and she was pretty close to it. Or at least she wasn't as selfish and unstable as I was. I was impossible to compete with in that department. Maybe that would be enough for him. I hoped it would be.

I'd love to say Jake and I lived happily ever after, that everything between us was easy and painless. But it turned out it was unreasonable for me to expect a seamless transition from disassociating during hookups with strangers to having passionate, sweaty sex with my husband.

On our wedding night, I only came back into my body in time to roll off Jake, who was apologizing for something. I was so livid with myself for not feeling any of it, for not even being there, that I rushed to the bathroom, shut myself in, and locked the door. I filled the bathtub and turned on the fan so Jake wouldn't hear me crying. When I leaned my hands on the rim of the porcelain, I noticed semen dripping down my thigh. He hadn't used a condom. Right. That was fine. We agreed not to since I had an IUD and was somehow disease-free.

It was fine. It was fine. *It was fine!* It was Jake all over me this time, not Jeff. Right? Still, I needed to get it off me. I sank into the hot water until it covered my face, weeping silently below the surface.

When I came up to gasp for air, Jake was knocking on the door. His voice was muffled when he said, "Sawyer, I'm sorry. It's just been a long time, and I didn't expect it to go so fast without the condom. Maybe we can do something else? Or try again—"

I climbed out and swung open the door, naked with a puddle forming at my feet. "Jake," I breathed. "I'm not mad at you." How could I ask the man who had forgiven me of so much to do something for me, to give me what I needed when I needed it because I hurt him? "Remember when we first started sleeping together, and I couldn't really deal with..."

His face fell.

My eyes teared up. "I'm sorry."

He glanced past me and then into my eyes. "Bath okay?"

I closed my eyes and nodded. "Thank you."

Jake took my hand and led me to the tub. He sat behind me, his legs on either side of me, my back against his bare chest. I combed my fingers back through his hair down to the nape of his neck, letting him stroke up and down my arm with his rough fingertips. I shut my eyes to feel his warm tongue and lips on my throat, then his hands on my waist. "Is this okay?" he whispered in my ear.

I nodded and guided his hands over my breasts, then waited to see if my mind would flee the scene. It didn't.

Jake reached my thighs, starting to ease his hands between them. "Still okay?"

"Um..." I shut my eyes tight, feeling his touch less as it slid toward my hips. "I think so."

"Sawyer, you're tensing up. We should take a break." He shifted behind me, and I heard his arms rising from the water. I assumed he was getting out, pissed off at me for ruining his wedding night. Instead, his hands kneaded into my shoulders and neck.

I ran my wet hands over my face to wash off the tears and said, "Thank you. I'm sorry."

Jake brushed his lips against my ear and murmured, "Stop that. I love you."

Never Touched

I sighed and wrapped his arms around me so I could nuzzle into his shoulder, my cheek against his bicep. This would get easier. It had before.

September 2018

*W*E PACKED UP AFTER OUR HONEYMOON AND trekked to the City of Angels to move into our new apartment. I restarted classes at the end of September, the same month Jake had his first professional match. The fight wasn't the most brutal I had watched, but it was a waking nightmare for me. As soon as the first punch was thrown, I huddled into a ball, shivering in my seat, my eyes peeking above my arms. Each jab, each hook, sent me back to December in the VIP room. I could smell Allen's leathery skin. Felt the sharp pain in my arms and legs where his knees pinned me to the couch. I saw the drywall crumble behind his head as I slammed him into it. And I couldn't shake it. I couldn't leave that VIP room for days.

The next week, I stayed in bed under a cozy fog thanks to a few bottles of tequila. Jake found the booze when I was asleep. He didn't say anything, just dumped it down the kitchen sink. He left three empty bottles on the counter so I'd know he was on to me.

Joke's on you, Jake. I could get more. I was in the

checkout line at the store when I scanned my wallet for my fake ID. It was gone. Just my stupid legal one with my real birth date that put me squarely at the age of nineteen. I sped home furious and sober and empty-handed, then tore the house apart searching for the fake: turning couch cushions over, flipping through books, sifting through every drawer. My hands in the trash, I glanced up at the tequila bottles on the kitchen counter. Jake, that book-burning ass I was hitched to for life, had cut the card into thick strips and slipped the pieces into one of them.

I turned it upside down, shaking and banging the glass, but only got two strips loose. The rest were adhered to the sticky insides. I raised the bottle behind me and smashed it against the edge of the countertop, closing my eyes against the thick shards flying across the tile and into the sink and onto the pretend wood floor. The soft pads of my fingers brushed the glass off the counter, clearing a space for me to reassemble the card. Bloody fingerprints smudged the plastic. I licked my fingers clean and kept at it. That was when Jake walked in.

There was nothing but a silent stare between us for a minute, him standing in the open doorway, the warm sun on his sweaty back, gym bag over his shoulder, and me—dizzy and desperate and bleeding while I pieced my ticket to a soft-lensed life back together. He scanned the books thrown from the shelves, the couch in disarray, and the debris on the floor. The mess was humiliating, sobering, like I had been caught screwing someone else. He finally said, "I'll get the broom."

I shut my eyes in relief, in that pain that only forgiveness stabbed with. There I stood frozen, barefoot, surrounded by glass, drops of blood drying on my skin. Jake returned with a broom, his shoes crunching on the shards on his way to me. He shifted his eyes down to my hands, then took them in his, running his rough fingers over the cuts, holding them up to the light to check for any pieces still stinging in my skin. He wrapped my arms around his neck, and he scooped me up to carry me into the bathroom. Silent tears rolled down my cheeks as he ran cold water to clean off the excess blood, then sat me on the closed toilet. He kneeled in front of me and tucked a shock of hair behind my ear. His fingers trailed to my wrists and wrapped around them, his tactile way of telling me he thought I was too skinny. "When was the last time you ate?"

"I don't know." *Jake, come on, alcohol had calories.* That counted for something.

Jake reached into the shower and turned on the faucet. "Take a shower. We're going out for dinner."

I nodded.

"I'll be back in a minute." He shut the door behind him, which was odd since he was going to shower with me. I listened at the door as I took off my clothes. He was talking, but I could only hear half a conversation. He must have been on the phone.

"Sorry to bother you with this—"

Pause.

"She's done this before but never like this. I don't know if I should try to get her to go to AA, or—"

Was *her* me? Me in *Alcoholics Anonymous?* Weren't those poor suckers not allowed to drink? Ever? Over my rotting corpse.

"So, it's some kind of PTSD thing?"

Long pause.
"No, she hasn't left the apartment."
Pause.
"Okay, yeah, I'll make sure she makes an appointment."
Even longer pause.
"No, she doesn't have any meds. Is she supposed to?"
Pause.
"Yeah, that'd be great. Anytime. I'm off this week."
Pause again.
"Thanks, man."

I was still in bed at ten the next morning when Jake welcomed someone into our home. Jerk. "Sawyer! Someone's here for you!"

I forced myself out of bed, my hair tangled, Jake's baggy shirt over his boxer briefs rolled at my hips. I squinted into the sunlit living room to see a familiar tall frame at the door. Cash crossed his arms and shook his head when he saw me. "You have therapy in an hour." He tipped his head toward the hall. "Get dressed."

Excuse me? Not even a good morning? Come on, Cash, your mama raised you better than that.

"No, I don't. It's Wednesday." As if the day of the week made a difference. I hadn't been to therapy in weeks.

"Jake scheduled it."

I glowered at Jake. He crossed his arms, too. That really pissed me off. I went to get ready, and by that, I meant I put a sports bra on under Jake's shirt and brushed my teeth, all while slamming dresser drawers and bathroom cabinets.

Jake drove me to my appointment, a car ride where I flipped him off with my unbreaking quiet. When we got home, there were six pill bottles on the kitchen counter next to a note:

Sawyer,

THESE are your medications. (Big, fat arrow included pointing toward the prescriptions.)

THESE are not. (Bigger, fatter arrow pointing to the empty bottles.)

We're here. We love you.

Cash

Bursting into tears, I curled into Jake's chest. I had Cash. I had Jake. I had everything. And I was an idiot.

I had both when I had to drop two of my classes that quarter because I couldn't take the stress. I had both beside me at church when I was afraid, to keep me from drinking, to push me to therapy twice a week.

And I had Jake every sleepless night. When I was afraid those men would find me or when I couldn't stop thinking about the videos they were still watching, I'd roll over, rest my head on his chest, and feel his hands glide through my hair. I closed my eyes to listen to his heart, that familiar *thump-thump* as I fell asleep. And when I was surrounded on Third Street, I'd listen for that sound and follow it to him, to a safer place.

About the Author

Growing up with poor reading comprehension, Laney Wylde avoided books at all costs. But after reading Francine River's Redeeming Love for the first time in high school, she fell in love with literature. It was then she realized broken anti-heroines and impossible love stories were the stuff of heart-wrenching, binge-worthy novels.

Afraid her slow reading pace and lack of writing skill would inhibit her from becoming a successful English major, Laney pursued her B.S. in Mathematics from Biola University, graduating in 2014.

Laney gathered the courage to write honestly and diligently in 2017, producing Never Touched, a passion project that sheds light on the uphill battle that is healing from sexual abuse.

She lives in Southern California with her dashing husband and precocious little boy.

Acknowledgements

THOSE WHO KNOW ME KNOW THAT I WASN'T A writer four months before I started Never Touched. Those who know me well know that it was because I was scared. Here are the people who lifted me from chicken to published author.

Grandma Audi, thank you for having an art project ready for me each time I came over to your house growing up--how did you do that?--for telling me, "there are no mistakes just opportunities for creativity," and for reminding me that I had a right brain even when I had given up on the idea.

Uncle Paul and Aunt Robin, you showed me adults read fiction, watch artsy fartsy films, and don't have to grow out of their dreams just because they grow up--not that I'm saying you guys have grown up. I'd never say that.

Mr. Brown, my AP American Literature teacher, your ominous advice still haunts me: "You will look back at your life full of regret if you don't write." Thanks for believing in me despite all evidence to the contrary.

A writing-in-the-sky thanks to my best friend, Stacey McCain, for reading Never Touched chapter by chapter in its roughest form and for saying sweet things like, "What's the hold up with Chapter 13?" It's no exaggeration that I wouldn't have had the courage to tell Sawyer's story without your constant, though blind, encouragement, your willingness to pick up the phone every time I called with a melodramatic "creative crisis," your laughing at my twisted humor. You're the reason Jake had a fighting chance with Sawyer. All the Team Cashers can take that up with you. I love you. I look forward to winning an Oscar with you one day.

My altruistic guinea pigs/beta readers--Whitney Brammer, Abbey Thomas, Andrea Ellfeldt, Kelli Frazer, Anna Brown, Sarah Mossembekker, and Lizzie Gardiner--thank you for making Never Touched what it is now. Andrea, thank you for helping me with the title. I suck at titles.

Aunt Jenny, thank you for listening to me go on and on about my writing, for paying for my RWA membership without me even asking because you knew I was a starving artist, and for introducing me to Rebecca Forster.

Speaking of Rebecca, thank you for telling me to rewrite Never Touched. I had no idea what I was doing, and no one in their right mind would have signed me without the changes you helped me make to my book and query letter. You hadn't even met me, but replied to all my emails promptly and with patience. I'll forever treasure your kindness and advice.

Ethan Gregory, for whatever reason you plucked Never Touched out of the slush pile and jumped up and down for it. Thanks for taking a chance on a new writer.

Melanie, Rebecca, Marya, Courtney, and Cynthia, thank you for turning my pipe dream into a reality, for your patience with my unprofessionalism, for your excitement about my silly little story. Working with you is a joy.

Chase Ellfeldt, thank you for your free social media advice and for not teasing me about how incompetent I am with hashtags.

Sarah and Josh Mossembekker, I love you artsy weirdos. Thank you for the marketing tips, taking my headshots, and for shamelessly promoting me. Sarah, I'd be lost without you making my Instagram posts and basically telling me how to use the internet.

My incredible parents, without you taking care of J when I was desperate to write or edit, my dream of becoming an author would still be a dream. You never doubted my aspirations or tried to curb my reckless enthusiasm. Thank you.

E, hubby, you told me not to write anything dirty in the acknowledgements to you, which I feel is no fun, but you said it would be inappropriate considering the content of the book, the fact that anyone could read this, because I don't know how to use euphemisms, blah blah blah. Fair enough. I know this whole writing thing hasn't always made sense to you. I know sometimes you and J miss me because my mind is somewhere else when it should be with you guys. And I know you don't have to support me. For some reason, you do. Thank you for loving me through this often emotionally-draining journey, for answering to my medical questions and letting me process my imaginary world out loud, for picking up my slack when I've been in writing-land. I love you.

J, your creativity and unrelenting confidence makes me want to be like you when I grow up. You'll always be my little squish. I love you, baby.

To my God, my Savior, the Source of my inspiration, the Author of the most heart-wrenching romance. Thank you for including me in your love story.

Lastly, thank you to all the Sawyers who have shared their stories with me directly or indirectly. Particularly, Digene Farrar, thank you for writing a memoir that gave me a special insight into the daily struggle that is recovery from sexual abuse. Sawyers, you are brave. You are fighters. You are survivors. You're my inspiration.